THE
LODGE

BOOKS BY SUE WATSON

THE
LODGE

SUE WATSON

bookouture

Published by Bookouture in 2023

An imprint of Storyfire Ltd.
Carmelite House
50 Victoria Embankment
London EC4Y 0DZ

www.bookouture.com

ISBN: 978-1-83790-441-9
eBook ISBN: 978-1-83790-440-2

To Kim Nash,
Thanks for those lovely nights in the winter lodge,
where we drank gin, shared our stories and started this one...

PROLOGUE

The oncoming darkness shrouded me as I stood in the freezing wind staring at the body before me, blood seeping into the cold, white snow. The ripped jacket exposing bare flesh on the frozen ground, and the silence, the deathly, tortuous silence.

Suddenly an arm reached out, fingers stretched in shock and pain. A pointless move, a final twitch of life, then nothing. I had to look away. It was hard to see what I'd done, the mess I'd made, but this was the only way I could move on and live my life. This was my revenge.

Standing in the winter wonderland of white, with only twisted skeleton trees as my witness, I called out to see if anyone was there. I waited and waited, but only the wind and the sea answered. Then I walked away.

ONE

FIONA

Friday afternoon

Looking back, it was naïve to think we could make it work. Me, my ex-husband, his new wife, his mother and various offspring, all under the same roof for a long weekend. What could possibly go right? But when my former mother-in-law, Angela, had called and begged me to go to celebrate her seventy-fifth birthday, I'd found it hard to refuse.

'I've rented a luxury lodge in a beautiful cove in Cornwall,' she opened with. 'I'd love you and the children to come along, all expenses paid.'

It was difficult to talk as I was at work. I'm in HR, and was about to go into a heavy meeting, so without knowing the details, I thanked her and said I'd love to celebrate her birthday in Cornwall. From that moment, she bombarded me with photos of sparkly winter landscapes under snowy skies, the lodge in question glowing from within, like it was on fire.

This was just like any other sales pitch from Angela – it began with my wedding dress choice and ended in the post-divorce home she helped me choose. I didn't mind, I was fond of her and grateful for her support. Money was tight and Angela was offering to pay for me and the children to have a little holiday, in a lovely place. But as is often the case with great offers like that, there was a catch.

'I just want us all under one roof, so we can forget all the problems and just be a family again,' she'd said that evening when I called her back to discuss plans.

'When you say "all of us" who do you mean?' I asked, knowing the answer already, feeling it in every nerve ending.

'Scott and Danni, and the baby of course.'

My stomach made its final descent, dropping with a thud. Even all that wintry loveliness and free food wasn't worth spending a night under the same roof as my ex-husband and his new wife. I was about to politely decline Angela's kind offer, but as I was trying to come up with an excuse she moved in before I could work out how to say no. And Angela didn't take no for an answer.

'Fiona, I know it isn't ideal – being around Scott, and Danni might be a little...' She paused, clearly wondering what to call this horrible, twisted menage of past meeting present.

'Hellish? Tortuous? Unbearable?' I offered.

Silence, then: 'It might be a little *uncomfortable*,' she replied, relaxing into the word.

'*Uncomfortable?* That's an understatement,' I replied. 'It's a very kind offer and thank you, but no thank you.'

I hated saying no to her, but Angela must have understood how impossible this would be for me. She adored her only son, and had been a great mother-in-law; even during the divorce she was as concerned for my welfare as she was for Scott and the children. But I couldn't accept.

'Don't get me wrong, I *am* over everything,' I lied. 'It was three years ago now, and I've moved on, but I don't think any of us will ever be ready to *holiday* together.'

After a long silence, she said, 'It would mean a lot to me.

Since Jack died, you're all I have – you and the children, Scott...
and Danni,' she said her name quickly in what I assumed was a
vain attempt to bury her in the conversation. But the name of
my husband's mistress-turned-wife could *never* be covered up,
or erased. It had been seared into my flesh, and each time I
heard *Danni* the scars flared red again. I could never forgive
either of them, but my feelings for Scott were more measured.
He was my children's father, we had a shared history and those
memories of our past continued to bind us and would always be
precious. I didn't want to erase the past with my own bitterness.
Scott still came around to take the kids out or pick them up on
his weekends, and was still in my life in a way Danni never had
been, so we'd stayed civil, and recently a warmth had returned
between me and my ex-husband. But after all the pain and
indignity, I asked that he keep Danni out of my world, so I could
pretend she didn't exist. Sometimes it worked for me to pretend
that I was still married, that Scott was just working late, or away
on a course. But I still woke every morning with a jolt, remembering that the husband I'd loved was now with a new wife in a
love nest paid for by the sale of our family home.

Angela just seemed to understand, she knew not to mention
the other woman or what was happening in my husband's new
life. She was so alert to my feelings she hadn't even mentioned it
to me when their baby had been born, for which I was grateful.
In the early days I had to protect myself, to find a way to live
with the new status quo.

Scott was living the mid-life-crisis dream, and initially
believed that the start of his fresh new family would wipe clean
all the mistakes of the past. I'd envied him, because, back then
as a forty-two-year-old mother of two teenagers, my ship had
sailed when it came to fresh starts and new babies.

'I can't do it, Angela,' I said. 'Why don't I take you out for a
birthday dinner with Sam and Georgia instead?'

'But I've booked the lodge now, it's in a beautiful Cornish

cove. Jack and I stayed there a few years back,' she said, brandishing the dead husband card again. I was surprised she'd booked it for all of us without consultation. Did she really believe I'd forgiven Scott and Danni? If so, she must have mistaken me for someone else.

'I beg you, Fiona.' Again the cracked voice, the slight pause before my name. 'Please. I *need* everyone there.'

'The kids can go along without me. I can celebrate separately with you.'

Silence.

'Why is it so important that *I'm* there?' I asked.

'Because it could be my last birthday.'

'Don't be silly.' I forced out the words. 'You're only seventy-five, that's young these days and... are you... ill or something?' I felt a sudden rush in my chest.

'Let's not talk about it now,' she replied mysteriously. 'Just say you'll come?' So I agreed to go on the holiday, how could I not? I put down the phone, concern fluttering at the back of my mind. Was there something wrong with her?

Angela had been more than a mother-in-law to me, she'd been my friend. It couldn't have been easy for her when Scott first left us and she had to listen to me ranting and crying. I'd made vile remarks about her treacherous son and the new woman in his life, but Angela had borne it, and seen me through some of my darkest days – now it might be my turn to see her through hers?

That's why, on a cold afternoon in early December, I found myself driving four hours from my home in the landlocked midlands, to the beautiful, rocky coast of Cornwall. Here I would spend a long weekend with the woman who stole my husband and ruined my life. I felt physically sick at the prospect.

As I drove along through the dark, wintry afternoon, the radio added to my dread: 'The Met Office have issued a severe weather warning...' Another stark reminder about the oncoming snow that threatened to cause travel delays, road closures, power cuts and chaos. My car was old, not the most reliable, and I was seriously worried about breaking down in the big freeze. The roads were empty, everyone else seemed to have taken heed of the warnings and stayed safe in their homes. I thought about the kids driving on their own to Cornwall. Georgia, my youngest, had spent a couple of days at Bristol University where Sam, my eldest, was in his first year of Law. He was now driving them both to the lodge, but I worried about him going too fast, or giving in to Georgia's demands to take over the drive – she'd only just passed her test but was desperate to get into the driving seat. I'd made Sam promise he would drive slowly and not allow his sister anywhere near the wheel especially in this weather, but she was bound to put pressure on him.

The evening was quickly closing in, and the coastal road had long ago been abandoned by any kind of lighting. Visibility was poor, and to add to the oncoming darkness, sleet was now landing on my car window, frosty little splatters knitted together like a blanket making it almost impossible to see beyond a few feet ahead. The windscreen wipers were doing little to clear the thick veil but *were* providing my nervous heart with a pace-making beat as they thudded from side to side. *Thud, thud, thud.* I thought about the kids again and wished they'd taken a train, but the lodge was so remote there was no train station nearby.

I had to stop worrying about them, that way madness lay, but as my mind flailed around trying to find something easier to focus on, my phone pinged, again. I was sure it was Nick; why couldn't he leave me alone?

I'd met Nick a few months before on a dating app, and he seemed like the answer to my prayers. During those first heady weeks, he was attentive, kind, loving, and made me feel attractive again. Soon, long-forgotten feelings began to blossom and I even believed I might be able to move on from Scott, who'd destroyed me with his selfish pursuit of a woman ten years younger. Scott had walked out on us just before lockdown, and by the time we emerged from that, I hadn't moved on at all; for me life had simply stood still. I hadn't adjusted, and continued to be suspended in the no-man's-land he'd left me in before Covid and Zoom and banana bread and death. I had this insane notion that when lockdown ended, we'd all emerge from our darkness, blinking in the sunlight, and resume our lives and our marriage. I became obsessed with mending the break, getting him back and repairing our family, but by then it was too late. Danni was pregnant.

It was my friend Cindy who realised I was becoming slightly obsessed with the absurd notion of healing my marriage and suggested I at least *try* to move on.

'You have to get back out there,' she'd urged, showing me the apps and the swipes and the etiquette required for online dating. At first, I wasn't convinced, but Nick was the first man who winked at me, and after messaging for a couple of weeks, he asked me out. We met at a local restaurant. He was as good-looking as his photo, he was charming and funny and I was immediately smitten.

After about a month I mentioned to the kids that I was seeing someone, and though they seemed surprised, were encouraging. One evening when he came to the house to pick me up, Sam was home and I introduced them. I could see now that I was subconsciously hoping he'd tell Scott, and he'd be jealous, realise what he'd lost and come running home. But Sam must have been discreet, because Scott never mentioned it.

My old car continued to struggle uphill until I saw a sign for Kynance Cove, where the website promised 'a bay of turquoise waters hugging dramatic rocky cliffs and sweeping white sands.' I smiled to myself as I turned off the main drag, where the land-scape opened out under a darkening sky. No sign of those turquoise waters in December, all that lay ahead was greyness, a whistling wind and pale sleet landing weightlessly on the ground.

As the road meandered through hilly terrain high above a roaring sea, the few trees dotted around were black against the sky, forced by the wind to twist like tortured skeletons. I watched as I drove past, and for a horrifying moment thought one of the trees was human. It looked just like a tall man watching, twisting in the wind, causing my heart to go faster than the wipers.

I put my foot on the accelerator, trying to steady the car, and my heart as the tyres skidded on the slippery road. I peered through the windscreen, blurred from falling snow, desperate to keep the car on the road as the voice on the radio told again of the threat of snow, urging listeners not to take unnecessary journeys and warning of *the risk to life*.

But on I went along the icy road, wind howling, snow swirling, and my windscreen wipers screaming across glass, unaware of the horror that lay ahead.

Like an invisible, furious wind it was already rushing in across the sea, lying in wait on roadsides and scrambling over dark winter hills, consuming everything and everyone in its wake. And as I headed down that empty road towards the darkness, it was already too late.

TWO

DANNI

The timing of this so-called 'winter break' couldn't be worse. The baby's teething, and Scott and I seem to be going through a really difficult time. I don't know why, but recently he's changed, he's just not himself; he's snappy and on edge, and seems to find it hard to look at me. I asked him last night if there was anything wrong, but he just said 'life', which hurt, because *I'm* his life now. Is it me making him like this? I drive along the narrow Cornish roads knowing a long weekend with his ex-wife and kids is the last thing we need right now. My insides are churning, I have a really bad feeling about it, and as the skies begin to close in around me, I'm so tempted to turn around and go back home. But I can't, because Angela implied that it might be her last birthday, so how could I say no?

Scott says the place she's booked is amazing, and very expensive. It sounds lovely, but even if it *is* her last birthday, why does she feel the need to do a social experiment by putting the old wife and the new one under the same roof? It's weird, and I doubt it will be stress free, it might even have a negative effect on her health, not to mention the rest of us. If it was anyone other than Angela who'd organised this, I'd think it was some kind of twisted game. I mean what's the point? But I guess if she's just concerned about the time she has left, the point is getting her family together and trying to make the best of things. So despite the obvious horror of it all, I reckon we owe it to her to try and make the whole thing work, as much as we can anyway.

Angela has always been kind to me, even though sometimes I still feel like 'the other woman' in the family. She manages to strike the balance, maintaining her relationship with Fiona, the first wife, while having one with me, the new wife. Scott says she praises me just as much as she does Fiona, but I sometimes wonder if Angela's just sitting on the fence. Is it really possible to have genuinely loyal feelings towards *two* people on opposing sides? Does she *really* like us both as much as she makes out, or is she just pretending she likes me to please Scott?

I sigh and gaze ahead at the long, narrow road, the windscreen fuzzy with sleet. If she *is* pretending, Angela's not the only one who'll have to hold back on how she really feels this weekend. I only met Fiona once, when she dropped one of the kids off at school; she was just Mr Wilson's wife then and I didn't think too much about her. I remember thinking she was lucky to be married to a man like that. Weird how life works out, I'm now his wife and the mother of his youngest child. I find it hard sometimes to believe he chose me over Fiona. Despite being married with his child, I still feel threatened by her. For a start, she's elegant and sophisticated, never a hair out of place and she apparently sailed through early motherhood, something I struggle with. The very thought of meeting her properly scares me to death, partly because I don't know her and have no idea what she's like. Fiona's made it clear she wants nothing to do with me. I can't blame her for that, but we all have to move on and while she isn't letting me in, none of us can move forward. Her refusal to acknowledge my existence makes me feel like the cuckoo in the nest, like I need her approval before I can be validated. I have to remind myself that my relationship with Scott is as legitimate as hers, it just happened later, and despite being relative strangers, our lives are horribly entangled in such an intimate way, I feel exposed. Our respective relationships with Scott are what bind us, yet also rip us apart, and there's nothing we can do to change that. We can *never* be friends.

It's getting dark. I wish I'd waited for Scott and driven down with him, but he had an emergency at work. Again! I couldn't hang around waiting for him, I have to think of Olivia, our daughter, who at twelve months old needs a routine. God, I hate that word. It conjures up a rigid world of dates and times, calendars and obligations. But all these things come with motherhood, and instead of noting dates for drinks with the girls or holidays, it's all about childcare, playdates and doctor's appointments. I adore my daughter, but not necessarily the piercing screams of teething and nappy rash. I look forward to the day when Olivia becomes a little person and we can tell each other about our days, and have fun together. But these early days seem to be an endless loop of waking her, feeding her, changing her and waving brightly coloured toys in her face in an attempt to stop her crying. All this and even when she's asleep I worry she's too quiet so I'm constantly checking she's still breathing. Having a baby was such a monumental shock to my system, and the biological need for sleep and peace of mind throws up all kinds of shit. I'm now the proud owner of a set of intrusive thoughts, and a twice-monthly delivery of panic attacks, something I never subscribed to. It's probably down to lack of sleep and hormones, but since Olivia was born, I've had some very dark moments. I've even wondered if, perhaps, it would be kinder to her if I wasn't there. But there's this primal stuff that kicks in, and you can't leave, because the physical, visceral bond latches on and sucks away at you for ever. At least this long weekend will give me a break. Scott can bond with her while I sleep and relax. I even bought a face cream to apply while I do it; there's a blast from the past.

I take my eyes off the road for a millisecond to glance behind at Olivia sleeping soundly in her car seat, then turn back to the road. Perhaps it's a good thing that I'll arrive on my own, don't want Fiona to think I'm a weak scaredy cat who can't drive myself. I also don't want her to think I'm ashamed or feel like Scott's plus one in this situation. I belong there as much as she does. I admit I feel guilty about the way Scott and I got together, I wouldn't have *chosen* to fall for a married man with children. But love isn't always about choice, is it?

I feel the wheels skid a little; the surface of the road is the consistency of a Slush Puppie and when this freezes over it'll be even more dangerous. The car radio is telling me the temperature will hit below zero in the next few hours. I have to get to the lodge as soon as I can, but I daren't put my foot down in case it causes the car to skid. I continue to glide slowly along the slushy road, and after a couple of miles the headlights catch the sign for Kynance Cove. My stomach jolts – I've dreaded this for weeks, and now it's real. There are no rule books for situations like this and I don't know how to feel. My conflicting emotions aren't just around me and Fiona, because she's created a weird triangle that I'm uneasy about. I reckon Fiona thinks there's still a chance for her and Scott, which totally freaks me out. She calls him late at night just to talk, and the words she wrote in her birthday card to him were all about precious memories and shared times together. It made me feel like she was still his wife and I was the outsider, but Scott says she just needs more time to accept it's over.

I know Fiona has her memories, but so do I, and just because they don't go as far back as hers, it doesn't make them any less precious or valid. I think now about that first day Scott walked into my classroom and introduced himself. I was preparing my first lesson and sitting at my desk alone. He stood in the doorway. 'Miss Watkins?'

I looked up and saw this handsome guy, with a devastating smile, and realising he was my new boss I stood up, knocking a ton of paperclips onto the floor. He was immediately down on his knees helping me to pick them up and lightening the tension by joking.

'I don't always get on my knees when I meet new teachers,' he said.

'And I don't usually throw paperclips at the feet of head-teachers,' I joked back. And in that moment, our hands accidentally touched, causing the air to crackle with electricity. I melt all over again just reliving the moment, and wish we could go back to that, to us being just us, a secret in our own little bubble, before the world broke in. Once we were 'outed,' everything changed, and it still makes me sad that those early days of getting to know each other were so brief, before being caught up in something shameful. I'll never forget how wonderful it was the first time we slept together. We were working together on a report and with him it was fun. I knew we were flirting, and our eyes kept meeting. I was on the other side of the desk, the proximity was unbearable. His aftershave, his smile, the gentle way he spoke. I wanted him, and when he stood up slowly from his chair and walked round the desk towards me, I knew what was going to happen, and I was helpless. He reached out his hand, and I stood up to meet him, our arms suddenly around each other, our lips together, tongues eagerly seeking out what we'd both been imagining for weeks. And it was wonderful, we made love like teenagers, like he was single and there was no wife and children because everything that had been stopping us was outside that office door. I was on cloud nine for days after, and it felt like a game, an innocent game where all we had to do to win was keep our delicious secret to ourselves. While we remained a secret, no one was getting hurt, we had nothing to feel guilty about, because we could stop this any time, right? So, there were little winks in the corridor, a conversation in front of students where he addressed me as 'Miss Watkins' and I responded with a nod and 'Mr Wilson'. Later we'd relish the late nights making love on his desk, in the car, on a mat in the school changing rooms when everyone had gone home. It was wild and wonderful and as long as it stayed between Scott and me we weren't hurting anyone, and no one could hurt us.

But it turned out someone could hurt us, and that *someone* had been watching, and waiting. To this day we don't know who it was, but some sick bastard had taken blurry photographs of the two of us together in Scott's office. Not only had that person posted them on the school's online message board, but they'd plastered the photos on an anonymous Facebook page, tagging the relevant parties. The faces in the photographs had been covered, but apart from tagging me, Scott and his wife, there were clues in the captions, which for anyone who hadn't already guessed, gave away *exactly* who we were. I was mortified, and scared too, because whoever had taken and posted these pictures was out to destroy us and clearly had no boundaries.

After that, everything escalated. The school was inundated with complaints from parents who'd seen the photos, and those that hadn't seen them were soon enlightened by their kids, or at the school gate. The school governors were called in, and Scott and I were interviewed and had to face several education panels and committees, which was mortifying. He was the headteacher and I was head of department, but we were treated like criminals, and I cried before, during and after all the meetings. We'd been stupid, thoughtless and reckless, which we acknowledged to each other, but we couldn't afford to lose our careers, so were forced to deny everything. Our strategy, thought up by Scott, was to blame 'deep fake', saying it was obviously photo-shopped. 'The quality is terrible,' Scott said, as he gazed at the photo of the two of us sprawled on his office desk. 'It's nothing but an elaborate student joke, or revenge for punishment one of us has meted out.'

It was hard to prove either way, and Scott played the calm, intelligent but outraged headteacher so well we kept our jobs, by the skin of our teeth. I know we were in the wrong and it's hard to justify, but ultimately we are both good teachers, we care about our students, and it wasn't like we'd put a kid's life in danger, or caused them any harm. Later, of course, we probably looked very guilty, but Covid came along, and with lockdown the situation between us became as blurry as the photos. Parents were so grateful to get their kids back to school at the end of it they didn't care who was teaching them or what they did after hours in the headteacher's office. But I'll never forgive whoever it was who posted those photos for what they put us through. And Fiona too – imagine how hurtful and humiliating that must have been, to be tagged in your husband's treachery? Then again, sometimes I wonder, had she *already* seen them? Was it *Fiona* who took and posted those pictures online? I couldn't imagine anyone being so crazy as to expose their marriage and risk their kids seeing stuff like that, but who knows? I guess what scares me more is, what if it *wasn't* Fiona? Who else could hate us both enough to be hanging around outside at night, their face against the window ready to take that photo? I shudder even now just thinking about it.

Three years later, we still don't know who it was. I asked Scott once if he thought it might be Fiona but he said she'd never do anything like that. 'She had no idea about us,' he'd said confidently. I wasn't so sure. Spouses have a way of knowing these things... the same way I'm feeling now that something isn't right with Scott. Is he doing to me what he did to Fiona?

But whoever posted the pictures, if they were trying to break us up, it didn't work because the silver lining to all this was that Fiona now knew the truth. Scott begged her not to tell the children (or the school governors for that matter) and to her credit, she was discreet. It wasn't in her interests for Scott to lose his job anyway, they had two children to support, who were just a few years away from university and they needed the money. Scott said he'd explained to her that he loved me, and just before lockdown, he left and came to live with me. But at first, it wasn't happily ever after for us; we were finally together, but Fiona constantly called his mobile and our landline and when he picked up she just sobbed down the line, saying terrible things about me, about us. This went on for a while, until she seemed to realise their marriage was finally over, the divorce came through and after about two years together, I discovered I was pregnant. Scott said she still seemed shocked and upset when she heard the news about the baby, and I reckon that given the chance she'd have Scott back tomorrow. I understand it must have been hard to let him go after all those years together, but still, I wish she'd move on.

Sam, their eldest, was fifteen when Scott left, and he'd started to hang around with a group of kids who were known to be involved in drugs. Meanwhile, Georgia's eating became a bit erratic, which was a worry. She was fourteen and like her brother had been embarrassed and teased about the photos of her dad and me all over social media, but we just kept reassuring them that they weren't real. I'm sure they knew the truth; if they *weren't* real why were their parents getting divorced? I remember one of the school governors asking Scott the same question, but he charmed them as he had everyone else, insisting that we were a couple now, but we hadn't been then. I think the reason we got away with it is because Scott's so good at his job, he has a reputation for turning failing schools around, and is seen as a bit of a genius. But as a mother myself now, I still feel guilty about the potential harm that something like that could have done to their kids.

Eventually Sam and Georgia accepted the situation, and

when Olivia was born almost a year ago, they seemed to fall in love with their little sister. To Scott's joy, they started coming to the house to visit more, often staying over or even babysitting so Scott and I could go out.

Scott says they see me as a big sister they can confide in, and they do. I know all about Georgia's school crushes and Sam's problems at school, which thankfully ended when he left to go to university a couple of months ago.

So recently, I've started to count my blessings. We've come through the tough times, but now I'm feeling more positive about the future. I have to for Olivia.

My phone pings, and thinking it might be Scott, I decide to pull over. I take out my phone. He's texted to say he's about to leave. 'See you both soon,' he says and I feel a frisson of excitement. I haven't felt that for a while, and it lifts me, makes me realise that there is light at the end of the tunnel, and Scott and I might just be able to make it. We have a beautiful little girl, a good life, so perhaps if I'm careful, we can have a good future too?

I'm about to put my phone away and drive off, when I see a notification from Facebook. Someone I don't know has tagged me in a post. Flooded with dread and panic, my mind is back there again, the terrible photograph, the humiliation, the feeling that everyone is talking about me. I put my phone away, and start the engine. Whoever tried to destroy us last time has surely moved on? It's not like they *know* anything, is it? But I know this will kill me until I read it, besides, it might be nothing, an old friend I can't remember, a page I followed a long time ago. Yes, that's all it is, something innocent. I force myself to click onto the website and scroll down. Despite telling myself it's nothing, my eyes alight on the post, and I know that's not true. This is horrific. I want to be sick, as my stomach lurches and I have to take long, deep breaths to try and avoid a panic attack.

Scott has also been tagged – along with most of the teaching staff.

> *A senior member of our teaching staff has a BIG secret, and they're hiding it from their husband, who is also a senior member of the teaching staff. LOL!*

THREE

FIONA

By the time I pulled up at the lodge it was dark. I was cold, my nerves were jangling, but more than anything I felt numb. I sat in the car for a while, just gathering myself together and eventually felt calm enough to step out, despite my hands shaking as I took the keys from the ignition. Climbing from the car, I worried my legs might give way beneath me, so I leaned against the car to pull myself together.

It was only then I really saw the lodge more closely. It was even more stunning than the photos Angela had sent to me. A contemporary wood and glass building emerged like a spaceship from the wintry dusk. It looked other-worldly, glowing bright, like a ghostly apparition amid the filthy sea and sky. I was finally here, on the edge of England, relieved to have reached my destination, but rising panic filled my chest as I thought about what might lie ahead for me.

Everything seemed so quiet and dead; naked, bony trees loitered on the surrounding hills like crows waiting for carrion. There was a sense of dread in the air, or was that just me projecting my own fear?

I gazed for a long time at the lodge. It was weirdly spectacular and ignoring the biting cold and vague whistle of the oncoming wind and weather in the distance, I took a photo. My hands were still shaking as I took out my phone, which had been pinging throughout the journey. I clicked on and immediately spotted Nick's name on the screen and wanted to throw up. Nick's texts had reached out like a grasping hand in the darkness, and my fear was blossoming into full blown terror. He'd sent *thirty-six* messages in the four hours it had taken me to get here. Without reading a single one, I pressed delete. If only it were that easy to get rid of Nick. I finally did what I should have done weeks before: I blocked his number and deleted him from my phone. It wouldn't be easy, but I had to put him to the back of my mind now, and prepare for what was ahead – seeing Scott, and coming face to face with *her* and their baby. I tried to blot out what was waiting for me by taking pictures, and snapped away listlessly.

I took a few more photos then pushed my phone, and thoughts of Nick, back into my handbag. Instinctively, I looked around in the dusk. I had that all too familiar feeling that someone was watching me. It was so very quiet apart from the distant wind. But I looked around hoping there was no one lurking behind a tree, or in the misty distance, but I couldn't be sure. I stood for a long time in the cold, just me and miles and miles of white under cold darkening skies, hoping, just hoping for some respite from the fear. I opened the car boot, took out my bags, put on my 'happy' face and marched along the crusty ground to the beckoning light of the lodge.

The huge oak door of the lodge suddenly opened before I'd even knocked, and Angela's head popped out. She turned from side to side, preoccupied as if she was looking for something in the near distance.

'Angela?'

'Oh, it's you?' She jumped a little, obviously hadn't seen me.

'Is everything okay?' I asked.

'Yes, I'm sorry, I was just looking to see if... anyone had arrived?'

She seemed a little out of sorts, and my stomach twisted slightly that she'd said this might be her last birthday. She wasn't her usual relaxed self and I wondered if this had something to do with her 'illness', if that's what it was.

'Am I the first one here?' I asked, as she ushered me inside.

'Yes, you are. I'm just worried about everyone driving here. I hadn't considered the weather, which was silly really, it's December, so there's every chance of bad weather and icy roads.'

I touched her arm. 'You are always worrying about us, aren't you?' I said with a smile.

'I'm a mother, it's what we do,' she replied, taking my hand. 'You're the same.'

I nodded, and breathing a sigh of relief, I hugged her. Angela always understood. I felt lucky to have her in my life, and grateful to be included in hers. Some mothers-in-law might have abandoned me after divorce, but not Angela.

Leaving my bags in the hall, I followed her into the sitting room. She seemed to have composed herself, and was back to the old Angela, chatty and bubbly in crazy earrings and bright pink wellington boots.

'We only just got here,' she announced, as I took in the room, which was bigger than my sitting room at home. It was huge, with high ceilings, and an interior wooded structure that made it feel warm and cosy.

'It's beautiful,' I murmured, suddenly realising how terrible it would be if this *was* her last birthday. I instinctively reached out and slipped my arm through hers.

'Happy birthday,' I murmured, leaning into her neck.

'It isn't until tomorrow, I'm hanging on to every last minute, so don't make me seventy-five yet,' she chuckled. 'God, I hate growing old.'

'I know how you feel. I'm forty-five and feel like I've already been consigned to the oldies bin, especially when the kids start on me.' I rolled my eyes. 'My outdated references and inability to understand social media amuses them both no end. Having teenagers is a joy, but also a constant reminder of my ageing mind and body.'

She laughed. 'Wait until you're seventy-four, then you'll *really* know how old feels.'

I realised this kind of conversation probably wasn't the best given this might be her last birthday, so I moved on.

'So, you brought the dog?' I asked.

'No,' she replied, puzzled.

'Oh, it's just that you said *we* only just arrived, I assumed you'd brought Poppy?'

'No, she's at the kennels. I thought it might be too much for her.'

I nodded. It was too much for *me* and I was a grown woman. To expect a small Shih Tzu to survive this weekend from hell really was too much of an ask.

'When I said "we" I was referring to someone else,' she said. 'I booked us a gourmet chef, she came with me.'

'How lovely, so we don't have to cook?'

'No, we don't. Jenna is taking care of everything, she was taught at the Cordon Bleu cookery school no less.'

'Wow!' I was impressed. If nothing else there'd be some nice food that weekend.

'She's doing the cooking, the washing up and any cleaning we need done, she's also done *all* the shopping,' Angela continued.

'She sounds wonderful, where is she?'

'Oh, she's not here at the moment. Given the weather warning, she's just popped out to buy a few extra things. The lady from the company who owns the lodges called me, she said there's snow on the way and we should make sure we have everything we need.'

'So there are more lodges around here?'

'Yes, only about four or five dotted around, but not close enough to affect us, we don't want any stags or hens making a racket after midnight.'

'I can't imagine it would be that kind of place.'

'You'd be surprised, we have a hot tub on the decking with flashing lights,' she said with a wink.

'Angela Wilson, you *are* planning a wild birthday weekend, aren't you?' I teased. In light of what she'd said about it possibly being her last, I was following her lead and keeping up the pretence that this was fun, there was nothing to be sad about.

She giggled. 'Well, I hear young people like the hot tubs, I won't be getting in, that's for sure.'

I smiled. 'Nor me.' The very idea of climbing into a hot tub with my ex and his new wife horrified me, how weird would that be? But the kids would enjoy it.

I was relieved that Angela had organised for someone to cook for us. I didn't fancy the prospect of Danni and I being trapped in the kitchen together playing happy wives. I still found it hard to even think about her, let alone wonder what her culinary talents might be, but hopefully now we had a cook, the kitchen *wouldn't* be territory for two wives to fight over.

'Come on, I'll show you around,' Angela said, leading me through the main room towards the bedrooms. They were all along a short hallway, except the one she'd chosen, which was up a short flight of stairs. 'Mine is up there, it has an en suite, overlooks the sea. I can't wait to see the view properly in the morning when it's lighter.' She'd gone from distracted to suddenly quite childlike in her excitement.

She opened the door on another bedroom, and we both gazed inside. 'Lovely, isn't it?' To my joy, the spacious double room had a huge king-size bed and floor-to-ceiling glass windows.

'Yes, it's lovely, thank you, I love it.' I stepped in, and she put her hand on my arm.

'Oh... this isn't *your* room, I thought this was probably more of a family room?' she added awkwardly.

This hit me hard in the chest, like a physical blow on realising that I'd been demoted. 'But if you'd *like* it, I'm sure we could...?' It was clearly as painful for her to say as it was for me to hear.

'Oh no, it's fine, let Scott and... have it,' I replied, unable to say her name. I was so embarrassed by my stupid assumption that as the single woman I would have the master bedroom. As welcomed as I was by Angela, the fact remained I was no longer the wife, I'd been usurped and had to step down – in every way. Smiling now, Angela manoeuvred me across the hallway to choose one of the three smaller rooms.

Each one was lovely, but whoever stayed in these rooms was definitely further down the food chain and would have to share a bathroom. Of all the horrible things I'd considered, and tried to prepare myself for that weekend, the hierarchy of rooms wasn't one of them.

'I thought this might be nice for you?' Angela suggested, opening the door on a very pink room that was just one unicorn away from being an eight-year-old girl's dream hideaway.

'It's perfect,' I said, feeling empty inside, as she left me with the starry pink duvet, surrounded by fairy lights wondering how the hell I got there. This wasn't part of my plan. I'd had my future mapped out, and working in HR, I knew about pensions and had planned an early retirement. Scott and I were going to stop working at fifty and travel the world. How stupid was I to think that just because I'd planned it that would happen? We think we're in control of our lives, but we aren't, because something random can throw it all into the air and suddenly we're somewhere we never thought we'd be. Through no fault of my own, my ex-husband's mid-life lust had led me to this fairy lit room with a wall of anatomically incorrect prints of rainbow-coloured ponies. It wasn't on my bucket list, but the humiliation had to be endured in order that my husband and his new wife could enjoy 'the family room', with their baby.

I was surprised Angela hadn't considered the inequity involved in this mash-up of family past and present. She was usually so thoughtful, so in tune with people's feelings, and this was a stark and hurtful reminder of my place in the pecking order. I was sure my ex-mother-in-law's lack of tact was more likely due to age, or illness, than using it to put me in my place. The term 'the family room' was a smack in the face though, and I questioned whether she was as kind and thoughtful as I'd always thought her to be.

But in truth, I was finding it hard to be rational. Angela wouldn't hurt me deliberately, or pit us against each other. But as the minutes wore on, the seed of resentment towards Danni and Scott was growing like a cancer.

I gazed up at the fluorescent pink stars entwined with pastel rainbows on the ceiling and told myself I was being selfish. This wasn't about me, it was Angela's birthday and she'd been kind enough to include me. So, I stopped feeling sorry for myself, grabbed my bags from the hall and started unpacking.

I'd made Angela a birthday cake. I'd always enjoyed making the family cakes for special occasions and had continued to make Angela's for three years since Scott walked out. She loved my chocolate birthday cake. I always put a little coffee liqueur, her favourite, in the sponge and the icing. 'Fiona, it wouldn't be a birthday without your cake,' she always said.

Once I'd unpacked, I put the cake in its Tupperware box in a kitchen cupboard with the seventy-five birthday candles, hoping to keep it from Angela as a surprise. Returning to her in the sitting room, I found her in repose. She didn't seem to be aware of my presence. I walked closer to her and she remained still, the look on her face a strange mix of fear and melancholy. Though I might have been projecting, those were the exact feelings running through me too. I was dreading seeing Scott with *her*, and trying not to think about the alternative: that without Danni, we'd be just on a family holiday. Like old times, it would be me, Scott, the kids and Angela, nothing would have changed. How I longed for that again and wished I could just rewind everything to a time Danni wasn't there.

I walked over to the huge glass window and looked out. To the left was a huge decked area with the hot tub. It seemed lit from within, and I saw steam rising. 'Is it permanently on?' I asked, turning to Angela, who looked at me vacantly.

'The hot tub – it's lit and there's steam coming from it.'

Angela suddenly seemed to realise I was there, and picked up a large earthenware mug of coffee, and pointed to the one waiting for me on the coffee table.

'Yes, yes, they keep them maintained, clean them every day and they stay hot and ready for action,' she joked, slipping back into her usual self.

'Like me then?' I said, with a chuckle. This made her laugh, and she got up and went into the kitchen while I continued to stare through the window. The sleet had turned to snow, and it wasn't easy to see clearly, but while I watched the steam swirling from the tub, I thought I saw something else. I stared and stared, trying to make out what I'd seen; something or someone was on the decking. Then I saw it – a face in the shadows, lit from the bubbling water. My fingertips tingled with fear as the apparition seemed to stare back, then bent down, his face almost touching the water. I could hear myself whimper as I gasped in horror, reaching for the chair to steady myself. Then he slowly stood up and stepped back, his face disappearing into the darkness, and then he was gone.

'You look pale,' Angela was saying as she returned to the

room, brandishing a bottle of brandy, and splashing it into both our coffees.

I thanked her, and tried to smile as I lifted the mug, and told myself it was just my imagination. But I couldn't help but feel he was out there watching me, just waiting.

'So tell me what's been happening with you,' she asked, brightly, while I sipped on my hot, brandy-laced coffee, welcoming the heat, and hoping for oblivion.

I tried to relax, and folded my legs under me, both hands around my mug, but I felt uneasy, and wished I had something to defend myself with.

'I'm good, a little nervous about seeing Scott... and Danni,' I confessed.

'Oh, I'm sure it will all be fine.'

I wasn't convinced. I was desperately hoping they wouldn't arrive for a while. I needed time to calm down, to appear composed and relaxed and like I belonged. For different reasons, I also wanted them both to see how my relationship with Angela was still strong in spite of everything. I'd lost my kids to them every other weekend, and also lost a little of my mother-in-law along the way too. When a marriage ends, more than two people get their hearts broken.

Asking me to meet Danni was like asking an arachnophobe to meet a spider. I'd tried to work on myself, become the best me I could be, I'd even tried to *forgive* – but that was never going to happen. So I tried a different approach, to rebuild my confidence, repair my destroyed self-esteem and take my revenge cold. I was permanently short of money after the divorce, as everything was cleaved down the middle and we both ended up with half of what we had. But knowing I was coming face to face with my nemesis, I needed backup. I'd always tried to dress well, even though I had very little money now. I didn't want Danni seeing my tatty old nightie and a hundred-year-old dressing gown. So before the trip I spent several nights on the internet trying to find some nice, but inexpensive stuff to wear while away. I didn't want Danni showing me up with her younger, thinner body and better wardrobe, so managed to find a rip-off of The White Company loungewear. I needed the boost, I'd been wearing the shade of wronged-wife-bitterness for too long, I was ready for something more positive. So that weekend I would swathe my pain and rage in muted shades of grey. Exuding love, light and acceptance in winter white wool lounge pants paired with a dove-grey fluffy hoodie, I planned to slay – as Georgia would say.

'What time are Sam and Georgia due to get here?' Angela asked, her voice pulling me back into the room.

I rolled my eyes. 'God knows, I'm just glad they're travelling down together. I'm sure their journey will be eventful, not necessarily in a good way.'

'Is Sam driving?'

'Oh God yes. Georgia was dying to drive, but no way was I going to let that happen.'

Angela chuckled. 'I remember when Scott first passed his test, he was only seventeen and wanted to drive everywhere. He was suddenly so helpful,' she said with a smile, 'offered to give me lifts everywhere. "I'll collect you, Mum," he said. I'd only gone to the corner shop.'

We both giggled at this. The brandy had been so welcome, and it seemed to have soothed both of us.

'I hope the kids are okay,' she murmured, then looked at her watch.

'They'll be fine,' I said, immediately regretting my rather flippant comment about their journey being eventful.

'Hope Scott and Danni are okay, they haven't called.' She turned to look at me. '*You* always called if you and Scott were delayed.'

I didn't respond to this. There wasn't much I could say, but instead I offered to make more coffee and stood up to take our cups into the kitchen. It was then that I saw it: a tiny keychain in the shape of a cricket bat. It was lying on the floor, close to the sofa where I was sitting. I thought my heart would stop beating there and then. I knew that keychain, it was me who'd bought it for him in the summer, when he'd taken me to a cricket match. *Nick.*

'The kids are here,' Angela said, getting up, delighted at their arrival. I'd been so looking forward to seeing them, but suddenly a black cloud hung over me, choking and heavy like smoke. I stood up to greet my kids, but before going to the door, glanced again at the hot tub, bubbling away and exuding an eerie light in the darkness. No one was there, but I was now certain he'd been here...

FOUR

DANNI

It's almost dark when I arrive at the lodge. I pull up where the satnav tells me, unaware if I'm at the right address or not. It's freezing and snowing and I'm so worried about the message on Facebook, I can't think straight. I check the post again, and despite others being tagged, I *know* it's about me. Why this? Why now? I quickly click onto the school forum. Last time the incriminating photos were on there too. I scroll down to see the comments from parents. There are all the usual questions regarding exams and school events, until I see it, and my blood turns cold.

> *A senior member of our teaching staff has a BIG secret, and they're hiding it from their husband, who is also a senior member of the teaching staff. LOL!*

Exactly the same message has been posted here as on Facebook. It's all starting again. Whoever tried to cause trouble for us last time is back, and I'm terrified. I immediately call Charlotte, a friend who works in the school office. She should be able to delete the comment, as she has access. She isn't picking up, so I leave her a message.

I have to hope Scott hasn't seen it, and push it from my mind. I'll talk to him when I absolutely have to, when the time's right.

I must put on a smile and lie to myself and everyone else for now. I climb from the car and after taking Olivia from her seat as gently as possible so she doesn't wake, I walk towards the lodge on heavy feet. Angela opens the door and looks beyond me, 'Hello, Danni, where's Scott... is he with you?'

'No, he had to work, so I came down on my own with Olivia. He'll be here later.'

'Oh.' I wish she'd hide her obvious disappointment.

'Is everyone else here?' I ask.

'The kids are here, and Fiona,' she replies, and my heart sinks as she closes the door behind me. I take a deep breath before walking into the hallway, where Angela immediately takes Olivia from me. She holds her tightly and grabs my hand, guiding me into the room. My mouth suddenly feels dry with nerves, and I wonder if Fiona has seen the message on Facebook. I didn't check to see if she was tagged, but if she knows anyone who was, then she'll see it. Then my stomach drops again. What if they've posted the name of the teacher in the past few seconds since I last checked?

But before I can even process this thought, I'm suddenly face to face with the woman I replaced. There she is, sitting upright like a queen, all dressed up in The White Company dove-grey loungewear, sipping coffee and smiling benignly.

'Hi, Fiona.' I try to be polite, I'm not going to play games, even if she is. I'm trying not to think about how much she's paid for the loungewear ensemble, it must have cost a fortune. I can't help but feel a little resentful as only last week she demanded extra money from Scott for Sam's rent at university.

'Hey, Danni,' she replies, apparently unable to make herself smile.

'Good journey?' she asks. I realise it's hard for both of us, and I try to warm to her, but don't know whether to feel angry or guilty as she looks back at her phone. She hasn't even acknowledged Olivia in her blush-pink snowsuit being fussed over by Angela. I'd hoped my marital and mother status would give me protection, but her coldness has made me shrink into myself. This is a nest Angela made, and where Fiona has resided far longer than I have.

'Bit icy on the road,' I reply, but she doesn't look up. I'm addressing the top of her head, which makes me feel foolish, like I'm begging her to see me. Bright blonde and caramel gold stripes emanate from her parting. It looks good, she's probably had her hair done specially for this weekend. I haven't had the chance, haven't been to a hairdresser in months, and feel dowdy and plain in her presence. I try to reassure myself by remembering Scott's reply when I asked him if he still felt anything for Fiona. 'She's the past, you're the future. I don't even *see* her, Danni.' He says this a lot when he's trying to reassure me about their relationship. I may come over as confident, sure of myself with the opposite sex, but I'm not. I've been hurt and cheated on so many times, my mother says I have a knack for picking the wrong man and it's messed with my head. That's why I was drawn to Scott, ironically, because he was married with children. I knew he'd be responsible, and reliable. He's intelligent and kind and I've never been with anyone like him before, but I do hate the baggage that comes with him. I find it hard when he disappears for hours on end to spend time with Fiona and the kids, when he could be with Olivia and me. And it hurts when Fiona phones him and they talk for ages about the past, when the kids were little and they went on family holidays. I find it upsetting to hear him start sentences with lines like, 'Do you remember that Christmas when...' I try not to think about their past together. I try not to think about her at all. I find it easier to pretend she doesn't exist, but it's hard because she still figures in my husband's life through the kids, and as close as I get to Sam and Georgia, I'll always be excluded from that family unit. A few weeks ago, they took Georgia to open days at different universities she's applying for, and each time he came home late, once at midnight, with alcohol on his breath.

I don't understand it, but Fiona still has this weird hold, which I guess all ex-wives with kids do. But even now Scott and I are married she likes to pretend they're still a family unit, and I'm the odd one out. I'm excluded from the kids' birthdays or any kind of school or university event, which cuts like a knife. I'd love to have the chance to support Sam and Georgia, they're Olivia's half-siblings and given the opportunity I could be a good stepmother. But because of Fiona's refusal to accept me, there's a whole part of Sam's, Georgia's – and Scott's – lives, that Olivia and I will never be part of. It's one of the main things Scott and I disagree on, but I guess it's the price I paid for marrying a man who's been married before.

I'm now standing in the middle of the room like a spare part while my husband's ex continues to sip her coffee and gaze at her phone. Is she feeling awkward, or is she *deliberately* ignoring me? I don't know what to say or do, I feel scruffy after the journey, with no make-up on and my hair in need of a wash. I'd been up most of the night with Olivia and hadn't had chance to prepare myself physically or mentally for this encounter. My plan had been to arrive early having had a nap on the journey and the chance to put some make-up on in the car, but at the last minute Scott was delayed at work. Having to drive here alone had thrown me into a tailspin, and I'm now feeling abandoned by him. It crosses my mind that he might have deliberately let me come here alone, and be thrown to the wolf in The White Company loungewear...

Angela's now relieving Olivia of her padded snowsuit, and

I'm starting to sweat in my big jacket and scarf as I stand near the blazing open fire. Fiona's already won this fight by arriving earlier than me, and making herself at home with Angela. I feel anxiety creep through my chest, and desperately trying to ground myself, say, 'So, Sam and Georgie are here then?'

'Sam and *Georgia* are here, yes,' she replies slowly, correcting her daughter's name. Realising she doesn't approve, I make a mental note to continue to call my stepdaughter Georgie. Fiona doesn't control *everything*, as much as she'd love to.

'Where are they?' I look around, like they might pop up from behind the sofa, as she stares at me with barely concealed loathing.

'They arrived about ten minutes ago, they're in their rooms, emergency TikToking probably,' she murmurs, going back to her phone.

I smile at this. I think she might have made a joke. Or not? But I push on regardless.

'Oh great, I'll knock and say hello, are their rooms down here?' I move to go towards a little hallway off the sitting room which I imagine is where the bedrooms are.

'Oh, don't disturb them, they've had a long drive,' she says, like I'm a tiresome six-year-old bothering the older kids.

'I'll just...' I walk towards the doors, about to challenge this, when Angela steps in.

'Danni, I think it might be better if you give them a little breather, they're probably both having a nap after the drive. I'll keep an eye on Olivia while you grab your stuff from the car before that weather comes in from the sea.'

This stings me slightly; perhaps Angela *does* take sides after all? By keeping me away from my stepkids, she's obviously Team Fiona.

'Okay, I'll just try Scott first, see where he is,' I say, taking out my phone to call him. Scott will be driving, and hates using the phone in his car, but I'm dying here and he's all I have. I stand for a few seconds while his voicemail clicks in, as I knew it would. His voice usually reassures me, but instead it just makes me feel even more lonely.

'He must be driving,' I mutter, putting my phone in my jacket pocket. 'I'll grab my bags then and start unpacking,' I say, taking on Angela's instructions that she'd dressed up as a suggestion. Is she different with me, or am I simply seeing her differently because Fiona's here? I walk to the door reminding myself it's her birthday, she might be ill and I need to stop imagining that everyone hates me.

'That's yours and Scott's room.' Angela smiles and gesticulates with one hand while bouncing Olivia on her knee.

I put my thumb up to acknowledge this, then head out through the door to heave my bags and extensive baby kit from the car, with, I note, no offer of help from Fiona. Walking back in with the first load of stuff, I have to pass through the sitting room to the bedroom, and neither woman looks up. Fiona's still scrolling on her phone, while Angela sits on the floor with Olivia who she's now placed on a rug.

The bedroom is gorgeous, and from the moment I walk in my heart lifts. There is a spectacular floor-to-ceiling window, which I peer through, but as it's dark, all I can see is a greyish landscape of snow. I can't wait to see it tomorrow when it's light.

Once I've finished unpacking, I remember Angela's birthday cake in the carrier bag on the bed. One of the first times Scott took me to meet his mum was on her birthday, so I'd made a lemon and elderflower cake, and she loved it so much I've made her cake in the two years since then.

'My birthday isn't the same without Danni's delicious cake,' she always says. That means a lot. It's become a new family tradition, something I'm keen to establish. I want to belong, I hate feeling like the outsider. It's not easy going into a family as

I have, everything feels second-hand, like I've inherited the marriage, the kids, the family from someone else. I sometimes feel like I'm being punished for falling in love, and trust me I self-flagellate about that often enough. So to have a connection with Scott's mum is important to me, and my annual cake is a symbol of that – it's from me to her, and no one else from the past is involved.

I open the carrier bag and lift out the box with the cake in. Opening the box, I'm pleased at the result of all my hard work. It's the usual elderflower and lemon, Angela's favourite, but along with the lemon frosting. I spent ages making little sugar lemons which I arranged on top around the intricate icing that I did in between Olivia's naps, it took me ages. Though I say it myself, it looks professional, and I can't wait to produce it tomorrow evening with all the candles lit. It will be quite a moment. I need to find somewhere cool to hide it as I want it to be a surprise, so when I leave the bedroom, I go into the kitchen with it, and place it on a high shelf in the larder.

I'm suddenly aware of movement and laughter in the sitting room, and on entering I'm surprised to see that Scott's arrived.

He's beaming from ear to ear, and laughing loudly at something Angela just said, and I'm guessing this means he hasn't seen the message on Facebook about the senior member of staff's BIG secret. In the meantime, I've texted Charlotte asking her again to delete it, as she may not get around to listening to the voicemail I left. She's always been really supportive in the past, she was the one who eventually removed the original photos when they were first posted. We've become good friends since then, she's a good listener, and very discreet. I lived in London for years, and it's taken me time to make friends in Worcestershire where I moved to take the Head of Department job. I guess that's why I fell so easily into my friendship with Jenna, but we got too close too soon and I really didn't know her. But Charlotte's been a godsend, a true friend who I can talk to, we tell each other everything, and now I need her more than ever. I'm comforted in the knowledge that the minute she gets my messages she'll be straight onto it, I just need to hold my nerve and try not to get too stressed. This weekend will be difficult enough without the added threat of being exposed all over again.

'You were only a few minutes behind me,' I say quietly. 'You weren't working *that* late, we could have driven down together after all.'

Taking his attention from Angela and Fiona, he looks at me, his smile fading. 'I *was* working late, but managed to get everything done.' He walks towards me, brushing my cheek with his face like I'm merely an acquaintance. '*And* I drive a lot faster than you, even in bad weather.' Am I imagining it, or does he seem flustered?

'Scott, you should be careful on these icy roads. You always drive too fast,' Fiona teases, and my hackles rise, seeing her sudden interest in what's going on. It seems the phone she was so fixated on just seconds ago has been abandoned.

'*Scott!*' she says, her voice raised. 'You always *do* that, you're so naughty!' She's laughing, Angela is shaking her head, and I try and work out what they're talking about so I can join in. But no one lets me in, the word 'always' is implicit of their shared history and I immediately feel alienated. Alone.

Scott's placed his snow-covered jacket on one of the sofas, that must be what Fiona's referring to – it's the kind of thing that obviously irritates her as much as it does me. I'm about to add to the affectionate chorus of dissent and tell him to move it because it's making the sofa wet. But before I can say anything Angela picks it up and walks to the front porch to shake it. He doesn't even seem to notice, I guess it's just expected. Sometimes I think she doesn't realise he's a fully grown man. She's always done everything for him, she absolutely dotes on him, and for Angela her only child can do no wrong.

'Aren't you warm?' Fiona suddenly asks me, I'm not quite sure what she means and must look confused.

'You still have your jacket on, are you cold?'

'Yes, er yes,' I lie, pulling it around me as she gets up to stoke the fire and make the place even warmer. I'm sure she's done that deliberately. It's like the bloody Sahara in here, but I won't let her see my discomfort, besides, my jacket is my emotional comfort blanket. I feel raw and exposed in this beautiful, lofty living room in the company of my husband and his former wife. Fiona and Scott have known each other such a long time, I feel excluded. I'm surprised how easy they are with each other, almost affectionate, it makes me uncomfortable.

They seem to know what the other is thinking, there's this easy camaraderie that surprises me.

'Hey, how was your journey?' I ask, telling myself to stop being petty.

'Good, good. And how are you?' He adds in a soft, loving way, and I'm about to respond when I realise he's not talking to me. He's now getting down on the floor addressing Olivia, who's gurgling and kicking out her legs.

'She's good, she slept all the way here,' I announce.

He looks up, horror on his face. 'Which means she'll be awake all night,' he murmurs, gazing back down at her. I can't seem to do anything right these days as far as my husband's concerned, so looks like it will be my fault if she keeps us awake tonight.

'Sorry, I was too busy driving to entertain her and keep her awake.' I say this good-naturedly, but there's a prickle of sarcasm.

I feel like Fiona is observing me, *us*, and I don't want her to think we're having problems, so bend down to get closer to him. Smiling at Olivia, I put my hand on his back, and brush a kiss on the side of his cheek, hoping he'll respond. I want him to turn around, kiss me back, but he won't, probably because he's concerned about Fiona's feelings. He walks on eggshells to make sure she doesn't feel hurt. But what about me? He's barely acknowledged me, and done nothing to include me or make me feel welcome in this tight little group. And now he's pulling away from me to pick Olivia up, abandoning me half bent over the tableau of father and daughter like an unwanted gate crasher. I see the fleeting smugness on Fiona's face and it kills me.

'The kids have arrived,' she remarks, a reminder to Scott that Olivia isn't his *only* child.

'Oh great. Are they okay?'

'I think so, you know what they're like, they arrived just after me, barely spoke.'

'I'll go and see them,' he says, pushing Olivia at me.

'No don't,' I say, 'they need a rest.'

'What?' He turns to look at me, like I've just said something disgusting.

'Fiona said...' I point vaguely at her, but she doesn't rescue me, neither does Angela, who's now returned from outside with his jacket.

'Go ahead, they'll be pleased to see you,' Fiona says to him, while looking directly at me. 'Their rooms are just there.' Apparently, the instruction not to disturb the kids was meant only for me.

He walks towards the hallway.

'I'm sure you'll get a better reception, they certainly didn't want to join Grandma and me for Irish coffee and idle chat,' Fiona adds lightly.

'Can't say I blame them,' he jokes. I wait for her to react, and to my surprise she hurls a fur throw at him.

'Cheeky sod, me and your mum are great company,' she chuckles. 'And we offered them coffee with whisky in, I don't recall you ever turning that down.'

'Or you for that matter,' he says with what looks like an

indulgent smile, as he places Olivia back on the rug and moves back into the room, picking up a cushion from a sofa and throwing it right at Fiona.

'Bastard!' she hisses, ducking dramatically as they both giggle.

I don't even smile, just stare ahead, like I haven't noticed. I hope he's picked up on my frostiness and that's the end of their playful banter, but then Fiona hurls the cushion back, and they're both now flinging mock insults at each other. I'm alone again in the middle of something I'm not part of, and the bloody cushion is going backwards and forwards while I'm standing there like a fool.

'Mind the baby with that,' I say to no one in particular.

'It was nowhere near *the baby*,' she murmurs, 'but you're right, Danni, best to keep an eye because his aim has always been shit.' She's addressing him, like I'm not there. Standing up, he walks towards her, and she curls up in a ball playfully, her arms out defensively. 'I didn't mean it, don't, Scott, you'll ruin my hair.'

Don't *what*? What on *earth* is she expecting him to *do* to her? I'm horrified, I thought they hated each other. If this is what they're like in front of me, what are they like when they're alone?

I'm disturbed. This isn't at all what I'd expected from two people who've just come through a sometimes-bitter divorce. He's told me she can be unforgiving, that their marriage was tired, that they were bored and he didn't love her anymore – it must be true or why did he pursue me?

'I think Angela's going outside again with your jacket, Scott?' I say, watching his mother opening the door. I'm concerned about Angela, but equally I'm hoping to stop this childish display between them. They remind me of sixth formers messing about in class.

'Angela?' Fiona calls, her demeanour changing in an instant, the smile slipping from her face.

'Scott?' She turns to him, concerned, clearly indicating that she'd like him to go outside and see if Angela's okay.

But he isn't moving, he's holding Olivia and looking at Fiona like she's mad. 'I'm sure she's fine,' he replies, turning back to our daughter.

'I'll go,' I say, and march across the room to the front door. Angela is now standing in the porch, still clutching Scott's coat, and I brush my palm across it, surprised at just how wet and snowy it still is. Why is it so wet? Scott only got out of the car and walked a few metres to the door, he'd have to be out a lot longer to cover it in all that snow and make it so damp.

'Is everything okay?' I ask her.

'Yes, yes of course.' She seems overwhelmed, and I guide her back into the lodge. I recall the same confusion in my own mother's eyes, and it crosses my mind that whatever prompted this gathering might have little to do with my mother-in-law's birthday, but something to do with mental decline.

'Everything's fine.' She suddenly seems to compose herself, and we walk back into the lodge together. 'I've just realised I haven't told you and Scott about the Cordon Bleu chef we have for the weekend.'

'Oh wow. Lovely,' I reply, walking back into the warmth of the lodge, relieved I don't have to share a kitchen or have cooking competitions with Fiona. I'd lose.

'Yes, she's so talented, and was keen to come along. She's doing it for a fraction of the price she'd usually charge.'

'Is she in the kitchen?' I ask, excited to meet her.

'No, she's just outside, unloading the car. She's been to the lodge shop, it's about ten minutes away, but it's the nearest place to buy anything, she said she needed herbs.'

As I walk back into the room, I turn to see Angela now fussing at the door.

'Here she is!' she announces as her Cordon Bleu chef struggles to get in through the door. She's carrying a crate of wine, but I can't see any herbs. Her hair's plastered down, she's obviously been caught in the snow.

'Goodness, you really got caught in it, didn't you? Did you walk all the way?' Fiona asks.

She looks up. 'No... I drove.'

She's looking directly at me, thick, black eyeliner, a slash of red lipstick, the familiar twisted smile.

My eyes slide over to Scott, who from the colour of his face has also realised who she is.

I don't say anything else, and neither does he, but my heart's beating, and I want to leave. She looks me up and down, staring at my jacket that I haven't yet had a chance to take off. She touches the front of her bright yellow jacket, which I realise is identical to mine. The thin red lips widen. 'Snap,' she says.

I discreetly turn to Scott, who can't look at me. He just gazes ahead, and then I realise – he *knew* she was coming.

FIVE

FIONA

What the hell? Danni waltzed in, dumped the baby on Angela expecting her to immediately take over the childcare, and barely acknowledged me. The baby was wearing a designer snowsuit that must have cost a fortune, and Danni was looking pretty pampered too. Her short, choppy blonde hair looked achingly cool, and she had that no make-up look, no one has skin that good. She was certainly living her best life since she married my husband, but I have to say I felt a bit sorry for her when she brought out that blingy pink phone and tried to call him. Scott's voicemail was something I'd become accustomed to during the last few months of our marriage, when he couldn't answer because he was with *her*.

She was so uptight and seemed really on edge even after handing the baby to Angela. I found it a little odd the way she stood in the middle of the room staring at me while I checked my phone. I was making sure I'd deleted all Nick's emails, I didn't want any distractions. But still she stood there staring, like she was expecting me to say something. I had nothing to say to Danni Watkins; to me she would *never* be Danni *Wilson*.

What did she want from me? Hadn't she already taken everything, including my kids?

I kept thinking about the keychain, imagining him going through the lodge, touching everything, sitting on the beds in our absence like a sinister Goldilocks. When Scott arrived I was relieved. Call me sexist, but given my fears, I felt happier knowing we had a six-foot man in the house. I tried desperately to appear happy, like my usual self, teasing Scott, just trying to shake off all the fear, but Danni was throwing daggers at me. And when we threw a very soft, very light cushion at each other, she virtually accused us of hurling it at baby Olivia.

I did feel a twinge when Scott and I were laughing at nothing and she looked on, helpless and excluded, but it was nothing compared to what they did to me on his office desk. I'd expected the two of them to be more affectionate, if only for Angela's benefit. After all they had to prove their love was worth breaking up a family for. But there did seem to be some tension coming from Scott, because when she reached out to touch his back, I swear he pulled away.

And as if that wasn't intriguing enough, I couldn't believe Danni's face when Jenna, the Cordon Bleu chef turned up. In the exact same jacket as her. What was that about? I was tempted to say something like, 'Oops, who didn't get the memo?' to try and make light of it, but something about the look on Danni's face, stopped me. Why was Danni so obviously upset when she saw Jenna? Danni's eyes were sliding over to Scott's, and he looked really uncomfortable, and the two women stared at each other too long, until Jenna said something jokey about them wearing an identical jacket. But Danni didn't laugh. I was beginning to think the dreaded long weekend might not be so bad after all.

It wasn't just the bright yellow jackets that were identical. Jenna also had very short, bleached-blonde hair, just like Danni's, but her make-up was quite heavy, thin red lips and loads of hard eyeliner. She seemed confident, unafraid to stare down Danni, and then she asked Scott to help her carry the wine she'd bought. Still no sign of the herbs she'd gone for though, which didn't surprise me. It was the middle of winter in the back of beyond, I doubted the little local shop even stocked herbs. I was glad to see the wine though, I reckoned I'd need it.

As soon as everyone else had gone to unpack and Jenna headed for the kitchen to start dinner, I tried to find out more about Jenna to see if Angela could shed any light on Danni's weird reaction to her.

'That's such a coincidence that Jenna and Danni have the same yellow jacket,' I said. 'Danni looked so surprised.' This was an understatement, both Danni and Scott looked horrified.

'Oh, the jacket? Fashion these days is all the same, isn't it? Homogenised. Young people all want "a look". What happened to being unique, individual?' She sighed at this. Angela had seemed so preoccupied I wasn't even sure she'd noticed the wardrobe clash.

'Did you book Jenna through a company?'

She shook her head. 'No, she works at the café where Margaret and I have lunch sometimes. It's very nice, lovely salads and sandwiches, Jenna's worked there for a few months now, she's very sweet.'

'Wow. She's wasted working in a café with Cordon Bleu training,' I remarked.

'Well, as I understand it, she *did* train in Paris, but ran out of money so had to give it up and come home.'

'That's a shame,' I replied. I was about to push on and try to find out if Angela had any more information that would explain Danni's reaction, but just then, Georgia emerged from her bedroom.

'Hi, sweetie, did you manage to take a nap?' I asked. She shook her head glumly and slumped down on the sofa next to Angela, who put her arm around her.

'It's a long old drive, isn't it, love? I feel bad making you all undertake such a journey, but I was desperate to come back here while I still can.'

Angela didn't offer any more clues, but Georgia and I caught each other's eye. She was as concerned as I was about her grandma. I think we were both afraid to actually ask her *why* she'd insisted on this gathering and why, at seventy-five, this might be her last birthday.

'Jenna's in the kitchen if you want to go and say hello, Georgia, she says you know each other,' Angela added.

'You *know* Jenna the cook?' Now I was really confused.

Georgia sat up. 'Yeah, she was a lab assistant at our school, she isn't there anymore.'

So *that* explained how Danni knew her. The kids had attended the same school where Scott was headteacher. In fact, the kids were already there when he got the job and Scott had told the school about them being there before he even applied. But they'd already decided Scott was the man for the job, he was considered to be a brilliant headteacher. So as both kids were almost finished at school, this was a short-term issue, and they didn't object.

'So she went from lab assistant to chef?' I mused. 'That's quite a career change.'

'Yeah, I guess so.' Georgia looked at me and seeing the expectant look on my face added, 'I don't *know* her, I just know who she is. She always seemed nice enough.' She shrugged.

'I tell you what, why don't you pop into the kitchen and say hi, perhaps she could do with some help?' Angela suggested.

I waited for Georgia's reaction to this with a secret smile, wondering which of her portfolio of excuses she'd use to get out of helping. My daughter was no one's helper, especially in the kitchen, I had to threaten her with phone confiscation just for her to unload the dishwasher. But before I could laugh at the prospect of her in washing-up gloves, she stood up enthusiastically, 'Yeah, okay.'

'Wow! I've never seen *that* before,' I remarked as she left the room.

'I think they'll get along,' Angela said, then changing the subject asked, 'By the way, how are things with that man of yours?'

She asked so bluntly this felt like a punch in the face. I'd almost forgotten I'd told her, but when I'd first met Nick a few months before, I'd been happy, and wanted Angela's take on it, her approval too. But now I just wanted to forget him. 'Oh it was nothing, ended before it began,' I lied, remembering the keychain again and feeling nauseous. I imagined him slowly sliding his hand along the sofa, caressing the cushions. I sat forward, feeling suddenly very uncomfortable. 'Angela, you know when you arrived this afternoon, was there anyone here?'

She thought a moment. 'No, why?'

'Nothing, I just wondered if anyone from the company came to greet you and let you in?'

'No, they leave a key in a metal box, you just need the four-digit code and you take the key and let yourself in.'

'Oh, that's good.' I heard my voice breaking slightly at this. 'What's the code?'

'It's 1234,' she said with a little chuckle. 'I don't know how they don't get burgled. Mind you, we're in remote Cornwall, I imagine you could leave all your doors open here and no one would bother you.'

I nodded uncertainly. I wasn't so sure, and thought back to that first month with Nick, when I'd been so happy, but so naïve about relationships. After being married for such a long time it was all so new to me and I thought this was what I'd been looking for. It started out as fun, a lovely, flirtatious friendship, followed by a few nights in hotels, or at mine when the kids weren't around. But it didn't develop into anything deeper, and the love and attention that I'd welcomed at first was beginning to make me feel claustrophobic. Nick's kindness morphed into neediness, his intelligence was limited to his own interests, and I wasn't sure I even found him attractive anymore.

But then when he started to behave like he didn't trust me, like I was using every free minute I had to cheat on him, I knew I had to make the break. He seemed surprised when I told him it wasn't working, and begged me to give it another go. 'I'll do anything you want,' he'd pleaded, which convinced me that this wasn't a healthy relationship. I told him firmly that it was over, but it was as if he hadn't heard me, or simply didn't want to. That was just a few weeks before the lodge holiday, and he'd been texting and calling me every day since, making me anxious and scared. Angela was looking at me, her head to one side questioningly. 'So are you still together?' she was asking.

'No,' I said with a sigh. 'I won't be dating again, it was a bit of a disaster to be honest.'

'That's a shame, I was hoping you might have found what you were looking for.'

'I already had,' I reminded her, thinking of Scott.

She nodded sheepishly. 'I know, love, and if I could turn back the clock—'

'It isn't your guilt to carry. I just need to find myself now and stop looking for someone who doesn't exist.'

'So, which one of you guys is going to get the brandy out?' Sam appeared in the doorway, all six foot of him, my son the law student who we were all so damned proud of. I smiled at him, I couldn't help it, my kids always made me smile. They filled me up when my tank was empty, and though they didn't realise it, they kept me going through Scott's betrayal and the situation with Nick. My kids were everything, sometimes I felt like they were on the end of a piece of string attached to my heart, and I wanted to hold that string tight for ever. That's why I understood Angela's dilemma with Scott; she didn't approve of, or condone what he'd done, but he was her son. She loved him so much that even when he destroyed his own family, hurt his own children, she stood by him and welcomed his *new* family into her life.

'Where's Georgia?' Sam asked, once Angela had handed him the requested glass of brandy.

'I hope that's a small glass,' I said warningly. He smiled at his grandma and she winked back.

'Georgia's in the kitchen with Jenna – Jenna's the chef that's staying with us to cook,' Angela informed him, like he would care.

'Jenna?'

'Yes, you probably know her, she used to work at your school, in the lab?' I replied.

'Oh yeah. Right, I don't *know* her – but I know who she is,' he said, repeating what his sister had said. 'Okay, I'll go and say hi then.'

We both watched him leave the room, brandy in hand.

Angela leaned forward. 'I know she can be a little anxious sometimes. But her heart's in the right place.'

'Who?'

'Danni.'

'Oh... yes.' I found Angela's vagueness a little disconcerting.

'She can be a bit much sometimes, but she's a good person,' she added, sounding more lucid.

'I'm sure she is, and as much as it pains me to say, I'm only tolerating her for you.'

I could see the pain on her face and instantly regretted my brutal honesty.

'It takes two, and I blame Scott just as much if not more, but it's so much *easier* to blame her,' I started. 'It's easier to tell myself she pursued *him*, the idea of him simply *wanting* her is still too hard to bear, Angela.'

She reached out, rested her hand on my knee, and almost whispered into the silence. 'You'll never get over it, will you?'

I shrugged. 'It's the kids...' I couldn't finish. I saw the tears in her eyes, and feeling them in my own, stood up and reached for a handful of tissues, passing one to her.

Taking the tissue, she clutched my hand lightly. 'I'm sorry,' she whispered. 'If I could change things...'

'No one can.' I shook my head, and gently pulled my hand away to wipe my eyes with the tissue, as she did the same. The silence that followed was heavy, neither of us knowing what to say to comfort the other.

'Angela.' Danni's voice suddenly penetrated the air like a shrill alarm, reminding us she was there, and *while* she was there, nothing would change. She came thundering down the little hall, bristling, flushed, sending a cloud of tension on ahead until it filled the room before she'd even arrived.

'There are two police cars outside.'

SIX

DANNI

'It's the police,' I say, staring out of the window in our room. Two vehicles have pulled up outside, their blue lights flashing. I turn to Scott who's lying on the bed. 'I bet it's got something to do with *her*.'

'Who?' he asks, feigning innocence.

'You know *exactly* who I'm talking about – Jenna.'

'Rubbish. I know you don't like her, but she's not a *criminal*,' he hisses back.

'That's a matter of opinion,' I snap. 'And in my opinion, she is!'

I seriously hope she's done something stupid and the police are here for her, because if it *is* her threatening to expose the teacher's 'big' secret, an arrest might just distract her for a while. But then again, is it her who's posting? My two prime suspects are Fiona or Jenna. It could be either of them threatening to reveal my secret during the first family holiday. After all, they're both here, and both have a reason to hate me.

I don't know who scares me the most – Fiona, who wants me out of everyone's life so she can get her family back together, or Jenna, who blames me for losing her career. I'm genuinely scared if it is her, because she's definitely deranged – and now staying with us in the lodge and calling herself a chef. But what doesn't make sense is, how can anyone know I even *have* a secret I'm desperate to hide? I haven't told a soul except Charlotte who I trust with my life, which reminds me, she still hasn't taken down the post on the forum, or texted me back. I hope she's okay.

As soon as I see the police climbing from their cars, I leave Scott in our bedroom and go tearing into the sitting room to see what's happening. Angela and Fiona are sitting there, chatting quietly, completely unaware of our visitors parking up in the snow. 'There are two police cars outside,' I say.

'Oh God,' Angela sighs. They both look terrified and they're just processing this when a loud banging on the door makes us all jump.

So I go and heave it open and two policewomen are standing on the doorstep, shivering, radios blaring.

'Sorry to bother you, but we're hoping you can help with our enquiries?' It's so cold, clouds of her breath disappear into the night as she speaks.

I look at her vacantly.

'It's about an incident that happened about half a mile down the road...'

'Oh. You'd better come in,' I say, and usher them through.

Alerted by the banging door, everyone is trooping into the living room with questioning faces. 'What's going on?' Georgia says, and she's followed by Jenna looking very worried.

After they introduce themselves as DCI Freeman and WPC Fry, Angela invites them both to sit down and, ever the hostess, introduces us all.

'There's been a traffic accident, about half a mile down the road,' Freeman starts.

'That doesn't surprise me in this filthy weather,' Angela replies, pulling her thick, wool cardigan around her protectively. 'Has anyone been hurt?'

'Yes,' Fry replies, putting her head down slightly, 'but it's a bit of a mystery.'

'Oh why?' Angela tilts her head to one side.

'Looking at the victim's injuries, and given several other factors that I'm not yet at liberty to share – this was a hit-and-run. The victim is seriously injured and currently being cared for in ICU, they are in a very serious condition.'

Everyone looks stricken, we are all apparently horrified at this.

'Whoever committed that crime,' she continued, 'whoever hit that person with their vehicle, may have been known to the victim, and there are strong indications that this wasn't an accident.'

We all murmur our concern, everyone's upset at this obviously. I don't know why, but I glance at Jenna and yes, I'm biased, but swear I see her eyes glittering.

'Well, this is dreadful, officer, thank you for letting us know,' Scott says, like she's made the difficult journey in terrible weather just to let us know the news.

'I'm hoping someone here might be able to shed some light on what happened,' she says. 'Did anyone see anything, or hear anything, because it would seem that the victim was hit by a car heading down the road that leads directly to *this* lodge.'

We all look at each other, and I can't help but wonder what everyone is thinking. Are they all wondering if the driver is one of us?

'So there are other lodges around here?' Sam asks. He's now lounging on an armchair, Georgia's perched on the arm, both still have their phones in hands. I have no idea why he asks this, probably because he's hoping there'll be young people in the other lodges. He is interested enough in this for a moment to stop looking at his phone, and even Georgia looks up, but I doubt the little flurry of drama will keep either of them off their screens for long.

'Yes, there are five lodges, all owned by Cornish Cream Leisure. The company has given us details about everyone's arrivals and departures today,' she replies, before going back to the matter in hand. 'Thing is, whoever hit the victim must have been aware, because it looks like they were thrown up in the air and onto the windscreen, and then the car reversed over them.'

Angela gasps.

'So as you can imagine, we have a *lot* of questions.' Freeman glances around the room. We all seem to have our arms folded defensively.

'Obviously forensics will be able to confirm some of what happened, but that's the theory we're working on at the moment until they can get down here. The weather's so bad the main road's blocked off, and we need to find that vehicle.'

Scott's been quiet so far, just watching and listening like the rest of us. But the headteacher soon takes over. 'Oh... this is terrible, when did this happen?'

'This afternoon, just a few hours ago, so it's important we get any information while it's still fresh in people's minds. The road is the only access to the lodges, so we need to make a note of the time guests arrived, today is turnover day, so...' She looks down at her notes. 'Checkout time was 10am, and all the guests left the site. According to our estimate the accident happened late this afternoon, between three and five, around the time everyone at the lodges would be arriving.'

'But we were *all* on that road between those hours,' Angela remarks. 'It could be any one of us.'

We all turn to look at her. She's right, but she might just as well have accused us *all* of knocking this person over, right there and then in front of the police.

'And how can you be so sure it's between three and five, offi-cer?' Angela is now asking.

Fry looks up from her notes, probably more used to asking questions than answering them. 'It's easier to make an estimate because of snow fall.' She keeps her eyes on Angela as she says this. I wouldn't be surprised if she thinks Angela's hiding some-thing, but she isn't. Angela drives so incredibly slowly, she'd be incapable of knocking anyone over, even in bad weather.

'So you're assuming the driver who did this is a guest from one of the lodges?' Scott steps in, saying what we're all thinking.

'Surely not?' Angela's hand flies up to her mouth.

She and Scott are playing good cop bad cop with the police. I find it amusing, they really are peas in a pod. They both take themselves too seriously. Angela was a teacher too, and I guess this is the result of a career spent talking down to children.

Fry half-shrugs. 'At the moment, that's the theory we're working on, whoever did this deliberately left someone to die in the snow,' she says. 'This is extremely serious, and we have reason to believe that they deliberately targeted this victim.'

She stops talking, allowing this to sink in. I felt a cold shiver run down my spine looking around at the people present. Surely it wasn't one of us? Was it?

'What about the people in the other lodges?' I asked, desperate to push this away.

'We are questioning them too.'

'If any of us *had* seen something, we'd have immediately called the police,' I offer, unsure what else to say.

Fry looks at me. 'Yes, I'm sure. But no one has.'

'No, no I see,' I reply, feeling stupid.

'So, in order to continue the investigation, we need names, times of arrival and car details from everyone. Starting with you, Mrs Wilson...' Both Fiona and I look up, about to answer, but of course it's Angela she's addressing.

'Jenna and I arrived about three-fifteen,' Angela says, 'and the next person was Fiona, who was about twenty minutes after us.'

It's Fiona's turn to wade in now. 'If you're looking for someone who *might* know something, I suggest you ask the stag party staying in the lodge further down the coast. They nearly ran me off the road earlier...'

'Oh really?'

'Yes, just about half a mile up that road, they came thundering down the road, driving far too fast. In heavy snow!'

'How do you know it was a stag party?' Fry asks, and we all turn to Fiona, who blushes and starts stuttering.

'I didn't mean it literally, I meant they were behaving like that. Yelling out of the windows and going too fast.'

'Thanks, Mrs...?'

'Ms... I'm Ms Penny,' she says, and my heart breaks a little bit for her. I even stole Fiona's name.

Fry then turns to the group, and starting with Sam, asks for arrival times and car details.

As the police ask their questions, Angela, ever the polite hostess, asks Jenna to make hot drinks for everyone. At this request, Jenna's face drops. She clearly doesn't want to miss anything.

'Now?' she asks, her mouth forming a pout. 'You want me to make *everyone* a drink?'

Angela smiles, nods in confirmation then turns her attention back to the questioning.

I avoid eye contact with Jenna. If she's the one posting messages, one word from me could have her straight there spewing her poison.

She spins around and heads for the kitchen. Jenna's one of those people who only ever does things that she will benefit from, and playing the Cordon Bleu cook gives her status, while at the same time ingratiating herself to the people she thinks might be useful to her. My husband and his mother.

She returns minutes later carrying a tray with cups of tea for the officers, apparently the rest of us aren't having one. I don't say anything. I'm struggling enough with Olivia who's wrestling to get off my knee, I don't need to add a cup of hot tea to the equation. Then she starts bawling, and I stand up and wander around with her as the police finish their questions and drink their tea.

'Until we know what exactly happened on that road this afternoon, I would ask you all to be vigilant,' Fry says before she leaves. I am trying to hear her over Olivia's crying. I'm walking up and down the room rocking her to no avail.

'Someone knows what happened on that road,' she's saying now, 'and I have to warn you the victim is in a very serious condition. Whoever is capable of doing that, may be capable of much worse, so do be attentive, and if anyone here remembers anything at all, or would like to speak to me in private, please call the station.'

'Wow, she wants us all to snitch on each other,' Sam says when she's gone.

'You might call it that, but if anyone here had done a hit-and-run, which of course they haven't, then we should be *snitching* on them as you put it,' Scott replies. He's tetchy, irritation singing in his voice, then he turns to me.

'Danni, why didn't you take Olivia to our room?' he snaps. 'I couldn't concentrate on a word the officers were saying with her screaming in the background, and you marching up and down, so bloody distracting.'

'Oh, I'm sorry *Detective* Scott Wilson,' I hiss. 'Why didn't you take her into our room? Or are you too busy trying to solve the mystery?' I snap, immediately regretting it as Angela, Fiona and Jenna all turn to look at me. Jenna's eyes are wide, she is clearly thrilled at this. I imagine her holding her popcorn.

'I'm sorry, Danni, I... it was just really annoying, and she was trying to make notes but couldn't hear what we were saying,' he replies in a conciliatory tone.

I'm so angry, I can't speak, I just keep walking round and round, rocking Olivia, who seems determined to embarrass me as much as my husband was by screaming even louder. But before I can do anything, Jenna starts walking towards me with her arms out. 'Come on, Danni, let me have a go with her, you're all stress and babies can feel that.' She's now touching Olivia, seemingly gentle, but trying to pull her from my arms, and the more she tries to pull, the harder I hold on.

'She needs a break, tell her, Scottie,' she's saying, clutching at Olivia, and for a moment I look at him, hoping he'll step in, support me, but my husband just looks helplessly on. I'm alone in this.

'No, NO,' I say louder, but our eyes meet, and I see the cold steel glaring back at me. Can no one else see this? I keep hold of my baby, but so does she, and she's pulling so hard I'm concerned that if I keep holding on, Olivia will be hurt. So reluctantly, I loosen my grip, and she whisks Olivia from my arms.

'It's fine,' she's saying to my child, looking down at her, cooing in this fake, soothing voice that I'm just not buying. Every nerve is tingling, I can't bear her touching my baby, I'm desperate to get her back to safety with me. But now she's cradling her, pushing her face into Olivia's and finding herself in a stranger's arms, Olivia is suddenly quietened, unsure, which gives the impression of calm.

'Oh, I think you have the knack,' Fiona announces pointedly. I could hit her, after I hit Jenna, who's waltzing around the room with my baby, everyone murmuring their approval at the way she's stopped her crying.

I try to bite my tongue and stay calm, and just walk up to her with my arms outstretched. 'I'll take her for her bath now,' I say, attempting to hide the fear and hatred in my voice.

'It's okay, Danni,' she says, looking right into my face, 'I can look after her tonight, you have some time off. You deserve it.'

'No I don't,' I insist. 'I want her back, I want Olivia back.' I reach out again, and this time she steps back, pulling the baby closer, like I can't be trusted.

'Danni, she's fine with Jenna,' I hear Scott murmur, and that does it.

'Jenna, GIVE her to ME!' I yell, causing Olivia to cry and Jenna to glance around the room in apparent surprise at my anger.

'Okay, okay if you really want her,' she says, like I'm doing this for show. I take Olivia, and despite her screams, relief floods through me. I walk on wobbly legs to our room. Closing the door, I lie on the bed with my child, and within minutes she's calm and asleep. I lie there for a long time listening to the sound of voices, the odd burst of laughter, someone telling a story, everyone listening. I'm not part of this, I don't belong here with these people, I fooled myself to think I could ever infiltrate this family with its rules of behaviour, its history, and its secrets. But then who am I to talk about family secrets, I have a big one of my own. I put Olivia into her cot and fall asleep for a little while, to be woken by Scott coming to bed about an hour later.

'You okay now?' he asks, like I should be ashamed of my earlier behaviour.

'Yes, I'm absolutely fine, and I will stay that way as long as she doesn't go anywhere near our child again,' I say, too loudly.

'Oh, Danni, please give it a rest,' he says with a sigh as he unbuttons his shirt.

I sit up on the bed, pushing some pillows behind me. 'No, I won't give it a rest. I genuinely believe Jenna's offer to cook this weekend is far more ominous than your mum, or anyone else seems to think.'

He doesn't answer, just climbs into bed wearily.

'I can't believe Angela *invited* her here. I reckon she's come here so she can get revenge on *me*. I know that sounds dramatic, and I doubt she'd actually harm me,' I add quickly, before he accuses me of being paranoid. 'I just think she's getting off on my unease at her presence. And that... that *performance* with Olivia was too much, she knew it would upset me to take her from me. She's evil.'

'Danni, you're overdramatising the whole thing, she was trying to help you.'

'She bloody wasn't, didn't you see what was happening, it was gladiatorial. She's so scary, I won't sleep tonight after that. I can't bear to think she's under the same roof as me and Olivia, I don't trust her, Scott.' I turn to my husband, hoping to appeal to him.

'Oh, Danni, you're overwrought. You aren't sleeping and it's making you paranoid.'

There he goes again.

'Rubbish, it's got nothing to do with that. I just don't see why else she'd cotton onto your mother of all people. And she definitely hitched herself a ride to this weekend.'

'Jenna's really not that divisive. She lost her job and now she's waitressing in a café, she needs the money, it's as simple and innocent as that,' he says firmly.

'Oh, so I'm meant to feel sorry for her?'

'No, but it's because of *you* she's in this predicament.'

'Not this again. You *know* what happened, Scott, and you agreed to it.'

'I had no choice, you were threatening to go to the police...'

'I don't understand why you aren't freaked out by her. She's turned up here looking like my doppelgänger, calling herself a Cordon Bleu cook, and trying to steal my baby from me, she is fucking insane!'

'I really don't think any of those things indicate Jenna is, as you put it, *fucking insane*.'

'She's bleached her hair, she's even had it cut exactly like mine!' I lean forward so I'm in his face. 'She wants my baby.'

'Danni, she doesn't.' He's amused by this.

'Are you laughing at me?'

'No, I just think you have some weird examples to illustrate someone's insanity. She tried to help you calm Olivia down, and it worked. You both bought the same jacket, and you don't have the monopoly on short blonde hair.'

'I'm not saying I do, but hers was long and dark until recently, and I had that jacket on in an Instagram photo, she must have seen it and bought one the same. Scott, she's suddenly turned herself into me.'

He just looks at me, shaking his head.

'What?'

'Stop, this is just silly, you sound like a Year Ten student! So she's cut her hair and dyed it, and who knows she may have had the jacket before you did. And if she is copying you, which I doubt, then see it as a positive. Imitation is the sincerest form of flattery.'

'I'm not flattered. I'm scared. And why is she now waitressing and calling herself a Cordon Bleu cook when she clearly isn't?'

'She might be. But whatever she's doing, I admire the fact that she's got back on her feet so quickly, and isn't too proud to work in a café to make a living.'

'Wow, you really *do* admire her, don't you? And how the hell did she find your mother, surely that's no coincidence?'

He starts slowly, to show I was testing his patience. 'She didn't know Mum was anything to do with me, my mum just *happened* to go into the café where she worked and they got talking,' he says. For an educated man, he can sometimes be very stupid, or perhaps he thinks I'm the stupid one and I'd believe him? Jenna's always had a thing for Scott, and having been the other woman, I know how easily he falls for a maiden in distress. But does she really think I'm so stupid as to let her worm her way in?

Perhaps I *am* paranoid. But I don't share Scott's faith in Jenna, or his seemingly high opinion of her. Whatever he says, he won't change my mind, because turning up on our family holiday, in the same yellow jacket, with a new haircut exactly like mine isn't a coincidence – it's *sinister*.

SEVEN

FIONA

Friday evening

'Well, Jenna, that was absolutely delicious,' Angela said, putting down her fork, picking up her napkin and dabbing her mouth.

'Yeah, it was really good,' Georgia agreed. I was particularly pleased at my daughter's enthusiasm for dinner because in the previous couple of years Georgia's eating habits had been sporadic at best.

But my slightly bigger concern that evening was Sam, who'd spent the previous two days at a rave and judging by his eyes, was still suffering the after-effects. My son had embraced the social side of university wholeheartedly, which I'm sure was a welcome distraction after his parents' divorce. But was his wonderful social life getting in the way of his academic commitments? I'd shared my concerns with Scott only the week before, but he'd said not to worry, Sam just needed to grow up and he would. Despite us often having long chats on the phone when Danni was out, or when it was late and she was asleep, it was quite different when she was around. I could often hear the baby screaming, Danni complaining in the background, and the stress in his voice.

'I'm on the bloody phone, Danni,' he'd hiss, and she'd hiss back. I would put the phone down on those occasions wondering again at the madness of a middle-aged man swapping our happy, peaceful life, for the raw, sleep-deprived madness of new wives and babies.

'Thanks, Jenna, the beef was delicious,' Scott said.

'There's plenty more,' Jenna offered and leaning towards him, she began ladling it onto his plate lovingly.

'Yes, thanks, Jenna, it was lovely. I'd love the recipe—' I started, but before I could finish, or Jenna could respond, Danni spoke over me.

'So what the hell happened on that road tonight?' She was addressing the table, bringing attention back to her, clearly not happy about Jenna being praised.

'Way to go to bring the mood down,' I murmured, wondering again what her issue was with this young woman who seemed quite pleasant and eager to please. Unlike Danni.

'Well, it might not bother *everyone*,' she said pointedly, taking me in with her sideways glance. 'But I feel guilty knowing that someone was knocked down just a few hundred yards away while we're all here eating *stew*.' She pushed away her hardly touched dinner like it was contagious.

An awkward silence followed. All you could hear was Scott's cutlery clicking on his plate – everyone else had finished, but he was now eating his second portion.

'It's not *stew*, it's boeuf bourguignon,' Jenna finally said, her face flushed with barely contained anger.

'And it's lovely, the best bourguignon I've ever had, Jenna, thank you,' Angela soothed.

'Let's not think about the accident,' I said calmly, 'this is Grandma's birthday weekend.'

I saw Danni's eyes roll and shot her a look, and she glared right back at me, challengingly.

'Yeah, well said, Mum,' Sam rallied. I was grateful, perhaps he'd picked up on Danni's nasty little dig at me and Jenna? My son hated confrontation, he'd heard a lot of that in the weeks leading up to his dad's departure. And now, like then, he was keen to smooth things over. Sam was one of life's fixers, there was nothing that gave him more satisfaction than making things right.

'Who's for the hot tub later?' he suddenly said. I almost laughed out loud. Freezing weather aside, did he really think a bubbling bath of jealousy and resentment would solve any of this tension? Now that *would* be a stew, I thought to myself.

'The hot tub, in this weather? It's freezing,' I exclaimed.

'That's the point, Mum,' he replied, amused. 'The clue's in the name. Hot. Tub.'

Danni sniggered, grasping onto Sam's amusement at my remark, and turning it into something negative and mean.

'I've never really understood the point of them,' I said, refusing to be drawn in.

'Well. For a start, you can sit out there all night watching the stars, doesn't matter how cold it is, the water keeps you warm,' he said.

'I'd rather sit by the fire,' I murmured.

'Me too,' Angela replied. 'When they told me there was a hot tub, I wasn't even sure what that was, but I knew you younger ones would like it.' She gestured to Jenna, Danni and the kids and I suddenly felt very old.

'Yeah, I'm up for the hot tub, Sam,' Jenna offered. The way she said his name and held my son's eyes made me wonder if there might be chemistry between them. It occurred to me that it could be good for Sam to have a nice young woman in his life. Jenna was a few years older with her feet on the ground and I could ignore the tattoo sleeve and heavy make-up if she cooked like that every night.

'Let's have dessert in the hot tub?' Jenna suggested. 'I made cheesecake.'

Angela and I pulled a doubtful face at each other.

'Sounds messy,' I joked.

'Well, I *love* messy,' Danni enthused, glancing dismissively over at me. 'Count me in!'

'Great, okay let's have dessert in the hot tub then?' Sam suggested.

'Yay,' she responded in a baby voice, the kind of voice I imagined she used when she was seducing my husband. Despite him now being married to her, I still thought of Scott as *my* husband.

'Angela told me there was a hot tub, so I've brought my bikini,' she added. No doubt she was keen to show off that post-baby body, it looked like she spent a lot of time in the gym, but Georgia said she'd started to work out at home now she had Olivia.

'She has weights and an exercise bike at home,' my daughter had told me in a rare lapse of discretion. Georgia was clearly impressed by Danni's commitment to fitness, but she tried to hide her admiration for her stepmother when talking to me. She rarely offered snippets from her overnight stays with Scott and Danni, because she was protecting me. Despite being just seventeen, my daughter was intuitive, and knew my innocent questions about the weekend were hiding a longing for information that might lead to hurt. I was desperate to know the minutiae of their loved-up domesticity and compare it to what we'd had. I wanted to know *why* he'd chosen her over me and the children and would take any kind of crumb the kids might innocently drop to use as evidence of what had gone so wrong for us and so right for them. But Georgia knew what I was doing, and how painful it was for me, so rarely gave any insight into their time with Scott and Danni.

Having not seen her with my kids, I'd often wondered what she was like as a stepparent. And observing her so far, it seemed she used her youth, and played the friend, and big sister rather than the strict stepmother. But despite her trying so hard to be one of kids, she seemed to be missing the subtext of what was going on here. Sam had probably mentioned the hot tub in his clumsy way of trying to get Jenna alone. I felt that he wanted to get to know her more, and what if she felt the same? Georgia had obviously picked up on this and said she didn't fancy getting in the hot tub, but Danni seemed to have missed this completely. She was happily and blindly going to play the third wheel, unless she was deliberately trying to come between them? After all she wasn't exactly a fan of Jenna. Whatever her reasons for joining them, now Sam and Jenna would be sitting under the stars accompanied by his stepmother!

'What about the baby?' I asked. It was a loaded question coming from me, especially after the drama with Jenna. I knew it would annoy her, but I couldn't help it, I hoped that reminding her of her baby might prompt her to give the hot tub a miss and let Sam and Jenna have some time alone.

But Danni's head whipped round and she glared at me. 'It's Scott's baby too. Didn't he ever look after Sam and Georgie when *they* were babies?' She smiled conspiratorially at Scott, like they were sharing a private joke about me.

'No, not really,' I replied. 'Scott's a good dad, but wasn't great with babies, were you?' I asked him directly. He shrugged, unsmiling. 'No,' I continued, 'he's better when they get to school age.' This wasn't meant as a slight to Scott, but of course it came over as that and he gave me a look that could kill. It was all so fragile, this conflict between past and present, the dynamic between two wives wrought with hurt and resentment. Every word, every action felt like a win or a loss, a stupid game presided over by the man who'd caused all this pain. I should have called a truce right then, because there was only one winner in this war of the wives – the husband.

'I'll happily look after the baby if you want to go with the others in the hot tub, Danni?' Angela offered, again a lifeboat in the storm, which was exactly what Danni had hoped for. She'd clearly viewed the weekend as a chance to unwind and dump the baby on Angela, as she had the moment she arrived.

'You are not going to spend the weekend babysitting,' I snapped, then tried to soften this. 'Look, Angela, this weekend is all about you. You were kind enough to invite us here, and pay for all this and I'm sorry but you shouldn't have to change nappies and put babies to bed on your birthday.'

I saw Danni sitting open-mouthed, pantomiming offence, but I just ignored her.

'I could look after Olivia,' Jenna offered. This landed like a bomb, and we all looked down at the table, waiting for Danni's reaction, until to everyone's relief, Scott stood up. 'I'll look after Olivia,' he said wearily, 'I'm used to putting her to bed. You go and get in the hot tub with the others.'

Danni scowled at this. I was surprised at his offer because in the past he'd have been the one in the hot tub while I looked after Sam and Georgia. He was obviously more involved the second time around. Then again, he was probably trying to avoid another world war between Danni and Jenna as they fought over Olivia. That had left a nasty taste in all our mouths.

So, while 'the kids' – Jenna, Sam and Danni – took their dessert out onto the decking, Angela and I sat by the fire with our dessert while Scott put Olivia to bed.

'This cheesecake is wonderful, so light and fluffy,' Angela remarked.

'Yep, I have to say, you definitely did the right thing when you booked Jenna. Not sure Danni is too keen though?'

'I did wonder. Danni barely ate any of the lovely beef. I think Jenna's more of a friend of Scott's.'

'A friend of *Scott's*?' This surprised me.

'Yes. I don't think she and Danni get along.'

'Mmm, I got the feeling that Danni doesn't like her. When she met her earlier, she seemed... I don't know, *upset* to see her.'

Angela gave a little shrug and smiled warmly, like she hadn't heard me, or was choosing not to.

We all gazed out onto the decking, silently watching the kids in the tub, the coloured spotlights changing slowly from blue to green to pink, the steam taking on the different hues, changing the scene minute by minute.

'She's finally settled,' Scott spoke into the silence as he came back into the room after putting Olivia to bed. He and his mother talked about Olivia's teething, while I had one eye on the decking, where Jenna and Sam were sitting in the water talking to each other. Seconds later, Danni appeared, slowly taking off her robe and revealing a very tiny bikini, which I felt was inappropriate for a family gathering.

'Danni looks good, the baby's only twelve months old,' I murmured, honestly. Scott didn't respond, and Angela was miles away.

I was fascinated watching Danni who immediately took Sam's attention from Jenna by saying something to him as she climbed into the tub. I watched him watching her and saw the look on his face as she stepped in, sitting down too close to him. Jenna obviously had now been made to feel the gooseberry and as Danni gazed into my son's eyes, Jenna climbed out of the hot tub. I expected Sam to climb out too, but he didn't. In fact he didn't seem to notice she'd gone. He just continued to sit in the steam in the semi darkness talking under the stars with his stepmother, like it was something they'd done many times before.

Within seconds Jenna was wandering into the living room wrapped in a towel.

'It's too cold for me out there,' she muttered, smiling at Scott. 'Push up, Scottie,' she said, squeezing next to him on the end of the sofa. I'd heard Jenna refer to him in this way before, and was surprised again at her informality. No one called Scott Scottie – he would have hated it, wouldn't he? But he didn't seem irritated, just moved up slightly on the sofa so she could join him and continued to gaze out at the hot tub like the rest of us. I found it uncomfortable to see Sam in this rather intimate tableau with his stepmum, and judging by the deathly silence, I think the others felt the same. I glanced across at Scott, but couldn't see his face because Jenna was blocking my view. I wondered why she hadn't joined me on the almost empty sofa. Was Angela right, were Scott and Jenna friends, or was it more – on Jenna's part anyway?

I was uneasy, and yes, a little hurt to see how comfortable Sam and Danni were with each other. I'd never imagined they shared this kind of closeness. Sam had never really spoken about Danni, only the basics if I asked, confirming she was there, saying yes she cooked dinner, or yes she was okay. It was never anything meaningful that I could create a picture with. Neither of my kids had ever provided me with any detailed accounts of their time with her and I should have been grateful, it made it easier. But now, what was unfolding outside, suggested a *very* close friendship that went beyond stepmother and stepson. I watched discreetly but intently as they talked, the conversation apparently so intimate, so secret their heads had to be close together. It was Sam who was doing most of the talking, and it was clear this conversation was nothing like the monosyllabic chats he sometimes deigned to have with me. I felt wounded; not only had Scott discarded me for a newer, better wife, but now my son had replaced me for a newer, better, mother.

We all continued to stare outside, silently like we were in a cinema, waiting to see what happened next. I had to grip the sofa to stop myself from storming out there and putting a stop to whatever was going on, this was unbearable. And when, through the rising steam and hot breath, I saw Danni touch my son's glistening bare shoulder, my heart dipped. Then she leaned in very close, and whispered something in his ear. The way their bodies touched, turned my world on its axis.

EIGHT

DANNI

Saturday

I wake up this morning feeling upset and angry. Last night I'd been as surprised as Fiona and Angela when Scott offered to take the baby while I went in the hot tub. I was of course relieved, because I didn't want another scene with Jenna playing Mary Poppins and trying to take her from me. But Scott was even worse, saying *I'm used to putting her to bed* in that voice, in front of Fiona and his mother was unforgivable. The implication that I was a neglectful parent and he did everything was simply untrue. I was so angry I couldn't speak to him, I just went to our room, put on my bikini and got into the hot tub. But later, when I got back to the room I was even more angry to see Olivia in her cot in just a nappy and T-shirt, while he was sprawled out on the bed fast asleep.

'So much for putting her to bed! You didn't even put her pyjamas on!' I yelled into his sleeping face.

I was standing over him, waiting to have it out. I was probably overreacting, but I'm under so much pressure in this place.

'Scott?' I said, waiting for a response, but he just turned over and pulled the pillow onto his head so he didn't have to hear me. I was hurt and angry and at this point if he just put his arm around me and told me to calm down I'd feel better, but he was ignoring me. It was like he didn't even *care*.

'You make out you're Mr Perfect, especially to Fiona and your mother... you want them to think you're father of the year!' I said through tears.

'Sssshhh, you'll wake everyone,' he murmured.

'I don't CARE!' I shrieked, making damned sure that *everyone* was awake. Unfortunately, I woke Olivia too, and had to tend to her, while he lay there half-asleep, trotting out the same old grievances.

'You've woken Olivia now, and probably everyone else too, you don't care about *anyone* but yourself,' he muttered. 'You really need to be more considerate around other people.'

'You're always so *considerate* around other people. *You mustn't wake them, you mustn't upset my mother or Fiona, you mustn't hurt Jenna's feelings.* But what about *my* feelings?' I cried.

'I can't do this, Danni,' he said from under his pillow.

'Neither can I, Scott. I'm your wife, but you care more about Fiona, she always comes first, and she knows it, she knows if she asks for something you'll give it to her, if she needs anything you're there. We mustn't upset Fiona at any cost!' I threw myself onto the bed, and sobbed into my pillow, thinking about how his inability to really leave his wife had impacted our lives. Just a few months ago, Scott and I were invited to dinner by some friends of mine. I'd lost some baby weight, bought a new dress and was really looking forward to a grown-up evening of nice food and conversation. We'd arranged for Angela to babysit but I'm convinced she must have told Fiona because half an hour before we were due to go out his phone rang. I remembered my heart sinking as he said, 'Oh hi, Fiona.' He wandered off into another room, as he always does when he's talking to her, and when he came back, he said, 'Georgia's due back from her school trip tonight, but Fiona has a headache, she can't collect her.'

I was so disappointed, I couldn't believe she'd stoop so low.

She really is an evil person, and if she can spoil something for me, she will.

And it isn't just the big stuff like nights out, it's also the little things. Fiona wants to ruin everything, and when I was sitting in the hot tub with the others I could see her glaring at me from the sitting-room window. She was looking at me with such disgust because I was wearing a bikini. Then as soon as I'd got into the hot tub, Jenna got out – and surprise, surprise, she joined Scott, Fiona and Angela who thought they were being discreet, but I could see them through the steam, watching, judging. I watched Jenna as she appeared in the living room and pushed herself next to Scott on the sofa while Fiona sat alone in a sea of soft furnishing. I knew Jenna's game, I knew Fiona's too. I didn't trust either of them, and my anxiety was rising. It was horrible staying under the same roof as two people who I knew hated me.

I turn to look at Scott now, in the dim light of the morning. He's moved the pillow from his head, and is now asleep next to me. In the semi-darkness I look at his handsome face in repose. I reach out and touch his dark, messy hair, pass the back of my hand along his face, an etching of bristle along his strong jaw, long lashes, and good cheekbones like his mother. I loved that face once, I would have done anything for him. I still love him, he gave me Olivia, but it's not the same.

He stirs, and I sit up in bed, touch his bare chest. He opens his eyes and I wonder fleetingly if we might have sex, but that spontaneity has gone, we both know Olivia will wake soon, we're always on borrowed time. We had rushed sex yesterday soon after we arrived. He seemed keen, but I said I felt weird with his wife in the next room. I swear that seemed to excite him even more, and before I knew it, I was sitting on the bathroom sink, my legs wrapped around him trying not to moan too loudly. But not now, I'm still dealing with the anger of last night. I need for him to listen and acknowledge how what he says makes me feel, so I tell him that making me look like a neglectful mother in front of everyone hurt me. But he just lifts the duvet then wanders into the bathroom and starts cleaning his teeth. So I give up and try a more positive approach. 'Shall we do something today, just the three of us?' I offer, as he spits toothpaste into the sink.

'No,' he replies, wiping his face on the towel.

I am smiling with incredulity at his rudeness. 'You can't just say no like that. We could go for a short drive?' I suggest. We only arrived yesterday and I'm already feeling claustrophobic.

'Have you seen the snow?' he asks, walking back into the room. 'No one's driving anywhere in that. And you may have forgotten, but today is my mother's birthday,' he adds, grabbing his clothes and throwing them on so quickly it feels like he's about to run away.

'I hadn't forgotten.' I point to a bag in the corner of the room. 'I bought and wrapped all her gifts. I made her a cake too.'

'So why are you suggesting we drive off and leave her on her birthday?' He's pulling on his socks with his back to me, doesn't even turn around to address me.

I throw my hands in the air in frustration. 'I'm not!' I hiss. 'I just thought it might be nice if you and I had some time together.'

'We will have all the time we want *together* once we're home, but right now we're on a family holiday, and it isn't about what *we* want.' He says this in the self-righteous tone he usually saves for school assembly when someone's 'disrespecting others,' by talking or using their phone.

'Oh shut up, you pompous knob!' I mutter under my breath.

He pretends to ignore this. 'Perhaps you can help Jenna in

the kitchen, I think you could at least try.' He finally turns to look at me. 'You were friends once, it isn't such a stretch, is it? I don't think you're being fair on Mum and it's causing an atmosphere.'

'Sorry, I don't want to upset your mum, but no way will I be going anywhere near that psycho in the kitchen.'

'Jenna is not a psycho—'

'She's a psycho and a liar,' I say too loudly, then turn down my volume as Olivia stirs. 'Cordon Bleu? More like Cordon ugh, she can't even make toast!' I say in a stage whisper. 'She needs to stick with the day job – drug dealing,' I add, unable to stop myself.

'It's comments like that that can ruin people's lives. She lost her job because you made unfounded remarks like that...'

'They were not *unfounded* remarks. God, Scott, you sound so bloody pompous sometimes, like a high court judge. I wish you could see through her, she puts it all on for you and your mother, plays the sweet little innocent, but she isn't, she's a—'

'Keep your voice down, everyone can hear you, you're hysterical, Danni. And as for her culinary training, you can say what you like but her cooking was wonderful last night.' He pauses as he stands up, pulling on his jumper. 'And I think it was rude of you not to eat it.'

'Well get used to it, because I won't be eating anything *she* makes. She is lying about being a trained chef. She'll probably put extra ingredients in mine – bloody anti-freeze.'

He rolls his eyes. 'You're going to starve then, because *she's* the cook.'

'Well, you don't need to worry, "I'll have a second portion please, Jenna."' I repeat his request in a whiny voice. 'Let's face it, none of that anti-freeze will be on your plate, *Scottie*,' I add, emulating Jenna's creepy, ingratiating voice. 'I don't trust her, I can't believe we were ever friends, but now I know she's a nasty piece of work, and the police need to know exactly what she is.'

I think back to when Jenna and I were friends, and it didn't take her long to get Scott involved in some so-called science project she was apparently 'passionate' about. I know he was trying to revamp the science curriculum, but why stay late at work to discuss this endlessly with Jenna? She was the lab technician, and as I said to Scott at the time, 'Why not talk to the *teachers* in that department?'

'Because Jenna's fresh blood, the new generation, and full of new ideas,' he'd enthused. I'd wanted to vomit, she was just some little wannabe who'd lied her way into the job as far as I could see. And I still felt the same about her now.

He stands there in silence looking at me, conjuring up the worst possible thing he can think of. I wait for it, preparing my response, so used am I to our game of mutual cruelty.

'*You* are the nasty piece of work, Danni. She's young and bright, she has her life before her, *that's* why you resent her so much.'

Ouch, and there it is, the stinging slap of words bounce off my cheek. So that's how he sees her, is it? *Young and bright.* I see her quite differently, she's a threat to me and my marriage and I know she's desperate, and desperate people are dangerous.

'How can you be so intelligent, yet miss what's right in front of you. I'm not *jealous* of her, I don't *trust* her, Scott!'

'Oh don't be so dramatic. She's just a kid. That isn't you, what happened to the strong, independent woman I married?'

'You *married* her, that's what happened,' I snapped. 'And it isn't just me who changed, Scott. You're now just like any other middle-aged man, seeking redemption through sex with someone younger, while clinging to the last few hairs on his head.'

He's now standing by the door. I can see by the twitch of a vein in his forehead this got to him, but on the outside he doesn't even flinch. He's so controlled and is now considering his volley back. 'God, you're mean,' he eventually says. 'Why did I never *see* that?' He's looking at me with such venom, such darkness, I feel a chill run through me.

I throw back the bed covers and grabbing my dressing gown, head for the en suite. I want to escape, to run away from his hate. 'I'm having a shower, why don't you take Olivia and show your mum and your ex how brilliant you are at giving her breakfast? Oh... you might need some help though, because you've never done *that* before!' I hiss, slamming the bathroom door so hard everyone in the lodge must hear it.

I turn on the shower and stand under the hot water. It soothes me, but not enough. I'm spiky with anger, but I'm also sad about the way things have turned out. There was a time, when he was still married to Fiona, that I would lie in my bath in my rented flat dreaming of him, humming love songs and *knowing* he was the one. I was convinced that all I needed was for him to leave her, make a life with me and I would prove to him what *real* love was. And after the divorce, the marriage and the baby, people moved on, new scandals erupted and people almost forgot I'd been the other woman, and we became Scott and Danni. We had finally erased Scott and Fiona, and weren't defined by infidelity and whispers of romps on the office desk. We kept our jobs, we had our baby and were well on the way to redemption and rehabilitation – or so I'd thought. But the reality of being married to Scott is a world away from the dreams I'd had when I was single, singing torch songs in the bath.

After I've showered, I get dressed, then click on the forum going straight to where the post about the big secret was. It's like an illness. I can't rest, I can't sleep, I can't leave it for a moment in case something has been said, because if I don't, who knows how long it could sit there, for everyone to see? Charlotte hasn't got back to me, I just hope she got my text and is checking it too so she can delete it the moment it appears – because it will.

I scroll down, holding my breath, just praying nothing has been added, and when I get to the bottom of the page, there are no updates. I can relax – for now.

Suddenly the landline starts to ring. It makes me jump, and after a few seconds Scott's voice is calling us all from the sitting room.

'It's the police on the phone. Can everyone join me? They need to speak to us all.'

'I've put the phone on speaker, the police have some news,' he tells us as we troop in and sit down on the sofas and chairs.

'This is DCI Freeman, is everyone there, Mr Wilson?'

'Yes, everyone's here,' he replies.

'I'm sorry to interrupt your morning, and indeed your holiday, but I'm afraid I have no choice. Some issues have arisen with both the investigation and the weather and I apologise, but both will have an impact on you and the other guests.'

'Okay,' Scott replies cautiously. Given the tone of Freeman's voice, this doesn't sound good.

'There are seven guests at your lodge, am I correct?'

He's holding Olivia who now gives a baby murmur right on cue.

'Yes... actually no, I stand corrected, quite right, Olivia, there are *eight* of us, including an almost one-year-old.'

We smile, and it defuses some of the tension, but I wish he'd let her get on with it, everyone's wondering what the hell this is about.

'Firstly, the reason I'm calling rather than *visiting* the lodge, is because there is now a red weather warning. The snow has come down so fast overnight, it's blocking all roads, in and out of the area. It's impossible to drive out of the cove, not to mention extremely dangerous, and we are asking that you stay indoors.'

We all murmur our concern at this. I want to scream; the very thought of being snowed in here with Jenna and Fiona is horrifying. I'm suddenly on the edge of tears, panic rising hot in my chest.

'But there's more. I'm sorry to have to tell you that the victim of yesterday's hit-and-run victim has sadly died. After making further enquiries it seems our suspicions have been confirmed... this *wasn't* an accident – we've now launched a *murder* investigation, and we are requesting that no one leaves until further notice.'

NINE

FIONA

When DCI Freeman told us about the death of the hit-and-run victim, we all just sat there, shocked, and upset.

I thought Danni was going to hit the roof. 'I can't...' she said, 'I can't stay here another minute.'

While the rest of us were processing the fact that someone had died, Danni was making it all about her. For once Scott wasn't pandering to her, he just ignored her drama and continued to bounce Olivia on his lap with the phone in his hand. But to my dismay, Sam got up from his seat and sat down next to her and put his arm around her shoulders, sending a prickle of concern through me.

'We will need your full co-operation, and will be speaking to *all* the guests at the lodges over the next forty-eight hours...' Freeman was saying, as I watched Sam's hand massage Danni's shoulder.

I looked away, obviously disturbed by the death but increasingly disturbed by the closeness of my son's relationship with his stepmother.

'At this stage, we're early in the investigation, and no one has come forward,' Freeman was saying. 'Though there are several lodges around here, and we've interviewed everyone, as I said yesterday, the road where the incident happened leads directly to *this* lodge.'

I looked around at the others to see their reactions, but they all seemed guarded.

'Hello, Detective, can I say something?' Angela asked.

'Yes of course, but would everyone please introduce your-selves before you speak?' Freeman instructed firmly. There was none of the 'sorry to trouble you,' air she'd demonstrated the previous day, this was now serious and she'd become far more businesslike.

'Angela... it's Angela Wilson. I just wanted to point out that it wasn't just *us* who drove down here yesterday.' She sounded defensive.

'You saw another car?' Freeman immediately asked.

At this, Angela deflated slightly. 'No, just because the cars came down that road doesn't mean the driver arrived *here*. One of the other guests may have started down this road then taken a turning and found an alternative route to *their* lodge?'

'No, the road turnings are all dead ends from that road. Just a few yards on and you're in a forest, there's no way out, unless you turn around and come back and head to the main road or this lodge.'

'Shit,' Jenna murmured under her breath. We all turned to look at her, and she blushed and pulled an awkward face.

'Someone might have driven down the road, then turned around and gone back?' Scott suggested, setting the conversa-tion back on track.

'There are no signs of cars turning,' Fry said. I had the distinct feeling she was testing us. Her voice was solemn, her words sparing, and her silent pauses made us all tense.

'What if they drove down, knocked the victim over and then turned around and went the other way?' Sam asked, which I felt was a reasonable question.

'Impossible. Unfortunately, the snow has covered most of the tyre marks, but from what we can see, the vehicles that came down here yesterday all drove straight on to the lodge from that road. As yet we can't pinpoint *which* vehicle it was, or *who* was driving...'

'I told you, a car full of lads whizzed past me in a Ferrari,' I offered. 'They were heading for our lodge.'

There was silence on the end of the phone, then she asked, 'Did the occupants of that car turn up at your lodge?'

'No one turned up at our lodge, just us,' Angela said, which kind of knocked what I was saying.

'Yes, but they drove past me,' I said, 'at great speed.' My voice faded, not quite sure what point I was making now.

Freeman didn't respond, they clearly thought I was mistaken – or making it up.

'No CCTV?' Scott asked.

'No. But what we *can* ascertain at this early stage, is that the vehicle that killed the victim drove straight to your lodge.'

We all looked down at the shiny wooden flooring. I think we were all trying to look innocent, trying to check for others' reactions, while not meeting each other's eyes. It probably made us *all* look guilty and I was glad this was a phone call rather than Freeman in the flesh, dripping snow everywhere and scrutinising us.

'But, with respect,' Scott wasn't letting this lie, 'it snowed overnight, surely that's covered all the tracks?'

'Perhaps? But we hope that the forensic team's swiftness in arriving at the scene yesterday means we have plenty of information that would have been lost overnight.'

I sighed. Thanks to the weather and the hit-and-run death, we were now completely locked in together. Panic filled my chest, I couldn't think of anything worse.

Eventually, after more questions than answers from Freeman, she said goodbye, and that she'd call back the following day, with any more information. 'If anyone knows something, or discovers something in the interim, do call us, again in strictest confidence if necessary.'

'She's convinced it's one of us,' Sam said flippantly once she'd hung up. No one else spoke, we all continued to sit there in the silence looking shifty, until Angela broke the silence.

'It's very sad,' she offered. We all nodded and murmured our sadness.

'Yes, it's bad news,' Scott replied. 'To think someone died just a few hundred yards from here, makes me feel uncomfortable.'

'Me too, and I'm sorry for them, whoever they were. But this means that the police can keep us all cooped up here under suspicion for as long as they like,' Danni replied.

'We have to co-operate, Danni,' Scott said, in a tone laced with mild reprimand.

'I am *co-operating*,' she hissed. 'I just feel like I'm in a goldfish bowl and everyone's looking at us. Sam's right, they think one of *us* did it!'

'They may *think* that, but we *know* we didn't, so let's just stay calm and do as they ask.' He was tetchy, and unusually for Scott he was letting his feelings show.

'I can't do this,' she muttered, sounding near to tears. She pulled away from Sam and standing up, took off into her bedroom, slamming the door behind her. Angela gave me a look and raised her eyebrows. I mirrored this and suggested we all take a break.

'This is terrible news,' I said, 'and difficult for us all to process, I think we need to take some time out.'

'What about tonight's dinner?' Jenna asked, looking from me to Scott.

'I think we should just carry on as we were,' he replied. 'You heard what the detective said, we aren't able to leave, and it's sad that someone's died, but doesn't change anything for us.

Mum invited us here for her birthday and I think we should honour that and celebrate, appropriately.' He turned to Sam. 'No balloons or fireworks, mate.'

Sam shrugged. 'Next year.'

No one responded. Wasn't the whole point of this travesty that Angela had told us this might be her last? I watched the others get up from their seats to go about their daily business. Just Angela, Jenna and I were left.

'Happy birthday?' I offered Angela with a smile.

'Thank you.' She looked sad. 'Doesn't feel very celebratory. That poor man.'

'If it *is* a man?' I offered.

'Yes, yes of course – we have no idea *who* it is, and so random.'

'It wasn't random if it was done deliberately, that's what the police said, didn't they?' Jenna remarked.

I shrugged. 'Who knows? The police interpretation isn't always right, I find it hard to believe anyone would deliberately do something like that.'

'You'd be surprised,' Jenna replied.

'What do you mean?' I asked.

'Some people will stop at nothing to get what they want,' she said mysteriously before standing up and heading towards the kitchen to start on one of her complex French recipes for dinner later.

'Can I help?' I offered, before she left the room. I was hoping to get her on her own and find out who she might be referring to who'd *stop at nothing*.

'No thanks, it's science, I can't be disturbed.' She leaned on the doorframe. 'My cookery is like brain surgery, and I can't let anyone in the kitchen while I'm in theatre, it ruins my concentration.'

She giggled and curtseyed before disappearing. Angela and I smiled after her as we drank our coffee and watched the morning lift its curtain. For the next hour or so, we enjoyed the slowly transforming landscape turn into a blueish white expanse, from ground to sea to sky. Snow was still falling like blossom in slow motion, landing lightly onto the huge white glittery blanket. Just beyond was the grey ruffle of sea.

'It's spectacular, the seaside in winter,' I remarked. Having lived in the landlocked midlands all my life, I'd only enjoyed sea coves in summertime, with ice cream, and the tingle of sunburned shoulders.

'A seascape this time of year has a rather cruel beauty,' she replied, nodding as she spoke. We gazed out at the beautiful, treacherous landscape. She sounded reflective, and I wondered again if she was contemplating the end of her life.

'Are you okay?' I asked tentatively.

She turned to look at me, slightly startled.

'I just... you said this may be your last birthday? Do you mind me asking, are you poorly, Angela?' I said gently.

'I don't know. I don't want to talk about it really.' She seemed upset, and I regretted being so pushy.

I decided to leave it, see if Scott could perhaps talk to her. We needed to know if she was ill because we would want to be there for her. I wished she'd share this more openly with us and felt a shimmer of guilt because this wasn't how she'd planned her birthday. It should have been a time for celebration, instead we were stuck here, contemplating someone's death.

* * *

Over the next few hours, the whiteout continued, and inside everything seemed grey and without meaning. We would regroup now and then to examine the evidence, to debrief and make sure everyone was okay. Or were we simply checking on each other to see if anyone had confessed yet?

Everyone seemed flat, even baby Olivia sat drowsily on her

father's knee, with none of the fussing she'd displayed the previous evening. The morning quietness seemed fitting in the circumstances, and I think it helped us all to begin to process what had happened. But Sam, as always, had his earphones in. He wasn't a fan of silence, and soon Danni appeared and managed to find enough room to sit close to Sam. She leaned on his shoulder and reached up to one of his ears, carefully taking out the earbud and pushing it into her own ear while smiling at him. He grinned back, obviously happy to share his music with his young stepmother. I felt sick.

'It could have been me, driving alone down that icy road, and stopping to check a tyre, or take something from the car boot,' Danni suddenly said. She was never far from her own thoughts.

'Not if it was deliberate,' Angela pointed out. 'If as the police say it was deliberate, then the killer knew him, and *you* wouldn't have been of any interest,' she added dismissively. In this close situation people's real feelings had already begun to emerge, but now there was no end date, even Angela couldn't hide how she felt. I liked her feistiness, Danni deserved to be slapped down, everything always seemed to be about her.

'We don't know, it might have been the deliberate murder of a stranger?' Danni volleyed back at her mother-in-law.

'That doesn't make any sense,' Jenna butted in as she walked in from the kitchen. At this, Danni turned around. She was about to say something back, but I stepped in.

'Look, I really think we need to stop going over and over this,' I said. 'None of us know what happened, let's leave the investigation to the police. Shall we make pancakes for breakfast?'

'Breakfast? It's almost lunchtime,' Danni replied.

'Okay lunch pancakes then.' I wasn't allowing her to spoil this. The others greeted my suggestion with some enthusiasm, especially Georgia, who'd always loved pancakes.

'You guys used to make us pancakes every Saturday morning when we were younger.' She looked over at me and Scott.

'Come on then, Fiona, for old times' sake?' he asked, standing up and handing Olivia to Angela.

'I'll give this trip down memory lane a miss,' I heard Danni mutter to herself, and standing up, she wandered back down the hallway to their room.

'I'll help.' Jenna jumped up from the sofa like an eager puppy dog, bounding after Scott.

'I'm not sure I'm needed,' I said to Angela. 'He has plenty of helpers.'

She smiled, holding the sleeping baby. She seemed okay, but aware that she wasn't quite herself, and seemed to drift off a little now and then. I decided to stay with her to keep an eye on the baby.

'Jenna seems fond of Scott,' I said. Having watched her with him the previous evening, I was keen to understand the dynamic. 'Do you think he's a father figure?' I asked.

Angela shrugged. 'Let's hope so.'

My stomach twisted at this. It wouldn't be the first time my ex-husband had been involved with a much younger woman.

'I doubt she sees Danni as a *mother* figure,' Angela said with a chuckle. 'Danni isn't even maternal with her *own* child,' she murmured under her breath as she gazed into the face of her sleeping grandchild.

And there it was. As loyal and neutral as she tried to be, and despite her recent bewilderment, she'd seen Danni for what she really was.

I was waiting for her to say something else about her new daughter-in-law, but she moved rather irrationally back to Jenna.

'Jenna's a lovely girl, you know.' She said this like I might think otherwise.

'Yes, she seems nice, I replied, seamlessly adjusting to the new subject matter. 'Did you know her before she worked at the café?'

She put her finger to her lips. 'Don't tell Danni, but it was me who got her the job at the café.'

I stared at her in total confusion.

'Scott felt sorry for her, he'd had to let her go and asked me to ask around to see if anyone was looking for staff, and the café needed a waitress. So I put her forward, and he gave her references, without Danni knowing.'

'But why didn't he want Danni to know?'

'He said Danni was jealous of Jenna and told everyone she had a drug problem. Apparently she told Scott if he didn't get rid of Jenna she'd go to the police – or something like that.'

'And so he got rid of her, as in fired her?'

Angela nodded.

This didn't sound like Scott. He wouldn't fire someone just because Danni told him to, he was his own man, and would do what he felt was right. There was more to this, but Angela either didn't know, or wasn't telling.

'Do you think perhaps Jenna *did* have a drug problem, and *that's* why Scott fired her from the school?'

'No, Danni just *said* she did, but from what Scott says I think Jenna was very popular with the kids, and doing well – Danni didn't like it. No one could prove there were drugs, none of the kids reported any issues, but Danni kept on and on until he said he had no choice.'

'Oh?' This still didn't make sense to me, but it was *very* interesting. Before I could quiz her further, she was back to Jenna again, her mind like a grasshopper's.

'Jenna, she's a good person, and I feel sorry for her. Scott says she's had a hard life, spent time in care and I think that's why she's, well she's sometimes a little *intense*,' she half-whispered.

It couldn't have escaped Angela's attention that Jenna was friends with both my kids, and she lifted her hand in defence. 'Nothing to worry about, she's perfectly fine,' she was keen to reassure me, waving her hand dismissively like I mustn't give it a second thought. I could see why Jenna might need some kind of support, and admired Scott for helping her, meanwhile I was more intrigued that Danni had somehow managed to get Jenna fired. Danni was obviously dangerous, and now the tension between them made sense.

Before we could discuss this any further, Georgia wandered into the room with plates, cutlery and napkins, and began setting the table.

'How are those pancakes coming along?' I asked brightly.

Georgia rolled her eyes. 'Taking forever. Jenna thinks she left the eggs in her car boot, so Dad's helping her bring them in.'

Georgia clearly wasn't happy about this, and I wasn't sure why, but something bothered me about the scenario. Had Jenna asked Scott to help her and was Georgia feeling pushed out? Or was there something else going on? I saw the way she looked at him, and it bothered me.

'Does it take *two* of them to get a couple of dozen eggs from the car?' I asked with a smile, trying not to reveal my own doubts and alarm to Georgia.

She shrugged. 'Dunno. I said I'd go with Jenna so Dad could carry on with the pancakes. But no one listens to *me*.'

'Oh, sweetie, that's not true,' I replied, feeling her hurt.

'Darling, everyone listens to you, because you're lovely and clever and interesting,' Angela remarked, with a big grin.

'You're my mum and you're my grandma,' Georgia responded, in a mock sulky voice, 'you're both biased.'

'Not at all,' Angela joked, and we smiled, while I tried not to think about Jenna and Scott, and death, and being snowed in, and the red flags waving in my face about Sam and Danni. I'd been there before. But this time I wasn't going to sit around and

let my life be messed around in my absence, I was taking
control. So on the pretext of going to the bathroom, I slipped out
into the hall. I wanted to check where Sam was and was about
to go into the kitchen to see if Scott and Jenna really were at the
car, getting the eggs. I checked my watch, it was just after 1pm.
I heard voices, and my heart sank like a stone. One thing worse
than Scott having a thing for Jenna, was Sam having a thing for
Danni, and after their closeness the previous evening in the hot
tub, that was still playing on my mind.

I stood around in the hallway for as long as possible, desperately trying to hear what was said. All I heard was 'I would die
if you told Dad,' and then Danni suddenly appeared in the
doorway. Her face was like thunder, she obviously thought I'd
heard something I shouldn't have. I wished.

Meanwhile, it took Scott and Jenna seventeen minutes to
get the eggs, despite the car being parked right outside the
kitchen door. Before they returned, I checked the kitchen
cupboard – and it contained six full boxes containing in total
thirty-six eggs, which in my estimation would have been plenty
for pancakes for everyone.

* * *

'These are *delicious*, Scott,' Angela commented proudly, about
half an hour later. We'd sat down to breakfast pancakes at the
table in the open-plan sitting room.

'You really are quite amazing, darling,' she continued, like
he'd just discovered the cure for cancer. Scott was a precious
only child and Angela adored him, but had always over-praised
her son. Consequently, he grew up expecting adulation for
everything he did, from getting a promotion to taking the bins
out. And watching him beam at the pancake praise made me
smile.

I had to remind myself that Scott wasn't my husband

anymore. At times, it still took me by surprise, and was made worse because I knew it was the kids' dearest wish for us to be together again. As if I needed proof, Georgia was now sitting at the table beaming at me and her father. Sam had joined us and despite being glued to his phone, seemed relaxed and happy, and was flirting with Jenna. Georgia seemed to like Jenna too, but was a little shy around her, which didn't surprise me. The older girl, with her scarlet lips, white-blonde hair and arty tattoos must have seemed achingly cool to my daughter. I'd been concerned that the kids might be a bit bored this weekend, but Jenna seemed to be providing entertainment for both of them, albeit quite different.

For me our pancake breakfast was a golden moment – no Danni, no drama, no tension, just a family around a table eating pancakes. It was like old times, and I dared to imagine a world without Danni. Baby Olivia could be our third child? I'd always wanted another one. I wished then that we could have frozen that snow-covered morning. It seemed that without Danni everything was pure and white, untainted. But not for long...

TEN

DANNI

Saturday evening

'Happy Birthday, Angela,' I say, as we sit down to the dreaded birthday dinner.

I'm trying not to think of how many times I may be forced to do this with fake Jenna and smug Fiona. The endless small talk and table runners are too much for anyone with a brain.

'It seats eight comfortably,' Angela keeps assuring us, but there's nothing *comfortable* about tonight. Jenna set the table – she's clearly googled 'birthday table-scapes,' because this 'snow-scene,' as she's calling it, is a *lot*. From crockery to candles, everything is white, the tablecloth and runner, napkins, there's even a bloody big piece of white netting hanging from the ceiling above the table.

'It represents snow,' Jenna announces, when Angela compliments her on the table.

'I just hope the "snow" doesn't catch on a candle because with this wooden frame it won't be snow it will be fire,' Scott points out. I hear the gentle chastising in his voice. I know it well because it's how he speaks to me and I can see by her face that Jenna's crestfallen. As I'd suspected, this display of Jenna's wasn't for Angela, it was for Scott, and without realising, he's just publicly rejected her. She smiles wanly at something Georgia says, then slides along the table pouring wine in our glasses, her tear-filled eyes going unnoticed by everyone but me. She's worked hard for this birthday meal, and whoever it's for, whatever her motives, I can't help but feel sorry for her. Georgia and Sam have been *helping* her, but all they've done all afternoon is blow up balloons and yell at each other over a game of Monopoly. They were so noisy I couldn't get Olivia down for an afternoon nap so Scott took her out for a wander and a little play in the snow which helped calm her – and me. She's now in her cot in our room and we're just hoping she'll sleep for a couple of hours at least.

'So, the starter,' Jenna announces, bringing in a large tray and placing it down on the table.

There are seven small plates, and as she brings them round to each person, she places them carefully on the table.

'Starter? Since when was a starter big sausage?' Sam's having a little joke, but like his father he's sometimes a little heavy-handed with his humour. He's now looking around the table, waiting for one of us to laugh, but even I don't want to openly laugh at Jenna – how would that look?

'It's black truffle white sausage,' Jenna responds, a little low-key now, but trying to smile through it. 'I made the sausage myself, from a French recipe,' she continues, as Sam mutters, 'Where's the mash?' going in once more for a laugh and again not getting one.

'The truffle sausage is accompanied by caramelised apple, celery root puree and calvados sauce,' she continues, more loudly, to not only ignore Sam, but drown him out. There's no love lost there, it's clear he really gets on her nerves. Sam's that bit younger than her and he's fun and kind and lovely, but she's obviously irritated by him.

'Please start,' she instructs, standing slightly back from the table, no doubt awaiting the applause.

The starter is surprisingly good, though the specks of black truffle taste suspiciously like black pepper, but what do I know?

My mind is on other things, like is Sam okay and who do I resent the most between Fiona and Jenna, and how long will we be forced to play this pantomime? What are the chances of being at an intimate, eternal dinner with the two people you hate most in the world?

I'm sitting between Fiona and Scott, how symbolic is that? I know this isn't a random thing, because Jenna did the table plan. It's a circular table, and she's sitting on the other side of him. She's completely monopolising Scott, and he seems fine with that, but as Fiona and I don't engage, it's awkward. So, I make a boring comment about the weather to Angela, desperately hoping she'll respond, and rescue me. But Fiona manages to say something even more banal about the food that Angela responds to immediately.

I look across the table wanting to scream 'help me,' but there's no one there, this is awful. Sam's still making sausage jokes in an attempt to impress his father, while being ignored by Scott who's put the baby alarm on the table and turned up the volume. It breaks my heart. Sam desperately wants his father to be proud of him, and because of that he's scared to tell him the truth, but Scott seems oblivious to his son's needs. He once told me he feels guilty because as the headteacher, he's always looking out for other people's kids, and his own have taken second place. He doesn't want to make the same mistake with Olivia, but as I pointed out, it isn't too late for Sam and Georgia. Meanwhile, Georgia's gone into her shell again and I wonder if it has something to do with the inscrutable Jenna, who I can see in my eyeline smiling slyly, while sitting snugly next to Scott.

The starter is followed by cassoulet (more sausage!), and Sam is now asking, 'Is it stew?' It isn't like him to be annoying, but as long as his father ignores him, there's potential for much more. I'm surprised he hasn't made some Freudian reference to the sausage... oh, spoke too soon, there he goes.

I try to throw him a life jacket and giggle at his joke. He's a funny guy and I love him. But Fiona's looking uncomfortable. 'Thanks, Sam, we don't need your running commentary, or your dad jokes,' she snaps, which is actually quite funny for Fiona.

Cue Jenna now, who's asking every two minutes if my husband is enjoying her food, and picking up on his weakness for unadulterated praise, is enthusing over the wine he chose. I have to stop myself from telling her to shut the fuck up and stop flirting with my husband under my nose. I also want to ask Fiona to stop calling my husband late at night to discuss the past and the kids and asking him to take the car to the fucking garage like they're still married. I want Angela to acknowledge me as the current wife and not some irritating girlfriend she has to tolerate. I take another mouthful of food to stop myself saying how I feel, because this truly is the dinner from hell. And after hearing the news that we could be trapped here together for days to come, I realise that if Jenna is putting anti-freeze in my portions of food, then bring it on, because death would be a blessed relief. So with nothing left to live for, I eat heartily, while Fiona or Angela or someone mentions the weather again, and the blandness of the evening is restored.

Over dessert, the conversation finally turns from the weather to the hit-and-run, courtesy of Angela.

'The police said that the victim was thrown into the air and hit the windscreen,' she suddenly says. Mid-mouthful, we all turn to look at her, surprised at this sudden change in tone. After an awkward pause Scott puts down his spoon and pushes his half-eaten mousse away. It's chocolate mousse, one of his favourite desserts. I'm surprised he isn't finishing it, but Angela's comment has reminded us that in the midst of dinner we are in death.

'Yeah, I keep thinking about it too.' Scott's shaking his head, he *wants* to talk about this.

'I wonder if he suffered?' Angela asks, her voice now croaky with emotion. My heart goes out to her. This poor woman just wanted a last birthday with her family, and there's a murder investigation, a lockdown in a snowstorm, and her son's two wives are ready to kill each other. *Happy birthday, Angela!*

'I *think* we should try not to dwell on it,' Fiona says piously, and looks to Scott for support.

He shrugs. 'It's hard *not* to dwell on it. What the hell was someone doing wandering that road alone in freezing cold sleet?'

'And why would anyone want to mow them down?' Angela exclaims in fresh horror.

'Perhaps the victim was pushed out of the car first?' I offer, warming to the subject. It's far more interesting than weather for God's sake.

'Oh God, I can't *even*...' Georgia throws down her spoon, abandoning the chocolate mousse. 'Can we *not*?' Silence lands on the table like an ice cap. The teenage daughter, who's clearly wound like a coiled spring like the rest of us, is unable to keep up the pretence under the layers of tension.

Fiona starts fussing. 'Sorry, sweetie, we were just talking it through, it's been a shock. But you're right, let's *not*.' She shot a warning look in mine and Scott's direction, like it's *our* fault her daughter's upset. If it's anyone's fault that she can't deal with this, it's Fiona's; she micromanages Georgia's emotions, and is always so scared of upsetting the girl. And in my view Georgia doesn't know how to feel until she's run it by her mother; she feels obligated to have an emotional tantrum just to please her. It isn't pleasant to talk about a hit-and-run, but shit happens and children need to hear difficult things, to get an understanding of life before it comes head on at them.

'Georgia, I know the subject matter is difficult, but I do

think you're being a little oversensitive,' I say soothingly, but before Georgia can respond, Fiona turns to me, raw hate in her eyes.

'Oh that's what *you* think is it, that my daughter's being *oversensitive?*'

'I do actually, *yes!*' I snap back.

'Well *I'm* her mother, and I know her far better than you do, and she most certainly is *not* oversensitive. So please keep your unwanted, ignorant remarks to *yourself!*' she hisses.

'You might *think* you know her, but...' I start, about to tell her everything I know about Georgia, but stop myself just in time. Angela's face crumples. She's staring at me bewildered, shaking her head, preparing to disbelieve whatever I have to tell, and I can't do it to her.

'Please, let's not spoil tonight, it's my birthday.' Her voice is breaking and I could slap Fiona for turning this into a fight.

'You're right, Angela,' I say. 'Sorry.'

I put my head down, push my mousse away and try not to glance at Fiona. If I do I will say something I regret, and that would come between me and Georgia. I've worked too long and hard to turn that relationship around and I'm not going to throw it away with an angry revelation at the dinner table. My relationship with Georgia started out very rocky when her dad first left. Fiona blamed me, and no doubt made her feelings clear to her kids. But after that difficult start, things between my stepdaughter and me have changed. Georgia is now a regular at our house for dinner, and I welcome those evenings, because that's when we really get to talk. She shares everything with me, and last week I almost cried when she told me I was more like a best friend than a stepmother. I feel the same, I value our friendship, we see bands together and go shopping for trendy clothes, I've even met up with Georgia and her friends, who remember me as their teacher from Year Seven. The only tricky thing is that Georgia's asked that we don't tell Fiona about us going out together because she might feel hurt. I understand, and it's really sweet of Georgia to protect her mother, but I think Fiona should know how close we are. That way, perhaps she'll understand when I offer advice, or my opinion about my stepdaughter that it's done with knowledge and love and friendship. Only when Fiona sees how close I am with the kids will she understand that I'm in their lives to stay, and she can wish me dead all she likes, but I'm going nowhere.

She's now gone into the kitchen with Jenna to make coffee, and I remember the cake I made for Angela, so quickly follow them in. Neither of them acknowledge me, so as they chat and the kettle boils, I go into the larder, where I'd stored the cake yesterday. I lift it from the shelf, and take it into the kitchen, placing it on the kitchen counter, then I find a large plate to put it on and place that next to the box.

When I open the lid, I expect to be greeted by my beautiful lemon masterpiece, I gasp. It looks like *someone* has opened it up and punched a great big hole right in the middle. I want to cry. I put so much into this cake, it was made with love for Angela.

I look at it with my mouth open. The other two have gone quiet, and they're looking at it with their mouths open too.

'What is it?' Fiona asks.

I'm sure she knows exactly what it is, but I go along with the charade.

'It's Angela's birthday cake – she's expecting it, as she always says, "My birthday isn't the same without Danni's delicious cake."'

I tell them this in the hope that whoever did it might feel guilty, but it seems to annoy Fiona, who says, 'Really, is that what she says?'

'Did it sink?' Jenna asks, stepping forward, gazing into the lemon cream abyss. 'Did it happen on the journey?'

I look at her. 'No, of *course* not, the cake was intact when I left it on the shelf in the larder yesterday.'

'Okay, I only *asked*.' She feigns hurt for Fiona's benefit, and I glare at both of them.

'Don't look at *me*, Danni,' Fiona says, her palm on her chest defensively. 'I didn't even know there *was* a larder.'

This didn't just happen. *Someone* has done this. I want to cry, but I will not be cowed. Whoever did it is definitely in this kitchen with me now, I just don't know who it is. But I am so desperate to serve this bloody cake, I blindly open a kitchen drawer and seeing a palette knife there, attempt to repair some of the damage. Instead, I manage to make it worse.

Jenna leans over, I can feel her looking over my shoulder.

'Oh shit,' she says, and I look up from the cake into her face. I just can't work out if she's pleased or surprised, her face, as always is a mask.

'No need to worry, I made one, I always do,' Fiona says, as she steps forward, holding a big chocolate cake, covered in lighted candles. 'Angela's expecting it, as she always says, "My birthday isn't the same without Fiona's delicious cake."'

ELEVEN

FIONA

I actually felt sorry for Danni; whoever had wrecked her birthday cake for Angela had meant business. I knew she thought it was me, especially as I'd also made one, but it gave me no pleasure to see her cake sabotaged, because it could just as easily have been mine. She completely overreacted, but I understood her frustration because Angela is the kind of woman you want to please. I remember feeling that myself as a young bride, I still did. She was a kind but formidable woman, and you wanted her approval, it guaranteed your inclusion. And seeing Danni's reaction convinced me that she was the same.

She was panicking, desperately trying to resuscitate her lemon sponge, sobbing and slapping it with a palette knife which was simply making it worse. She'd snapped Jenna's head off, and was giving me daggers, so I felt it probably diplomatic to leave the kitchen and get my own cake to safety. She seemed so unhinged I wouldn't have been surprised if, in her devastation, she'd lunged for me and my cake, and we didn't need *two* cake casualties. I felt sorry for Danni, but again this wasn't about her, it was about Angela and I just wanted to get on with the birthday celebrations, there'd been enough delays. So, I lit the candles, and walked into the sitting room, leaving her in the kitchen with Jenna and her cake carnage. Walking slowly back into the sitting room, Scott turned out the lights as I presented my cake to Angela. She squealed with delight, her face glowing in the birthday candlelight as she made her wish.

I watched her, eyes closed, hands clasped together in apparent joy, like every other year. But this was different, because apparently she'd said exactly the same thing to Danni about *her* cake, and all the years I'd baked one for her seemed to have been erased. This was about more than cake, this was about Angela keeping her place in the family. It was a case of same family, same rules – and it didn't matter if it was a different daughter-in-law, we were interchangeable. As she blew hard on the tiny flames, leaving only small plumes of smoke in the semi-darkness, I finally saw Angela for the first time. Her feelings for Danni and me were superficial, to her we were both extensions of Scott, she only *really* cared about him and her grandchildren. Everyone else, including me and Danni, was a piece of Lego, to be clicked on the family when needed, and then clicked off again.

In the aftermath of singing 'Happy Birthday', still in almost darkness, I suddenly became aware of a sound coming from the kitchen. I was about to ask Scott to turn the lights back on, when Danni suddenly appeared in the kitchen doorway, streaky mascara, crazy eyes, her face lit by the glow of candles. She looked like something from a horror film, clutching the bashed-up cake that she'd randomly spiked with flaming candles. Everyone turned to look at her, and hoarse from crying, she started singing 'Happy Birthday'.

It was the most unsettling, embarrassing scene. I looked over at Scott, and even in the dim light I could see the expression of alarm on his face. We all stared, not knowing what to do, how to handle this, until after she'd taken a few wobbly steps, when Sam stood up and walked over to her. Then he quietly joined her in the singing, followed by Georgia, and when they'd finished, Sam guided her and the cake to the table. Angela hid what must have been sheer horror at the flaming mess that was laid before her and said nice things about the mashed-up cake.

* * *

The morning after Angela's birthday we all found ourselves congregated in the sitting room. We were all pretending this was like any normal lazy Sunday morning, eating toast, drinking coffee, just shooting the breeze, but I think we were all waiting for the phone to ring. We'd been due to leave for home on the Monday, this was to be our last day, and as lovely as the lodge was, none of us wanted to stay past Monday. But what now?

'We could still be here next week?' I said, trying not to reveal my inner panic.

'Don't, just don't,' Danni groaned. She'd been prowling around the lodge like a caged lion all morning and was now pacing around the sitting room with Olivia on her hip.

'So, Mum, let's talk about how very old you are today,' Scott teased, bringing a welcome respite from the gloom. This made me smile. I saw the same cheeky humour in Sam. He was so like his dad, always trying to make things better, attempting to solve everyone's problems, sometimes with a silly joke.

'As of yesterday, I'm seventy-five years young, you cheeky sod,' Angela replied with a giggle. She could take it from her only child, because along with Sam, Georgia and Olivia he was everything to her.

'You look great for your age, Ange,' Sam said, smiling warmly.

'And it's *Grandma* to you,' she said affectionately, and chuckled. He smiled at Danni who was still pacing the room.

She smiled back, and I tried to watch them discreetly and work out what was going on here, because *something* was.

'Angela, Sam's right, you don't look seventy-five, you're gorgeous!' Jenna said, blowing Angela a kiss.

'Thank you, love,' Angela glowed, as we all murmured in agreement.

'What about me, am I gorgeous too?' Jenna asked.

Sam flushed slightly and my heart broke a little. 'Yeah, yeah, beautiful, mate,' he muttered, embarrassed.

I immediately looked at Danni, whose smile dropped.

'I'm not beautiful. Stop teasing me, Sam,' Jenna replied.

'Oh, he's always teasing,' Danni said, in monotone, unsmiling. She was staring at them both until Jenna couldn't look at her, but Sam was holding her eyes with his. There was so much going on underneath the surface, if only I could have worked out what it was, but it was beyond me.

Earlier that day, I'd walked in on a conversation between them in the kitchen that was clearly not meant for anyone else to hear. He was talking about something he'd said to her the night before, but as hard as I tried I couldn't even get the gist of the conversation. But then she saw me loitering (which I denied) and went mad, and I wondered if I'd ever know what he'd said. Now I wondered again just what had gone between Danni and Sam to cause this rather tense encounter. It wasn't like my son, he was the joker, the pleaser, I'd never seen this side of him before. Had Danni toyed with him and he was hurt and now paying her back? Or was this something to do with Jenna, who Danni obviously had issues with? Were these two women fighting for my son's attention in some weird way? I couldn't work it out, but was surprised to see Jenna discreetly touching Sam's forearm with the back of her hand. It was a moment, and so swift, so gentle. Was this comfort, or encouragement? Either way it had meaning that I couldn't work out.

'Well, I'm loving it here,' Jenna suddenly announced. 'But

it's such a shame to be cooped up on your birthday, Angela, especially as you were kind enough to bring us all here.'

'I can think of *worse* places to be locked down,' Scott tried reassuringly.

I didn't share his optimism. The place itself was beautiful, but we were stuck here because of treacherous weather, and a murder; however he tried to frame it for Angela, it wasn't the stuff birthdays were made of.

'Yes, we shouldn't complain, and obviously my sympathies are with the victim and his family, but for God's sake, it was an accident. I doubt anyone planned it. The weather was terrible, it was getting dark and someone decided to go for a walk, which was just silly.' Angela shook her head in disbelief at the silliness.

'The police told us we can't leave the site, but does that mean we can't *drive* anywhere?' Danni asked, looking anxiously around the table.

'Given the weather, we won't be able to drive anywhere,' Scott replied. He sounded exasperated with Danni.

'Surely we're allowed to go for a walk nearby, get some fresh air?' Sam offered.

'Yes, we can do that, can't we?' Jenna looked at Scott like he was the oracle.

'Yeah, I imagine we *could* go for a walk,' he replied with a shrug. 'It can't do any harm, as long as we don't go alone – it isn't just the weather we have to worry about,' he added. 'There's apparently someone out there using their car as a murder weapon.'

I felt the hairs on the back of my neck prickle at this.

'I was planning to go for a drive, have a look around Lizard Point,' Danni was saying.

'What? Are you crazy?' Sam said.

'Danni, Lizard Point is the edge of the world. People get swept off the cliffs in places like that,' Scott said. 'I wouldn't even try to go there in a snowstorm.'

'*Wouldn't* you?' she replied sarcastically, before adding, 'I *would.*'

This kind of crashed onto the table and bounced around a while. The rest of us seemed to find something fascinating in the bottom of our coffee cups. It seemed there was trouble in paradise for the honeymoon couple. I tried to hide my delight at this.

'The snow is so pretty out there,' Jenna was saying, as she stood up from the table, and turned to face the window. 'I want to go outside and play snow angels,' she announced, turning back to the table and looking straight at Scott.

'I think after breakfast we *should* go outside,' he said, smiling indulgently back at her, 'I don't know about anyone else, but I need some fresh sea air.'

Georgia brightened at her dad's suggestion. 'Yes, let's all be snow angels, you too, Dad?'

'I'm not sure about that,' Scott said gently.

'Let's *all* go,' I said, keen to keep an eye on my son and his stepmother.

'I hope I don't regret this,' Scott said, with a smile.

'You will,' Danni replied, her face like thunder. There was a vague threat in her tone and I suddenly saw a dynamic here that I hadn't seen so far. Danni was *angry* with Scott. Now I was keen to know why, just *what* had he done?

I glanced back at Scott to see his reaction. He didn't respond verbally but gave her a hurt look. Was this the tail end of some disagreement they'd already had in private?

I put that away for later, and listened politely as Angela and Scott talked fondly of their family holidays at Kynance Cove when Scott was a child. We all smiled at the right time and asked questions, allowing the birthday girl some attention. The hit-and-run and weather had set the tone, and it hadn't been much fun for Angela, who'd just wanted her family around her. But being locked down here was hell, and when Danni and I weren't competing, Danni and Jenna were, and these difficult dynamics had created such tension. It hovered over the table even now, as the family sat together. Fortunately, Danni soon became bored, and interrupted Angela and Scott's reminiscing to say she was taking Olivia to get her changed for the walk.

Danni leaving the room instantly eased everything and I could breathe again. Without her I felt free to speak without feeling judged. I could laugh with Scott about something from the past, make a reference to when the children were small without worrying that I was excluding her. In Danni's presence I felt like I had to erase my own life, and I resented that. But now as we chatted and drank coffee and talked about the day ahead, there was a rare easiness around us all. Just like it used to be before she came along and spoiled everything.

To anyone on the outside, this would have looked like a normal family scene, a film montage of people laughing, chatting, listening. In that moment, with the fire crackling, the smell of fresh coffee and the sound of my children's laughter, I wondered if there was a chance that we might all one day come together in the ashes that were left. But something was already circling around that family scene, and despite the smiles and shared violet creams, resentment and hate still bubbled underneath the surface. Past and present collided, and if we'd listened carefully we might have heard the distant rumblings of a storm coming in from the sea. It scuttled under doors, and slid through windows, bringing with it something so awful, that none of us would ever be the same again.

TWELVE

DANNI

I still feel a bit weird about last night. I got myself into a real state about Angela's cake, and this morning when I saw everyone, I felt embarrassed. Everyone seems to be avoiding me, or being weird around me. Jenna's glancing over more than usual, and I'm not sure if it's disgust or pity on Fiona's face. Even Sam's giving me a wide berth, which hurts most.

I am desperate to leave this place, I feel so trapped. And despite the cold outside, I'm even finding the open fire too much. The constant heat chokes me and I mentioned it to Angela and Scott who keep stoking it and adding more fuel, but they just ignored me and Angela said, 'It isn't just you, Danni – everyone else likes it.' But that simply isn't true because Sam and Georgia both said they found it too warm. Anyway, there's this awful plan for us all to go out into the snow together, so much for escaping them all. But I'll be glad of the fresh air and to get away from the stuffiness in here.

Meanwhile, I have to get out of the sitting room, they're all politely listening to Scott and Angela's endless reminiscing about childhood holidays. Once I would have loved my mother-in-law's memories about the lispy way Scott demanded ice cream when he was two, or how he always took his baby elephant on holiday and had to photograph him. But I've heard it all before, and besides I can't stop checking my phone, I can barely have a conversation anymore. So I say Olivia needs a rest, and just as I'm escaping, Scott reminds me about the family walk, which makes my heart sink. I promise him I'll be back in ten minutes.

I'm now in the sanctuary of our bedroom and have just minutes to get myself and Olivia dressed for outdoors, but first I have to check my phone. I click on, then click through the school website and start scrolling and to my deep, but temporary relief, nothing has been posted – yet.

I have this wonderful fantasy that the troll has forgotten, or moved on, but perhaps that's what they *want* me to think? I feel like someone's constantly watching me, in the car behind me, standing close to me in the checkout at the supermarket, but when I slow the car down, or turn around, no one's there. I'm not even sure I trust Scott anymore. I mean, who could trust a man who calls his wife to say he's working late then has sex with you on his office desk? I still shudder with embarrassment at that candid shot, my blouse open, my legs splayed. I will forever cringe with embarrassment and shame, and long to know who the hell was standing outside the headteacher's office window at 9pm, close enough to take those photos.

We were always careful, waiting until everyone had gone, the lights were out. We'd even move our cars from the car park so no one would know we were still there. Was it, as Scott says, pure chance that a mischievous kid, an angry parent, or even a random dog walker was passing that night? I find it hard to believe, but the alternative – that someone knew about us, and waited around to get their pictures – is a creepy thought. But unlike Scott, I believe someone found us because they were looking for us, and that scares me.

I dress Olivia for the outdoors, then climb into my snowsuit, and finding it hard to zip up, curse my life. I used to be able to eat what I liked and do what I liked, but not anymore. Now my life is about baby fat and milk and early nights. I resent that Scott still goes to the gym and out for drinks after work spontaneously while all I get to do is snatch the odd ten minutes to work out in front of the TV when Olivia's sleeping.

I fling my snowsuit on the bed, and after pulling on a vest and jumper, grab my jacket and head out of the door with Olivia. There's no one in the living room, they're all getting changed to go out. But where's Scott? Because he isn't in our room. Still holding Olivia, I wander over to the window to see if he's already outside, but no sign of him, and he isn't in the kitchen either. There's nowhere for him to be unless he's in someone's bedroom.

I think again about Fiona and the weird way she was looking at me, and, more importantly, the way Jenna was looking at Scott. Unease crawls through me, turning my veins cold, forcing the blood to pump harder and I wonder if he's with her.

I know he isn't here, or outside, and he wasn't in our bedroom, so he has to be in someone else's room. I stand in the middle of the room so I can see all the bedroom doors down the small corridor. And every time I hear a door opening, I watch, on red alert. One by one a door opens, first Angela's, then Sam's, then finally Fiona's. One by one everyone emerges from their respective bedrooms. Except Scott, Jenna and Georgia. And so I wait.

I need to know he hasn't already left me for someone else – Jenna.

Such is the plight of the mistress-made-wife; the shadow is always there, the past shapes the present, nothing can be erased after all. I concentrate on the two closed doors to see which one he comes from. It's fifty-fifty that it's Jenna's room. And even if he does emerge from there with her, his hair a little roughened, her lipstick smeared, he'll say he's been helping her fill in an application form, or mentoring her on a future career. He'll sound plausible and she'll nod vigorously in agreement at his side. But I know how he works, I watched him lie to Fiona.

So when Georgia's door slowly opens and she walks out alone, my world starts to spin. If she's alone then there's only one other bedroom that Scott can be in. Georgia suddenly leans back into her room, says something, and there he is, stepping through the door, putting his arm around her shoulder. And as they walk down the hallway his head down as he talks gently to her, I'm so relieved, I only briefly wonder what's going on and if she's okay.

Georgia is often having minor crises, and they always blow over. It might be that a friend has been brusque, or Sam has teased her. I worry these things are made bigger by her mother who encourages the drama, thus causing Scott to run back to his first family – and her.

They walk into the room and I see the gentle concern on Scott's face as he looks at his daughter. I find it endearing and hope that one day he shares the same kind of relationship with Olivia, and that he still has the energy to be a good father by then. He certainly doesn't seem to have the will for being a good husband lately.

'Where's Jenna?' Sam is asking, as he walks towards her bedroom door and bangs on it.

'Sam, she might be napping,' Fiona says, slight chastisement in her voice.

'Jenna never naps,' he replies with a smile.

'Come on, let's go, Jenna probably doesn't fancy going out into that cold,' I add, marching towards the front door, knowing Jenna does want to go out, but not willing to wait for her. I am reluctant enough to go walking in Fiona's company, but to have Jenna there too will be unbearable. She's been banging on about playing bloody snow angels all morning, and the prospect of a twenty-five-year-old woman lying on the floor waving her legs around is not something I'm keen to watch.

As soon as we open the front door, the wind comes howling in and I hear Jenna's voice. 'Wait for me, guys!'

My heart sinks. God, I wish I hadn't agreed to this, but can't refuse because Scott will sulk, and at the same time, I don't want him out there with Jenna. But my fingers are crossed she might not come anyway. So, I wander over to Angela, who's wrapped in several layers of fleece and jumpers topped with the padded waterproof she's so pleased with. Even in sub zero temperatures nothing will penetrate her cold weather garb. She's brandishing her walking stick, which she says she doesn't need. But she does.

'You should be warm and dry in all that, Angela,' I say, hoping to start a conversation I can conduct on autopilot while keeping an eye on Jenna's bedroom door.

'Yes, thank you,' she says dismissively with a smile that doesn't reach her eyes, then turns to say something to Fiona, who laughs at her comment. I can't hear what she says, but it's clear even Angela isn't into me today.

'I'll take Olivia in the baby sling?' Scott offers, which I'm relieved about, I don't feel completely safe walking around on the icy ground with her in case I should fall. At the same time I'm irritated because he'd normally leave me to carry Olivia in the sling, so it looks like he's still playing this hands-on role to impress. But who? His mother? Jenna? Fiona?

But I soon dismiss that idea when he dumps Olivia on the sofa to help Jenna on with her jacket, the exact same one as mine. Looking at her now, she *has* changed her style recently, and she's become more assured, more mature, I guess? It's quite the transformation, because the last time I saw her she was sobbing and pleading with me not to tell the police.

THIRTEEN

FIONA

It wasn't easy to watch Scott grab Danni's hand and help her across the snow. I found it difficult to comprehend that the man who cared for me and our children just a few short years before, was now caring for another woman and another child. The kids and I had been everything to him, and yet how easily he'd slipped into the same role with someone else. How could he do that? I'd found it hard to become involved with *anyone* else since the break-up. I'd seen Nick for about six months, and initially I'd hoped he might help me move on, but it was quite the opposite. Would I ever be ready to give up what we had? I stood alone in the whiteness watching Scott put his arm around Danni protectively while cradling the baby in the sling. It filled me with so much pain I had to look away. Angela was alone too, standing there in the frozen whiteness with her pearl-handled walking stick. She seemed bewildered, so I crunched through the snow towards her, and slid my arm into hers. She glanced over at Danni and Scott in a little huddle, obviously whispering sweet nothings, and she patted my hand, and smiled at me with such pity I wanted to cry.

We walked on further, to where Georgia and Jenna were

now lying with their arms and legs spread out in the snow. Angela and I smiled indulgently at the two young women, but looking across at Danni, she seemed so agitated by this. She clearly couldn't stand the attention not being on her, and within seconds she'd abandoned the cosy little huddle with Scott. I thought she was walking away, but quite the opposite, and in a rather frantic plea yelped, 'Make room for a little one.' More like room for a desperate one, I thought, watching her get down on her back and wave her limbs around erratically. All three were now moving their legs and arms from side to side creating the shape of snow angels on the white ground. Georgia and Jenna were just doing this for their own fun (okay, perhaps Jenna was also enjoying the attention), but I found Danni's involvement rather cringey. She seemed permanently wound up, and it stopped her from relaxing and melting into the snow like the other two. Despite the display of confidence, she seemed awkward and slightly self-conscious. I felt she was competing with the two younger women. I watched Scott watching her and had the feeling he wasn't too impressed by her performance. She really was too young for him, on so many levels.

Eventually it was over, and the girls stood up to take photos of the angel-shaped snow. But as they did, Jenna let out an almighty roar, and fell back onto the snow, 'Oh my God! I think you've broken my ankle, Danni.' Jenna was groaning in pain.

'What are you talking about? I didn't touch you.'

Jenna was lying in the snow, looking up at Danni with a pained expression. 'You know you did, you deliberately stomped on my *leg*!' Jenna exclaimed, outraged at Danni's denial.

Scott staggered over in the snow and immediately went to Jenna's aid. With Olivia still in the sling around his neck, he bent forward and offered her his hand.

'Scott, you'll *drop* her,' Danni yelled, her face flushed.

I hadn't seen what happened and had no idea who was telling the truth. Both seemed equally outraged and offended, and I felt it wisest to stay out of it, as did Georgia, who walked away from the scene.

Presumably Scott realised it was more than his life was worth to help Jenna, so stepped back, a little embarrassed, while Sam moved in to help. He grabbed Jenna by the upper arms, then seemed to dump her on her feet. 'Ouch,' she yelped, holding her ankle and looking at Scott.

Sam then went to Danni, asking her if she was okay. She suddenly started crying, and saying, 'I never touched her, Sam, you believe me, don't you?'

Sam didn't say anything to this, but the fact he had his hand on her back and let her rest her head on his broad shoulders, suggested to me he was Team Danni.

I glanced at Angela who pretended not to see, but I could tell by her pursed lips that she found this too much. Scott was busy placating Olivia, who was now crying. Her little nose and cheeks were red from the cold and she really shouldn't have been outside.

Sam meanwhile seemed cool with the situation, which of course he would be, wouldn't he? The woman hanging all over him might be his stepmother, but to an eighteen-year-old boy, she was also an attractive older woman. It bothered me how physically comfortable the two of them were with each other, and I wondered what Scott thought of this, but he was too distracted by Olivia. I noticed Jenna also seemed to distract him as she leaned against a tree, covered in snow, one leg lifted, staring at Danni and Sam with barely concealed hate.

'Danni?' she yelled accusingly, as she grasped her ankle in apparent pain. 'You stood on my ankle.'

Danni lifted her head from Sam's shoulder.

'You *know* I didn't.'

'You *know* you did! You *stomped* on it as you tried to get up,' she said accusingly, her eyes narrowed.

'Come on, let's stop arguing,' Sam said. 'Jenna, can you move your leg?' he asked her, turning away from Danni, and walking to the tree where Jenna was leaning dramatically.

Georgia walked over with him, and Sam suggested the two of them try to help Jenna to walk. She certainly seemed to be in a lot of pain, her face was deathly pale and she looked on the verge of tears.

Danni had now returned to Scott and their belligerent baby, ignoring the injury she might have caused.

'She did it *deliberately*,' I heard Jenna whisper to my kids. 'She *stomped* on my leg!'

'I think we need to get you back,' Sam said, tactfully ignoring what she said. At this I saw Jenna glance over at Scott, like she was hoping he might take her back, or at least get involved in helping her. But he was too busy trying to placate Olivia, while Danni, now emotionally recovered, checked her phone, again!

'I'm fine,' Jenna said, presumably realising that there was no mileage in this. I was no fan of Danni, but doubted very much she'd *deliberately* stomped on Jenna's leg.

'You sure you're okay, Jenna?' I asked. Only Sam and Georgia seemed to be acknowledging her injury, if indeed that's what it was, and even they weren't exactly being sympathetic.

Georgia bent down to touch her leg. 'I don't think it's broken,' she announced, and declared her fit to walk.

I could see her in my mind's eye in a white coat with a stethoscope, and felt so proud of her in that moment, wanted to give her a hug.

We all moved on a little further, and Jenna joined with Sam and Georgia, while I stayed with Angela. But then suddenly, Sam stopped to pelt snowballs at Georgia, who, squealing with surprise and joy, retaliated. Soon Jenna was joining in, and then

Danni ran from where she'd been standing with Scott and hurled herself into the middle of the action. Within seconds she'd wrestled Sam to the ground and was sat astride him trying to force snow into his mouth. I was horrified. My instinct was to march through the snow and pull her off my son by her hair, but I clenched my fists in my jacket pocket and held on to my rage. I looked over at Scott, who was also watching Danni. His eyes slid over to mine, and he gave an almost imperceptible raise of the eyebrows. We were both bystanders here, both adults, the *real* mother and father of the group, the *real* husband and wife.

'Come with me, Fiona, I want to see the sea from that high ground the other side of the lodge,' Angela suddenly said. 'Look at the lighthouse, it was flashing all night last night in my room, it's on all the time. Let's try and get closer to it.'

I took my eyes from Scott and smiled gratefully. My ex-mother-in-law was offering an escape, which I accepted gladly. I was desperate to remove myself from this snowy scene which was making me extremely anxious.

So we walked on, and as much as I longed to get away, I was also keen to see the lighthouse up close and the spectacular view that Danni and Scott enjoyed from their master bedroom.

'We'll follow you guys up,' Sam called after us, still in the middle of his snow fight with Danni and clearly in no rush to join us. I worried Angela might struggle as she leaned hard on her walking stick and I realised how steep the walk was. But despite some confusion that weekend, she showed no signs of *physical* weakness. She seemed on fine form considering she was seventy-five and this might be her last birthday.

The snow was pretty deep and crunchy underfoot, and in some places halfway up my calves, and even deeper for Angela who was a couple of inches shorter. Finally, we reached the top of the incline and gasped, both with exertion and wonderment at the sight before us. The lighthouse was white, and though it should have been a beacon, it was lost in the equally white landscape, save for the constant, flashing light warning ships of the perilous currents.

The sea roared over the rocks beneath, and the high, perilous waves could be seen through the snow, a gigantic lace curtain softening the danger below. I realised, in our keenness to see, we'd moved dangerously close to the edge, and I held on to Angela for both our safety. One slip and it could have been the end.

'Let's stand further back,' I said, the wind biting at my face. We were on high ground with no shelter, completely exposed to the elements. 'You're close to the edge,' I warned, but Angela didn't seem at all scared, which bothered me.

'Angela?'

With her eyes now half-closed, she slowly raised her head to face whatever was coming towards her, towards us. Panic swept through me, but I didn't want to scare her, she might fall.

'Angela?' I said her name again quietly, so as not to alarm her, while attempting to manoeuvre her gently away from the edge. She didn't respond. The only sound was the constant roar of the waves smashing hard on the rocks, freezing snow and sea spittle hitting my face. She suddenly grabbed my arm with her hand and turned to look at me. Her stare was that of a stranger, no light of recognition in her eyes.

'Angela, are you okay?'

She reached out and clung to my arm, leaning towards me, looking into my face.

'Are you okay, Angela?'

'Be careful... don't trust her, Fiona.'

I felt the hairs on the back of my neck raise.

'Who, love? Who can't I trust?'

We were alone on a cliff, the swirling sea beneath us, and Angela's eyes were wild, she seemed frightened.

'Tell me,' I said gently.

Wordlessly, she turned back towards the sea, succumbing to the white oblivion of snow now falling more heavily around us.

She was still clutching at my upper arm, and unsure of her now, I was scared she might jump.

And as much as I cared for my mother-in-law and wanted to keep her safe, the way she was clinging meant she could easily take me over the edge *with* her. I tried to step back, while looking behind me. There was no sign of the others, and we were alone here, the two of us. I was terrified.

FOURTEEN

DANNI

Everyone's drinking hot chocolate and playing happy families after our walk in the snow, but I can't join in. There's been nothing more online, but Charlotte hasn't removed the teasing question about which teacher has a big secret. She must be away on holiday or something, which makes me feel very vulnerable and exposed, anything could be posted there at any time. It fills my every waking hour.

What doesn't make any sense is that I haven't been at the school since before Olivia was born. I deliberately took a long maternity leave so that any issue around the photos was forgotten. So why has this psycho decided that now is the time to start trolling me? Is it because my maternity leave ends soon and I have to go back? As much as I want to return to teaching, I can't bear the thought of going back to that school if the troll is waiting for me.

I feel so alone, it's not the kind of thing you can share with just anyone. But I have a close relationship with Sam, and when he goes into the kitchen, I follow him. I tell him all about the post on Facebook and the website, and he looks concerned.

'And *do* you have a big secret you're keeping from Dad?' he asks, suddenly serious.

'No, of *course* I don't have a big secret I'm keeping from your dad,' I lie, already regretting this conversation.

'So what are you worried about?' He soon slips into his signature flippant, laid-back manner.

'I'm worried about what they're threatening to post, they'll spread lies about me again. This is my reputation, my career...'

'Is it the same person who posted the photos?'

'I don't know, I think it *must* be.' I blush, reliving the horror of my stepson seeing a picture of me in flagrante with his father.

'I guess you'll just have to ignore it,' is his advice.

'I can't, not until I know what they're going to post.'

'Might not be about you?' He raises his eyebrows hopefully, his sweet attempt to offer me something.

'I mean it's a lie, but I just know how these trolls work. Is it just a coincidence that this turns up online just as I'm due to go back after maternity leave?'

'No, I guess.'

'Whoever it is, they hate me, but *who* could hate me so much?' I ask, desperately hoping he'll come up with a name, a theory at least.

Sam just shakes his head, apparently baffled. I doubt he'd openly suggest his own mother is the troll, but surely it's occurred to him that she might have some skin in the game. She's still on my list of two along with Jenna.

But the rational part of my brain wonders how either of them would know I was hiding a big secret from Scott?

Sam leans against the kitchen cabinet and says under his breath, 'Talking of mysteries, any thoughts on the hit-and-run?'

I didn't expect him to ask about that. We've all talked and talked about who what when and why, but we go around in circles. I'm intrigued, does he know something?

'I haven't a clue,' I reply. 'I think it's probably more random than the police believe. I don't think anyone *here* did it, do you?'

He raises his eyebrows.

'Who?' I am positively salivating now. Well-meaning but bad driver Angela? Psycho Jenna mowing down innocent walkers? Fiona, her bitterness blinding her to oncoming pedestrians in the dark? Scott? Sam driving too fast? I'm always telling him about it. I guess it could be anyone, but then again, we aren't criminals (except Jenna) and surely whoever it was would simply have pulled over and called the police.

'Who, Sam?' I repeat impatiently, watching the cheeky smile play on his lips.

'I have my theories,' he replies tantalisingly.

'So you think it was deliberate? Do you think it might be one of us?' I whisper this, looking around to check no one's listening.

'I reckon it was those guys in one of the other lodges, they tore past us in a bloody Ferrari on Friday night. Mum said they almost pushed her off the road.'

I'm slightly disappointed, but hugely relieved he doesn't think it's one of us. Just then Fiona appears like a bloody apparition in the doorway.

'Sam, there you are. I was looking for you.' She walks into the kitchen and slowly picks up a kitchen knife.

'I've only been here with Danni,' he says, 'you didn't look far.'

'It's just that Jenna was asking where you were,' Fiona says, with a twinkle in her eye. Oh God, she must be so naïve to think Sam and Jenna – what the hell? Has she *really* no idea? Can't she see what's right in front of her?

Fiona takes a loaf out of the bread bin and cuts a slice. 'Toast anyone?' she asks, holding the knife in what I perceive as a threatening manner. I am hyper paranoid at the moment, but you never know.

'No thanks.' I shake my head at her offer, while Sam, who never stops eating, nods vigorously. Fiona jams more bread into the toaster.

Then to my surprise, she walks towards me and stands directly in front of me. I don't know whether to run or stand my ground. We both stare at each other for at least thirty seconds, which is a long time for a new wife and an ex-wife to stare at each other. And when she reaches out her hand quite close to my face, I half-close my eyes in anticipation of the slap she so wants to give me. I hold my breath, grit my teeth and just stand my ground, knowing that I probably deserve it.

'Are you okay?' she says, looking from me to Sam.

'I... yes, are *you*?' I say uncertainly.

'Yeah. It's just that you're standing in front of the fridge. I need to get butter for the toast.'

I feel such a fool, and my whole body relaxes like liquid as I slide across the shiny fridge door so she can open it.

I'm so embarrassed, I mutter, 'I'll just go and find...' then leave it there and leave the kitchen.

I go back into the sitting room where the others are still sitting around the fire drinking hot chocolate. We've just been out for what Angela optimistically referred to as 'a lovely family walk,' though of course it was nothing of the sort. Scott was sulking because I wouldn't for once take charge of Olivia, Fiona had stood around with that judgemental expression like the bloody snow queen and Jenna falsely accused me of assault! Some family walk that turned out to be.

And I'm finding it really creepy the way Jenna will do anything to get Scott's attention. She thinks if she wears clothes like me and has her hair cut the same, he'll be hers, but that's how childlike and superficial she is. I wish I could say Scott was unaware, but he is *very* much aware of Jenna, always engaging with her, sometimes chatting quietly together. But when I mention their little chats, he gaslights me.

'I hardly know the girl. It's your imagination,' he says. 'You're so wracked with guilt because of what happened between us, you imagine I'm now being unfaithful to *you*.' He tries to reassure me, but I'm not convinced, the dynamic between them bothers me.

I watch her now, her eyes looking at him over her cup of hot chocolate, listening intently to everything he says. It's a pretty blatant way to behave in front of me, but it's the way Scott encourages her that really pisses me off. He seems so kind and engaging towards her, when he must see that she's playing a game. It doesn't make sense to me. Well, perhaps it does, I just don't want to see it.

'Lovely hot chocolate, Jenna,' Angela says, and everyone murmurs their approval.

'The weather's getting worse,' Scott observes. 'The app on my phone says there's another weather warning. I'm concerned we might be here even longer than it takes the police to sort out this hit-and-run.'

'Oh no!' Angela's hands fly up to her mouth.

Fiona looks pale. 'No, we have work to get back for,' she says.

I'm on a sofa sitting with Scott and Olivia, when a few minutes later Sam joins us with his toast and plonks himself next to me. I'm tired and lean on Sam because Olivia's trying to take his toast and he's playing with her. She always laughs when Sam's around, I do too, he's funny.

A few seconds after Sam sits down, Fiona's in the room, and I can see she's unhappy about the seating arrangements. She hates that Sam and I are so close. She hates *me*. I wish for her sake she'd move on, but she can't. She sits next to Jenna who's sitting snugly with Angela, like she belongs here in the family. Why is no one else alarmed by her presence the way I am?

But the others don't know what I know about Jenna. And there's so much I want to say, so much I *could* say that would make them realise that she isn't the sweet young girl they think she is. Jenna has no moral compass, she's dangerous, but Scott will always defend her publicly. He stood by her at school, took her side against me both personally and professionally, something for which I can never forgive him. But if I said anything against her in this company, not only would it ruin Angela's birthday, it would look like I'm jealous of her bond with my husband. But things aren't always as they seem, and she's the one who's jealous of me, I'm not *jealous* of her... I'm *scared* of her.

FIFTEEN

FIONA

I finally got Angela down from the coastal path, but somehow, between there and the lodge, she lost her walking stick. I'd never known her to be so forgetful and was annoyed with myself for not realising she didn't have it with her when we walked back. Sam said he'd go and have a look for it, but came back shaking his head. The snow was so heavy it had probably been buried in the short time it had been left.

Once we were back at the lodge, we drank hot chocolate and I went into the kitchen to check what was going on with Danni and Sam. Just as I'd expected, they were huddled together, so I made toast for me and Sam, so I could hang around. But Danni was behaving really weirdly, standing in front of the fridge so I couldn't open it, she seemed very anxious. The situation was getting to all of us, but she clearly couldn't hide her feelings.

Later, in the living room, I saw Danni pull a face when Jenna mentioned dinner. They glared at each other in this weird stand-off, but I stayed out of it, I had enough problems of my own, and it wasn't in my interests to get involved in their drama. I needed to stay low on everyone's radar and just get through the weekend, but when Georgia went off to get changed into dry clothes, leaving Jenna alone in the kitchen, I went in offering to help.

'What can I do?' I asked, as I walked in.

'I'm fine really,' she said, stirring milk slowly in a pan, and adding butter, then flour, but it seemed to be splitting. I didn't say anything, I figured she must know what she was doing.

'So, how long have you known Angela?' I asked.

'About a year, I think.' She looked up at the ceiling like she might find the actual calendar date there. 'Yeah, it was November last year when I started working at the café, she was my first customer. She's lovely, isn't she?'

'She was a lovely mother-in-law,' I said.

'I'm sure she was.' She then seemed to hesitate before saying, 'I am a bit worried about her, Fiona.'

'Why?'

'She seems a bit... lost?'

'You mean like she's a bit confused?' I asked, remembering earlier when Angela and I were outside and she'd said, *'Be careful... don't trust her, Fiona.'*

'I sometimes pop in and see her at home, you know, just to check on her. And the other day I called in and she was asleep.'

'Oh? Do you have keys?'

'Yeah... she wanted me to have them, just in case she ever needed me, you know?'

'Yes, that's good,' I said, realising this made a lot of sense.

'So, the other day I walked in and she was asleep, but one of her cushions was on the floor and it had been ripped up, slashed. Feathers everywhere!' She waved her arms around like a child to illustrate the feather explosion.

'Who'd *done* that?' I asked, horrified.

'Angela, I suppose. I asked her when she woke up and she seemed confused.'

'Was she alone?'

'I think so, who else would be there?'

I didn't feel she could offer any more information, and as much as I liked Jenna, it probably wasn't fair on Angela to discuss this any further. I made a mental note to raise this with Scott, see if he knew anything. If Angela was having blackouts, it might explain a few things.

'I know you've come along to cook, but I hope you're enjoying yourself too?' I asked, moving in gently.

'Oh I'm having the best time.' She turned from the pan to give me the brightest smile. 'You guys are all really cool, and it's not like work at all, I feel privileged to be here.'

'We're lucky to have you,' I replied. 'Your dinners have been wonderful. You really have a talent.'

'Oh, I don't know about that. But you have a talent – the birthday cake you made was delicious.'

'Thanks, I enjoy baking,' I replied, realising this was my opportunity to introduce Danni into the conversation. 'I felt a bit guilty though, Danni having made a cake too, and it being... you know?'

She turned the heat down on the milk and sighed. 'I guess.' She leaned back against the cooker. 'I'm sure she thinks it was me who messed with her cake, but it wasn't.'

'Did she *say* you'd done it?'

Jenna ran her fingers through short, thick blonde hair, just like Danni's. 'No, she didn't say anything, but I know she doesn't like me.'

'Really?' I acted surprised.

'Yeah, she never liked me. From my first day at that school, Danni Watkins, as she was then, hated me.'

'But why?'

She shrugged. 'She thought I'd been spying on her and Scott, she thought it was *me* who'd taken that picture and...' She seemed to suddenly realise I was his wife at the time, and therefore impacted me too. 'Sorry, Fiona.'

'Oh, it's water under the bridge. It wasn't pleasant seeing that photograph, humiliating actually.' I lifted my head to face her. 'But it was a long time ago, and I'm over it,' I lied. 'But why would Danni accuse *you* of taking the picture?'

She just looked at me, then walked to the kitchen door, closing it gently, and lowering her voice before saying, 'She accused me of being a stalker, said I was obsessed with Scott – joke is it was *her* who was obsessed with him. I remember her first day, she was all over him.'

I nodded; I could imagine.

'Anyway, she told all the staff it was me, the kids heard about it and gave me a hard time too, and then when *that* didn't cause enough problems for me, she started telling *more* lies about me.'

'Like what?'

'Oh just stuff about drugs... lies.'

'Why do you think...?'

'Like I say, she was the one who was obsessed with Scott, and she hated that we were friends.'

'You and Scott?' This was intriguing, and a little worrying.

'Danni Watkins put me through hell.' She was shaking her head as she spoke, still distressed at what she'd been through. It seemed painful for her to tell me even now. 'She accused me of... of dealing drugs.'

'Oh...'

She was shaking her head. 'It wasn't just that, Fiona, she said I was dealing to the kids at the school.' Her big blue eyes were rounded in surprise as a tear made its way down her cheek.

'Jenna, that's awful.' I feigned surprise, even though Angela had already told me about this. I wanted to hear it from Jenna, because I had no idea whose version was the truth.

'She threatened to call the police and get me sacked, so I went straight to Scottie.' I cringed again at the way she referred to him like this. Again, I noticed how she referred to him in first name terms. 'I told him it wasn't true, that I *wasn't* a drug dealer, but then...' She looked at me, then looked away. '*Other* stuff came out and it got messy. Scott said it would be better if I left – and I *know* she was behind it.'

'Messy? What do you mean, did Danni report you to the police as she'd threatened?'

'No, Scott talked her out of it. She said if I agreed to leave she wouldn't tell the police.'

This didn't really make sense to me; surely if she was guilty, Scott would agree with Danni that the police should be called in. Equally, if innocent, why not let Danni call the police and simply prove she was innocent?

'Scott's so kind,' she gushed, 'he really helped me. He found me a job and gave me good references at the café.'

Scott was always trying to save the kids, and though she wasn't a student, Jenna seemed little more than a kid.

'He saved my life. I wanted to kill myself, Fiona.'

'I'm so sorry you had to go through that. Nothing is worth losing your life, Jenna. You're okay now though?'

'Yeah, yeah. I'm okay, it's lovely to meet you and spend time with Georgia and Sam, and be with a real family.'

I nodded in acknowledgement, it was awkward, we were more of a *fractured* family than a *real* one.

'Obviously I'd be happier if Danni wasn't around,' she added with a sigh. I could so relate. 'But I'm doing this for Angela, and Scott, of course.'

'Of course,' I repeated quietly.

Suddenly the kitchen door opened, Georgia came in, opened the fridge door and took out some orange juice. Our conversation was over. 'Come and play chess with me, Mum,' she asked. I was surprised she didn't want to hang around the kitchen with Jenna, but of course Jenna didn't like people around when she was cooking anyway.

'Come on then, let's leave Jenna in peace,' I said, noticing the yellow oil swirls on top of the pan of milk. The sauce had definitely split, and Jenna was panicking.

Georgia and I walked into the living room, and for my own sanity, I tried not to notice Danni leaning all over Sam. I found it hard to watch, it made me so uncomfortable, and I wasn't the only one; the disapproval on Angela's face was clear as she looked across at Danni pawing at her grandson. I sat down, Georgia brought over the chess box and we started to place our pieces on the board. I glanced around at the others who were now talking about the hit-and-run.

'It's all very distressing,' Angela was saying, wringing her hands, gazing ahead at nothing. We'd all been disturbed by the news that the victim had died, but Angela seemed to have taken it worse than the others.

I wanted to discuss Angela's odd behaviour with Scott, I wondered if he'd noticed it too. We hadn't had a chance to talk, and it wasn't a conversation I wanted to have in front of, or with Danni. We didn't need her getting involved and offering her stupid brand of advice. I watched her now, still sitting far too close to my son, and now disturbingly gazing up into Scott's eyes. Did she have to have *both* of the men I loved? Was one not *enough* for her?

* * *

'You realise we are breaking Dad's rules?' I said to Sam, as we stood on the back doorstep after dinner. We'd gone together to make sure the outside kitchen door was locked, but as the moon was full, we stood a while on the doorstep to admire it.

The view was stunning, though it was dark. The moon lit the snow with a milky blue hue, almost neon, I couldn't take my eyes off it.

'Jenna told me that Danni got her sacked from the school. Did you know that?' I heard myself say.

Sam turned to look at me, a doubtful expression on his face. 'Is that what she said?'

'Yeah, is it true?'

'I don't honestly know.'

'Do you think Jenna would *lie* about it?'

'Don't know. Not sure I'd trust Jenna, but Danni really hates her. They used to be friends, she came over a couple of times when I was at Dad's.'

'Oh really?'

'Yeah, but I think it got a bit awkward, I got the feeling that Jenna was only there to see Dad.'

This hit me right between the eyes. I was shocked, but at the same time, I wasn't. 'Are they close then, Jenna and Dad?' I posed this as a question, but he obviously didn't want to answer me and moved back into the house, opening out his arm to usher me back in.

'It's cold out there,' he said, the conversation apparently over. I wondered why my question about Scott and Jenna had provoked this reaction, but everything was erased the moment we were back in the sitting room. The TV was blaring out that evening's news, and we stopped in our tracks.

'Is there a killer at large in Kynance Cove?' the news reporter was asking, peering earnestly into the camera. Everyone was glued to the screen, including me and Sam; we'd stopped in our tracks to watch. Without taking my eyes off the screen, I sat down quietly on the edge of the sofa, desperate to see and hear everything.

'Police have launched a murder investigation after a man died following a "horrific and callous" attack in Kynance Cove, in Cornwall,' the newsreader started.

A murmur of horror echoed around the room.

'Officers were called to the scene on Friday evening. Paramedics from the Devon and Cornwall ambulance service were also in attendance.'

'Oh my God!' Danni groaned, holding her face with both hands.

Angela was white. 'Evil, pure evil,' she mouthed in horror, as Scott raised a hand in the air requesting silence.

Suddenly DCI Freeman was on the screen, at what looked like a hastily organised press conference. Everyone murmured in recognition, but I just watched open-mouthed as the horror unfolded.

'Shit,' I heard Georgia sigh.

'This appears to be a premeditated attack, the driver collided with the victim and after dragging him for half a mile reversed their vehicle over him before making off. It is one of the most horrific and callous incidents I have ever seen in over twenty-five years in the force,' she added, to the sound of more groaning around the room.

'The driver of the vehicle left the victim to die in the road, where he was discovered by a local man walking his dog. We are continuing the investigation in spite of the difficult weather and hope to make an arrest soon,' she said. 'We are appealing for anyone who was in the area at the time or who might have dash cam footage of the incident, to please contact us.'

Back in the studio, the presenter ended the report. 'Police believe they know the man's identity and have informed his next of kin. Formal identification of his body and a post-mortem will be arranged in due course.'

'Doesn't look like they've made any arrests yet,' Scott murmured as she moved on to another story. We all looked at each other, dread and fear on all our faces – this wasn't ending any time soon.

I felt my blood turn cold, but before I could join in on the speculation, there was a 'Breaking News' banner on the TV, and we were back to the studio, where the newsreader was holding her hand to her ear, listening to talkback. 'We have some breaking news regarding our earlier story about the murder investigation in Kynance Cove.' She paused. 'We've just heard that Friday afternoon's hit-and-run victim has now been identified by police as a forty-two-year-old man from Worcestershire. Police will release more details once his family have been informed.'

'Oh, he's from Worcestershire like us,' Angela remarked. 'Poor man, what a horrible death, can you imagine?'

'As the police said, that wasn't just a hit-and-run,' Scott said, horrified. 'That's someone using their car as a weapon to kill another person in cold blood.'

We all sat in silence for a few seconds taking this in, until Jenna spoke.

'So do you think they will be able to find the person who did it?' she asked. No one answered.

SIXTEEN

DANNI

I feel trapped. There's nowhere to be alone, if I go into the bedroom Scott follows me. If I go into the kitchen someone turns up, or is already in there. The only sitting room is like Central Station, with everyone coming and going and talking rubbish.

They're now all talking in fake sad voices about the man that was killed in the hit-and-run. It wasn't a hit-and-run after all, turns out it was a cold-blooded murder and looks to me like the driver was a bloody sadist! He not only dragged the victim along that road for miles, but then *reversed* over him. And just thinking about the state his body must have been in after all that, gave me a dreadful headache and I've had to sneak into Angela's room to see if she has any painkillers. Scott found mine and threw them down the toilet, he's such a bloody drama queen. He was so angry at me for taking them. But I needed *something*. So as Angela's room is in the roof, at the top of a small flight of stairs at the back of the lodge, I knew no one would see me going up here. Angela's downstairs chatting away with Fiona, so she'll be busy for a little while at least. And when

I walk in I'm quite surprised, it's a bloody suite! Angela certainly got herself the best bedroom, it's huge and leads onto another room with what looks like a small sofa and coffee table. I don't have time to go in and have a proper look, because despite walking with a stick, old Angela is faster than she seems, so I just run straight into the en suite. I don't want the embarrassment of her finding me in her room, she wouldn't be happy with me taking paracetamol either, and I'm sure she'd make a fuss and I'd feel like a criminal.

Once in the small bathroom, I rummage through Angela's toiletry bag, and when I can't find anything in there I try her bathroom cupboard. I just need something to take the edge off, but sadly she doesn't have any painkillers, just dental floss and mouthwash.

I'm just closing her mirrored bathroom cupboard, before leaving, and as I do, the mirror catches a movement. My stomach thuds, and I see her. Blonde hair, bobbing out of the bedroom behind me. What the hell was Jenna doing in Angela's room? I turn back to the mirror. She's gone, but just as I move away to leave, my eyes still on the mirror, I see his thick, wavy dark head disappearing from Angela's room. Scott! I run after him, but he's too quick, and when I reach the top of the stairs there's no sign of either of them. Jenna and Scott, together in Angela's room. Did I really see that? Of course I did, I don't imagine things. I think I'm going to be sick.

I feel so numb, like I have this wound that's wide open and it's bleeding as I walk down the carpeted stairs back into the main body of the lodge. I hear Jenna's stupid voice, and Scott's pompous one riding over hers, and I can't bear to see them. I knew, I just knew something was off, I never trusted her, and now I know I can't trust him. I need to escape to my sanctuary, and so I go to our room and lie on the bed for an hour, processing what I think I've just seen.

A little later, there's a knock on the door. 'Danni, you said you'd come and sit with me in the hot tub, I want to talk.'

Jesus, it's Sam. I don't really need this right now, life is complicated enough.

'I'll come out in a bit, I have a headache,' I say.

'Prosecco will cure that,' he jokes. 'I'm giving you five minutes, and if you don't come in, I'm coming to get you.'

I sigh. He means that. 'Okay give me five,' I say.

* * *

About fifteen minutes later, I'm sitting in the hot tub with Sam. I'm trying to work out what I'm going to say to Scott about seeing him in Angela's bedroom with Jenna. In order to confront it, I'm going to have to tell him that I was in her bathroom looking for pills, but surely that's not half as bad as him being in there with a girl half his age?

Meanwhile, I'm not really engaging with Sam, who's swigging from a bottle of Prosecco, and putting the world to rights.

'Mum's watching, she thinks I'm drinking too much,' he says, nodding his head towards the window where Fiona's staring out at us. Two big, evil eyes glowing through the whiteness. She's so damned creepy, God knows what Scott ever saw in her.

I shrug. '*Are* you drinking too much?'

'Mum thinks so. She thinks you must have been drinking too last night – well, everyone does.'

I remember the cake with a jolt. 'Yeah, I had a bit of a meltdown, didn't I?'

'True that.' He throws his head back, smiling.

'What are you smiling about?'

He shakes his head.

'Are you laughing at me?' I'm smiling, I love the way Sam

doesn't take things too seriously, unlike his sister he takes every-thing in his stride.

'I just... The vision of you standing there sobbing with this mashed up cake!' He starts laughing. 'It was just cake, but your face was all lit up with the candles.' He pulls a manic face, meant to emulate mine from the previous evening. It breaks my heart, but I smile through it.

'No! Tell me I didn't look like that.' I roll my eyes and half-heartedly slap him on his bare shoulder.

'All your make-up down your face, you were straight out of a horror film, it was like Carrie had a birthday.'

He throws his head back again, and it might look like we're both really laughing, but I'm crying.

'What's so funny? I could hear you two inside with the doors shut!' Georgia's wrapped in a big towel, shivering and smiling expectantly.

I put my face into the hot tub so they don't see the tears, and when I emerge after a few seconds, I feel a bit better. 'Your brother is being disrespectful to your stepmother,' I say, moving in the tub to give her room to get in.

I hold out my hand and she takes it. Her teeth are chattering as she climbs in cautiously, giving little yelps of shock at the pleasant sting of hot water.

'That's so good!' she exclaims, settling down into the bubbles, grabbing the bottle from Sam and taking a discreet swig as Sam repeats what he just said to me about my face and the cake.

'Sam, that's mean, Danni was upset,' she says, protectively.

'It's okay, Sam's right, I looked crazy. I was just stressed, everything got to me,' I say. 'My mascara was down my face, red lipstick slashed across my mouth. I must have looked like the Joker!' At this they both laugh loudly, and Georgia throws her head back just like her brother. They are so alike, both blonde, good-looking, bright, athletic kids. Sam's in the university rugby team and Georgia's captain of the school netball team. I'm proud of them, even though they aren't mine to be proud of.

As they continue to laugh, I catch Fiona's glare from the big window. It hits me in the stomach, instantly killing my joy, felling me to the ground. The kids don't see, but I feel her eyes everywhere.

'Can I have some more drink?' Georgia asks, reaching for the bottle.

'No way,' Sam shakes his head sternly. 'You'll get pissed, George, then you'll do something stupid – and it's me who'll be in trouble for giving it to you.'

As laid-back as my stepson is, he's the elder child, he looks after his sister.

At least Fiona doesn't try to join us in here. Jenna has, but I don't think she'll bother tonight – when I walked through the kitchen earlier she was busy showing Scott what a great little homemaker she is. Mispronouncing the names of French dishes and eviscerating poultry with great vigour seems to be about the sum of it. God only knows what she was trying to show him in Angela's bedroom an hour ago.

'This hot tub is the only place where I can sit without being annoyed by someone,' I say, a little unguarded given that they must know I'm referring to their mother and their friend, Jenna.

They both smile cautiously. They are as wound up as I am being locked down here, but I have to be careful, I mustn't say anything mean about their mother. She is just awful with her snide remarks and put downs, always looking for the last word, always competing and trying to out-do me, the cake being a prime example. Angela must have mentioned that I always make her cake, so Fiona not only made one too, but probably smashed mine, in a fit of temper. Or perhaps Jenna did it to make me think Fiona did it. I'm overthinking, and imagining everyone's out to get me. But they are, aren't they?

'Talking of annoying people though, did either of you guys see what Jenna was doing with that poor chicken?'

I'm taking a risk; they both love Jenna, but I think I'd noticed a distinct cooling off today. They haven't been hanging out with her, she's been clinging to Fiona and Angela and hiding in bedrooms with Scott.

Neither of them say anything in response to my remarks about the chicken, but they both smirk at each other knowingly. I hope they've finally realised what a treacherous little fake she is.

Eventually, we all climb from the tub, but I'm having trouble getting out, which makes me laugh – I think it's slight hysteria after everything. Sam tries to haul me onto the decking, and it's slippery so I'm clinging to him like a life raft, and when I look up, Fiona's still observing from the sitting-room window. Her fury is evident, even through glass. What is her problem? As a mum myself, if Olivia were ever to have a stepmother, all I would ask is that she's kind to my kid. And I'm kind to *her* kids, they *like* me, we have fun, so why can't Fiona just be glad of that instead of resenting me? We are still giggling as we walk into the kitchen, but the mood drops immediately when Fiona walks in. I sense the kids sobering up, in every sense.

It seems Jenna and Fiona are making coffee together and I wonder what my husband's posh, judgemental ex-wife and rough diamond Jenna can possibly have in common. Scott perhaps? Then I realise – it's me. The saying *my enemy's enemy is my enemy* was made for this 'friendship'.

As we walk through, Jenna ignores us and Fiona smiles only at the kids, then they go back to their small talk and coffee pods.

Being a lodge, there aren't many hallways – one room leads to another and we now have to pass the sitting room on the way to our bedrooms. Angela and Scott are together on the sofa with Olivia who's crying again, and they seem to be having trouble calming her down. Hearing her cries triggers something primal in me and I walk towards Scott and his mother on the sofa.

'She's tired, that's why she's crying,' I say. 'Let me take her to our room it's way past her bedtime,' I add, reaching out for her, but Scott pulls away, holding her protectively. I feel this like a slap. 'Scott?'

'No, you're not taking her anywhere in the state you're in!'

'What? I'm fine.'

'Have you had a drink?' he asks.

'No, of course not.'

'No pills either?' he asks. I'm assuming he's referring to the painkillers he stopped me from taking earlier.

'NO!' I hiss, wanting to scream at him, but aware this would upset Olivia. 'I'm not *drunk* and I didn't have any pills, you threw my paracetamol away, remember?' I take a step closer to him. 'So if you don't mind, I'll take my daughter with me, she's *tired.*' I again reach out, but he's still clutching her like I might hurt her. I'm devastated and confused, is he joking? I look to Angela for clarification, but she's glaring at me, and moves to the edge of the sofa, like she's ready to pounce should I dare take my child from her son.

'What is *wrong* with you?' Scott's saying under his breath.

'What's wrong with *you?*' I reply.

'Danni, I really think you need to go and sleep it off... whatever it is,' Angela says quietly, unsmiling.

'It's nothing. I'm *sober*, I didn't drink or take anything.' I look from one to the other. They're ganging up against me, implying that I'm not fit to be alone with my own child.

I feel like I'm seeing them both for the first time: Scott keeping our child from me, pretending he's scared for her, and Angela, this seventy-five-year-old woman in crazy earrings and rainbow trainers who's always smiling. The woman who welcomed me into her family with open arms against all the odds suddenly seems different. And I'm scared.

'You need a nap,' she's saying, her voice is strange, like she's trying to make it sound soft, but can't hide her anger. She's getting up and walking towards me, her hands reaching out to touch me, touch Olivia. Her stare is dark and cold, there's nothing behind her eyes.

'No, no I won't go for a bloody nap.' I quickly move away from her clutches. She glances at Scott, her eyebrows raised in disapproval; gone is the open smile, the bohemian *love is all you need* approach that's Angela's trademark. She's never judged me, never treated me like the other woman – Angela forgives everything and everyone. Doesn't she?

Perhaps Fiona has got to her after all, laying down her poison? Has Jenna said something to her, has she lied about what happened at school? Or is this who my mother-in-law *really* is? Was all the warmth and apparent acceptance just a façade to keep Scott happy? Did she ever *like* me?

And suddenly I see her in the corner of my eye. Jenna, standing in the kitchen doorway with a tray of coffee, her eyes glittering. 'Is everything okay?' she asks in that sing-song voice she saves for Scott and Angela.

No one answers her, the air is taut. I want my baby.

'What's wrong with you?' I ask. 'I've done nothing wrong. Just because I spent half an hour in a hot tub with my stepchildren does not mean I can't be with my child.'

Someone moves behind me. Fiona is now here in the room, she must have heard it all. I feel outnumbered, and turn to see if the kids are here. They'll stand up for me, they know I'm not drunk, they *know* I look after Olivia well. But they disappeared into their rooms when they saw Scott and Angela's faces, this isn't their problem. So it's just me against the four of them. And in a searing moment of clarity, I realise that no one here is on my side, I will never be fully accepted by *anyone* in this family. Even my husband.

'Now, now, dear, why don't you just sit down, Jenna's made coffee,' Angela offers.

'I won't be drinking her coffee,' I hiss, probably sounding crazy, but I wouldn't put it past her to dope my drinks. Jenna's now placed the tray on the coffee table and instead of discreetly leaving, or busying herself with something else, she's stood watching me, and apparently finding it hard to conceal her delight.

It's the unbridled joy on Jenna's face, and the fake concern on Fiona's as she walks towards the little group, that makes me realise, now isn't the time to fight this. I'll talk to Scott later, alone. In the meantime if he doesn't want me to be with Olivia alone, then I'll let him keep her in here until he brings her to bed. If I stay, I will say stuff I regret, possibly to all four of them, standing around me now like zombie security men, watching and waiting for me to kick off. I won't grab Olivia – not only will it distress her, it will also give one of these psychos the chance to rugby tackle me.

'Instead of providing the drama that Jenna and Fiona so clearly crave, I'm now going to bed, knowing my child is safe with her father,' I say, and wander towards the hallway to my bedroom. I can only breathe once I reach the sanctuary of the bedroom and close the door.

Here I take a long breath, looking out through the huge window, wondering what the hell to do next. I check the school website. The post is still there, Charlotte has obviously still not seen my message or voicemail because she hasn't deleted it yet. My only consolation is that I haven't yet been named. But with no text from Charlotte to say she's ready with her finger primed over the delete button, I hope she's okay. Now I'm worried about her along with all the other worries, not to mention the ongoing tension here in the lodge, I won't sleep tonight.

I walk towards the huge window. Even in the dark it's like an impressionist painting, a frozen snowy version of Van Gogh's

Starry Night. Apart from the navy sky, everything is white, with silver skeleton trees rising up through the snow like barely hidden secrets. Just beyond is a swirling mass of angry sea, lightening cracks the sky, and thunder rolls in the distance towards us, limbering up to thrash around in the oncoming storm that's heading our way. And despite trying to cling on to a flake of hope, I see my reflection in the dark window, already knowing it's too late.

SEVENTEEN

FIONA

I wasn't comfortable playing another night of happy families around the dinner table. The holiday was originally a long weekend, Friday to Monday, which would have been tortuous enough, but due to the weather and the hit-and-run, it was now Monday, and we were going nowhere. It had been the longest four days of my life, and everyone was crumbling. The air was taut with tension, we all had cabin fever, and I think we all dreaded the knock of the police at the door arriving to arrest one of us for the hit-and-run murder.

I was a mess, Angela was still out of sorts, being vague and forgetful. Jenna was okay, but finding it hard to hide her resentment if anyone so much as asked her to make a cup of tea. Meanwhile my kids had spent far too many afternoons drinking in the hot tub, or on the sofa, or even in their bedrooms, and it had to stop. Scott was stressed at having to keep Olivia calm and happy, and it seemed to me that Danni was on the verge of a breakdown.

I felt sympathy for her, she was obviously suffering, and wasn't happy in her new life with my husband. Perhaps the sizzle of an illicit affair with her boss hadn't panned out quite as she'd expected now the baby was here and real life had kicked in? I hoped so. But Danni's happiness wasn't of any interest to me, I just hoped to God she hadn't moved on from my husband to my son. The longer we were stuck there, living in that febrile atmosphere, the more intense Sam's attachment to Danni seemed to be growing.

My son didn't need someone like that in his life, he needed solid, reliable people who would ground him. He'd been in with the wrong crowd at school, and he was easily swayed, there'd been lots of drinking and late nights, and it had affected his exam results. I didn't want the same to happen now he was at uni; getting entangled in some weird relationship with his flaky stepmother was the last thing he needed. I knew from bitter experience that Danni would stop at nothing to get what she wanted, and Jenna had also suffered at her hands, losing everything through Danni's jealousy.

* * *

That evening, at dinner, I watched Danni playing with the food Jenna had worked hard to make and felt angry at her lack of respect.

'Is your food okay?' I asked her, in the same voice I'd have asked one of the kids if they were messing with their food. It was just rude, especially with the cook sitting there.

'It's *okay*,' she replied grudgingly, without lifting her head.

'You probably don't have much of an appetite?' Angela suggested.

'What do you mean?' Danni snapped, and we all collectively looked up. No one snapped at Angela, she was kind and gentle and her approach never warranted a bite-back. She looked surprised at this and raising her eyebrows almost imperceptibly, pushed away her empty plate and rested her chin on her knuckles. She had that faraway stare, but was looking directly at Danni. 'I mean you look tired and I think you have a lot on your mind, don't you?'

Danni's head shot up. She seemed genuinely shocked.

What the hell was Angela talking about?

Just then, Olivia's cries could be heard at the baby monitor sitting by Scott's elbow.

'Excuse me, everyone,' he said, no doubt relieved to be exiting at this awkward juncture.

'I was about to serve dessert, Scottie. Shall we wait for you?' Jenna asked, pertly.

He turned, looking harassed – dessert was clearly the last thing on his mind.

'Er, no, thank you, serve everyone else,' he replied tightly, then disappeared down the little hallway to where his baby was crying.

Jenna was looking around the table, smiling. 'Okay, are we ready for dessert?' she said in the voice of an entertainer at a children's tea party. It was bad timing, but I appreciated her clumsy attempt to lighten the mood, even if Danni didn't.

'Who are you trying to be now, Jenna?' Danni glared at her. Angela's remark had upset Danni, and she was now taking it out on Jenna, or using her as a distraction from whatever the hell Angela had been referring to.

Embarrassed silence descended on the table like a thunder cloud.

Jenna looked surprised and lost for words. 'Danni, I was asking who was ready for dessert,' she said, her face taut with frustration.

'Don't give me that innocent, wide-eyed face. You know *exactly* what I'm saying,' Danni spat. 'I'm surprised you didn't offer to go and help Scott with Olivia so you could be alone together!'

'I don't understand...' Jenna's eyes were suddenly damp with tears. She glanced over at Angela, then me. Despite the simmering tension between the women, we were all stunned by Danni's outburst. Was she just lashing out at Jenna, or did she really believe there was something going on between her and Scott?

No doubt feeling attacked and unsupported, Jenna picked up her napkin, stood up, and left the room. But before she did, she turned around and all she said was, 'Have you heard back from Charlotte?'

All the blood drained from Danni's face. 'Charlotte?'

'Yeah, we're best mates, we're always chatting. She's nice, a real chatterbox, she called me earlier, said to say hi.'

Danni was glaring at Jenna, her face pale, her lips white. 'You. Bitch.' She forced out the words, two guttural sounding breaths, and before anyone could do anything Danni was up off her seat and running at Jenna, who screamed and ran into her room, locking the door behind her. But that didn't stop Danni, she was banging on the door shrieking insults at her, until Scott emerged from their room, his face red with fury. 'What the hell is going on, Danni?'

Sam got up from his seat, and headed towards her. By now she was crumpling at the door, falling to her knees in floods of hopeless tears.

'Help me get her to bed, Sam,' Scott said, reaching out to pull her up, but Scott's presence seemed to reignite her rage and from somewhere deep inside she said slowly, 'Don't let *him* come anywhere near me.' This was enunciated with such fury, that Scott stepped back, looking shaken.

'It's fine, you go and deal with Olivia,' Angela said, getting up and walking towards Sam who was now attempting to lift Danni back onto her feet. 'Danni, there was no need for all that,' Angela said, bringing her back into the room. 'Jenna was only talking to you about her friend, a mutual friend I think too?'

Danni didn't respond, as with Sam's help, Angela sat her on

the sofa and placed a throw across her knees, as Georgia and I, the only two still sitting at the table, stared on, trying to process what just happened.

'You don't know her, Angela, you have no idea what she's capable of. She's been laying her poison here ever since she arrived.'

'What? What did you say, she's been poisoning people?' Angela seemed confused again.

'You're all taken in,' Danni was saying, now looking right at me, ignoring Angela's fussing as she pushed a cushion behind her. 'Think about it, she's twenty-five, she was supposed to have a degree and an MA in Education when she came to work at the school, turns out there's no record of that. And now she's suddenly reinvented herself as a Cordon Bleu cook!' Her breath shuddered, a hangover from the crying.

'She's a good cook,' I offered, defensively.

'Fiona, it's right in front of you, don't be *stupid!*' Danni jammed her finger to her head. 'She pretends to be whoever you want her to be, a lab technician, a friend, a big sister figure.' She gestured to Georgia. 'Angela needed a cook, oh look, there she was – and then she pounces. She did it with me, I was new to the school, to the town, and needed a friend. And she became my friend – we "happened" to like the same films, the same drinks, the same *clothes*.' She stopped to wipe her eyes with a tissue. 'She's no one's friend.' She turned to the kids. '*No one's*, you hear me?'

I expected them to reject this observation – Jenna was their friend – but strangely they didn't. They seemed to acknowledge what Danni was saying, Georgia even nodded in agreement, and Sam raised his eyebrows as if he felt the same way.

Then she leaned forward and lifted her finger in a warning gesture, her voice hoarse from shrieking, her eyes still wet. 'There's a reason Jenna Phillips came to this lodge, and trust me, it isn't to *cook* for us.'

Like a glass chandelier, this hung precariously over us as we considered what she'd just said.

A few moments later, Angela spoke and shattered it.

'She has come to cook for us, Danni,' she said, slightly pink with mild outrage. 'I *asked* her to come with us, I *invited* her here, she didn't force me to bring her.'

'That's exactly what I *mean*. You think it was your idea, but it wasn't. She's manipulative, and I bet if you look back, she's been angling for an invite for weeks. Sneaking around telling you how she's never been to Cornwall because she comes from a poor family, never had a holiday as a kid...'

Angela looked uncomfortable at this; Danni was obviously onto something.

'I can hear it all now, that Uriah Heep voice telling you how she's "never seen the sea, Missus,"' she said this in a cockney accent which made Sam snigger. 'But when you didn't immediately invite her on the family holiday, she worked out how to get here.' Danni continued to attack Jenna, then sat and stared at each one of us, waiting for a reaction. But Angela was shaking her head adamantly, and as Jenna wasn't there to defend herself, someone had to.

'Danni, I think you might have misunderstood her,' I said tactfully. 'You seem to find fault in everything she does, but she's just a young woman trying to do her best.'

She leaned back in her chair, took a deep breath. She was angry, frustrated that no one was buying into her meanness about Jenna. 'I thought *you* might have seen what she really is, Fiona, she's totally unhinged! But you're obviously as *naïve* as everyone else.'

I raised my eyebrows. 'Perhaps I am. After all, I didn't see *you* coming up on the inside, did I?' I stopped, regretting it the minute it left my mouth. I shouldn't have said that in front of the kids and Angela.

Not surprisingly, my remark seemed to enflame Danni even

more, her eyes wild with fury now. 'You really are *obsessed,* aren't you?' She was leaning over Sam, pointing her finger at me from the other side of the room, on her face an incredulous, angry smile.

I didn't respond. I didn't want her shrieking at me as she just had at Jenna. Angela looked equally shocked, while the kids just hung their heads, embarrassed.

'You can't bear to see me with Scott,' she continued to rant at me. 'You don't even like me being near Sam and Georgie. You're *so* jealous, I can feel your eyes on me all the time. You really need to move on, Fiona.'

Scott came out of the bedroom – he'd obviously heard the raised voices.

'This is ridiculous, I can't get Olivia to sleep with all this noise. What's going on now?'

'Have you left Olivia on her own?' Danni said, standing up suddenly, marching across the room and storming past him, towards the kitchen.

'You're stressed, you'll make her worse,' he called after, following her as she left the kitchen and marched to the bedroom, another tantrum about to erupt, no doubt. Their bedroom door slammed hard and we all sat in silence. I glanced over at my son, who rolled his eyes.

'That went well.'

'Mmm, she *is* stressed,' I said, making the understatement of the year.

Sam and Georgia seemed low after all the drama, and soon retired to bed, leaving Angela and me alone.

'I'm worried about her,' Angela was saying. She seemed lucid again. 'But obviously my first concern is with Scott and my granddaughter. Scott's at his wits' end, my heart breaks for him. I shouldn't say this – but Danni isn't the mothering kind.'

I agreed, but didn't respond, I felt uncomfortable hearing Angela say something like that. She usually kept her opinions on others close to her chest, so much so it could be frustrating sometimes trying to work out what she really felt. I thought then how much she must dislike Danni to say it, and I realised I'd known her more than twenty years, but really didn't know her.

'Scott told me recently, that he felt he hadn't married Danni, but adopted another child,' she announced, her words edged in bitterness. 'I think he regrets everything, Fiona.' She offered me this like a flower, a gift from her to me. I took it, but it was no surprise, I knew exactly how Scott felt about Danni. At least I *thought* I did.

* * *

Scott returned ten minutes later with Olivia and a duvet, but no Danni. 'It's just an impossible situation, she's so *angry*, always lashing out, and Olivia needs a calm environment,' he muttered, almost to himself as he dropped the duvet down on the sofa, and handed Olivia to his mother. Angela took her lovingly, cradling her and cooing as she once had with my kids and her own son.

She looked up at him. 'This can't go on, love.' He gave a slight nod, and the look that passed between them was knowing. I wasn't sure I understood. Danni was a bit of a nightmare, but she was triggered by Jenna, and let's face it, by me too. Didn't Angela or Scott realise that before the weekend? Were they really surprised at the way things were working out between us all? Angela was perhaps becoming confused, and a little forgetful, but surely she'd thought it through. Even if it was her last birthday, she knew the potential outcome of bringing Danni and me together, and was also aware there were problems between Danni and Jenna, so why did she want to spend her last birthday in a war zone?

'For the first time in my life, I really don't know what to do,' Scott said, standing in the middle of the room, a child talking to a parent. This was a mess, and though he was the one to blame for the situation he'd put himself in, the mother in me felt for Angela, the tiger mother protecting her son and grandchild from the crazy new wife. I couldn't imagine how I'd feel if I thought someone, a *woman*, might hurt Sam one day; like most parents in that situation, I'd want to *kill* her.

I had no reason to doubt Jenna's story about Danni falsely accusing her of supplying drugs to the school kids. But having not heard Danni's side, I had to be circumspect. It was easy to believe bad things about the woman who took my husband. I was only human and found it difficult to see *anything* from Danni's perspective or in her favour. But who was Charlotte, and why had Danni been triggered when Jenna mentioned that she was also a friend of hers? It was all pretty unfathomable, but I didn't doubt she'd lied about Jenna dealing drugs to get rid of her. How I'd wished I could get rid of Danni in the same way. How wonderful it would be if Danni didn't exist, and we could rewind the clock and get together and be a family again.

Recently, mine and Scott's friendship had started to re-emerge, after the long freeze, a warmth returning between us. But Danni was the mother of Scott's child, and in our lives for ever. Babies last a lifetime, and Olivia would bind them: her first day at school, her birthday parties, Christmases, and even when she was grown there'd be the boyfriends, the wedding, the grandchildren. As long as Danni was around, the mess and trouble and hurt would continue, and none of us would ever be free. It was like a stain you could never rub out. But Olivia was beautiful, and since we'd arrived here, I'd seen how my kids loved her. I knew I could get to love her too given the chance. Scott brought Olivia's travel cot into the room, and I helped him set it up, then I held Olivia, walking around, rocking her to sleep. She was just an innocent baby. It broke my heart to think of how difficult her life would be with Danni for a mother. She'd just handed everything over to Scott, who had, through a temporary madness, got himself into this, but now, with the baby, it was hard for him to escape. Even if Danni wasn't a life-time commitment, Olivia was, and as time went on, and she lost her looks and her options, Danni would only get more clingy. She was already accusing Scott of all kinds of things, she was paranoid and insecure, and I felt like she was heading for a breakdown. But it was no worse than what I'd been through, and I survived. I wondered how she would react when she discovered Scott's latest betrayal. What would she do when she found out that her husband had been sleeping with someone else for the past four months? And how would she feel when she found out that that *someone* was me?

EIGHTEEN

FIONA

'Has anyone seen Danni?' It was now Tuesday morning, a day after we should have left the lodge, but as the police still hadn't made an arrest for the hit-and-run, and the weather was still terrible, we were still there, going stir crazy. Scott was standing in the hallway, holding what looked like her dressing gown. I was keeping an eye on Olivia while he'd gone to the bedroom to have a shower, but he'd only been in there seconds and was now shouting her name and opening and closing doors looking for her.

'Scott, she's probably in the kitchen.' I nodded towards the kitchen while handing Olivia a pale blue ball.

'She's not in the kitchen,' he snapped, flustered, running across the room to the front door and heaving it open, allowing an icy blast to stream through the lodge. 'Danni? DANNI?' he called louder, but the wind and the sea were louder than any human voice, even if she had been out there, she'd never have heard him.

Sam looked up at me over his phone. I widened my eyes at him, he mirrored it and went back to his phone. God knows what was happening now.

'She's not out there.' Scott let the door close with a loud bang.

'But where can she *be*?'

'She probably just went for a walk?' Sam offered. 'Have you called her?'

'Yes, her phone is ringing, but she's not answering. I can't hear it in the house, so she must have it with her...' Scott seemed very concerned, he couldn't keep still, desperate for anything that could explain her absence.

'I'm sure she's fine,' I murmured soothingly.

'Oh her jacket,' he said, ignoring me, walking towards the coat rack. He started sorting through the outdoor stuff, absolute panic on his face.

'Scott, I'm sure she's *fine*. She seems to have had a difficult couple of days, like Sam says she's probably just gone for a walk,' I offered.

'But she *can't* have, her jacket's here?' He lifted the bright yellow jacket from the hook and held it out as proof that she hadn't gone for a walk.

'Does she have *another* jacket?'

'No,' he snapped, 'she only has *this* one.'

'Hang on.' I lifted my hand out in a calming gesture. 'She may be wearing someone *else's* jacket. I think I saw her with Sam's on the other day?' I remembered because it irritated me, it was such a 'girlfriend' thing to do. I looked at Sam.

'Yeah, she put one of my sweatshirt jackets on in the house, she was cold. But *my* jacket's there on the hook, she might have gone out *without* a jacket?' Sam shrugged, going back to his phone, clearly bored of the drama.

'In *this* weather?' Scott was still clutching her jacket. I followed his eyes to the window, a white sky, swirling snow, and frozen ground. We both looked at each other.

It was then that Jenna appeared in the doorway. 'What are you doing with my jacket, do you want to borrow it, Scottie?'

she asked, singing his name and smiling as she walked into the room.

He looked from the jacket, to Jenna and back again. 'This is *yours?*'

'Yes, why?' she seemed puzzled.

'Are you absolutely *sure?*' I asked, getting up and walking towards Scott and the jacket. 'Because Danni has one just like it.'

'Yeah, she does. But Danni's is an expensive one, mine's the knock-off.'

'And can you tell the difference, because I can't?' Scott said, holding it out to her, while she wandered over to inspect it.

'Yeah that's mine, the stitching is different. But I'd be happy to swap with Danni's,' she joked, seemingly unaware of Scott's distress.

'Her jacket's not here, that means she's gone out,' Scott muttered, ignoring Jenna's light-hearted comment.

'Good, glad we cleared that up,' she said with a smile. She really hadn't read the room and maintaining her happy mood asked, 'Breakfast?' Then without waiting for an answer, she turned and headed into the kitchen.

I glanced up at Scott, but he was staring out of the window, seemingly unaware of anyone else. Meanwhile Sam was still on his phone, and didn't seem concerned at all about Danni's whereabouts. Having been troubled by their closeness, I wondered if perhaps I'd got it wrong after all and perhaps he wasn't inappropriately attached to his young, bikini-wearing hot-tub-hopping stepmother.

'Don't take this the wrong way, Scott,' I said, 'but Danni might just have gone off like this to make you worry?'

'So what do we do?' Scott replied sharply. 'Punish her by allowing her to wander around out there until she dies of hypothermia?'

I quelled the urge to admit that would be my *preferred* option, and instead suggested that we call the police.

'What good would that do?' Scott snapped, answering his own question. 'The police can't get here, we're cut off, and even if they *were* able to come and look for her it might be too late.'

'Too late? I don't want to seem uncaring, but she's a grown woman Scott – and I think you might be overreacting.'

He was shaking his head. 'It's below freezing out there, we need to search for her,' he said. 'We all *have* to head out now and see if we can find her.'

'You're kidding?' Sam muttered.

My heart sank. 'It could be a needle in a haystack, Scott,' I added with a sigh.

'Yeah, especially if she's determined *not* to be found until she's ready,' Sam added, which was a fair point.

'Why would she do that?' I asked, knowing full well it was just what she might do for attention.

'She might *think* she can hide for the next few hours,' Scott said, without answering my question, 'but it's so cold out there and after a while... no, no I can't let that happen. I'm going to get changed and look for her, and would appreciate some help,' he called in Sam's direction.

When he'd gone, Sam looked at me, rolling his eyes. 'What was all that about?'

'Mmm, I know Dad's overreacting, but I think he's right, we should probably all go on the search, Sam.'

'Yeah, yeah okay...' he replied, reluctantly.

'After all, you and Danni are very close.'

'What's *that* supposed to mean?' He continued to gaze at his phone, fingers and thumbs flying around the keys.

'Nothing, I just wondered if she's ever *said* anything to you? I know that you guys talk.' They'd obviously had private conversations, I'd walked in on at least one, and as the mother of an eighteen-year-old boy, I was keen to know the nature of those conversations.

'I don't understand what you're trying to say?' He seemed genuinely confused, but perhaps he was just pretending to be confused?

'I just wonder what you two could possibly have in common,' I murmured.

'She's cool, I like talking to her.'

'I'm sure she is, and I'm sure that's all it is, but be careful, Sam.'

He finally took his eyes from the phone screen. 'Why? She's my stepmum. It's not weird or anything.'

'It might not be, but she seems anxious and unhappy, and I think you should be careful.'

At this he started laughing, which I found irritating.

'Look, Sam, it isn't funny. I don't trust her, and neither should you. I think you're playing with fire, hang around with her long enough and you're going to get burned.'

'Hang around?' He was smiling broadly, amused at this. 'She's my dad's wife, I *have* to see her.'

'I know, but I think she behaves *inappropriately* around you.' I tried to say this gently, but I knew it sounded judgemental. As someone who worked in HR, I was aware it sounded a little corporate, but I wanted to be clear, and not too emotional.

'I feel like Danni might be using you to get at Dad...' There, I'd said it, and I knew he wouldn't like it.

'God, Mum, I don't need this shit,' he muttered, closing down completely and looking back at his phone, 'and now there's no signal,' he murmured, 'God I'm starting to hate this place.' I'd obviously struck a chord.

A few minutes later, the phone signal returned, and Sam seemed to be responding to a text he'd just received. It was presumably an emergency due to the speed he was replying. I wished he'd reply to my texts so quickly. Then a thought occurred, was that *her* texting him? But before I could ask who he was texting, he got up and wandered to his room.

Olivia woke and started crying, which distracted me, and soon brought Georgia out of her bedroom. When I told her Danni hadn't returned from a walk, and we were a little concerned, she immediately burst into tears.

I tried to reassure her. 'She's only been gone a while,' I added, trying to rock Olivia back to sleep in my arms. But Georgia was inconsolable, and I realised then how close she really was to her stepmother, and I have to admit, it stung me.

A few minutes later, Scott came back into the room dressed in a woolly jumper, padded outdoor trousers and thick socks. He was just putting his boots on by the door when his phone pinged. I looked over. When he didn't say who it was, I had to ask.

'Is that Danni?' I asked, not actually expecting it to be her.

Eventually he replied, 'Yes,' in a defeated voice.

'Oh, so she's okay?' I asked, as Georgia looked up, hopeful.

'She says she's okay, but she's had enough, and I mustn't try and find her, or try to text her back. She wants to be on her own to think.' He was holding his phone, gazing at it. I wished he didn't care so much.

'You should do as she asks and give her some space, Scott,' I tried, soothingly. 'If she isn't back by, say this afternoon, then go and look for her?'

'Yeah, she needs her space,' Georgia said, wiping her eyes. 'I think I'll go and have a shower,' she said, getting up from the sofa wearily and wandering back to her bedroom.

Taking Olivia from my arms, Scott looked at me sadly, and said, 'How did I make such a mess of our lives, Fiona?'

'Apparently our life wasn't exciting enough for you. Predictable, you said. You certainly can't accuse your new wife of being *predictable*.' I rolled my eyes. I hadn't been exactly predictable myself recently, and thinking about this made my stomach twist.

He shrugged. 'You're right, she can be unpredictable, and difficult, but I'm worried about her safety, if she's slipped or – worse.'

'You mean the driver of the...'

He nodded, unable to even talk about the possibility that she'd been hurt or worse. I shuddered at the thought, pushed it away to make room for something else that had just occurred to me.

'Danni's pregnant, isn't she?' I didn't know, I *guessed*, and hoped I was wrong. But that would explain his panic, and the way he'd accused her of drinking, and she'd snapped at him for throwing away her paracetamol. Knowing Scott's disapproval of painkillers or any kind of alcohol during pregnancy, I think I'd half-guessed at her condition, but hadn't been able to bear the prospect, so hoped I was wrong. The fact she was carrying his baby also explained why he seemed so consumed with worry, when he knew there was a high probability she might just be playing games.

He didn't answer me straight away, which was in effect an affirmative.

'Sorry... I'm sorry,' he eventually replied, gazing into Olivia's face. 'I just wish she didn't have this hold over me, just when I think I have everything under control, she throws a curve ball.'

'But you told me that side of your marriage was over?'

'It happened a few months ago, it was just a one-time thing.'

'How... pregnant is she?'

'Three months, just.'

'And you didn't think to tell me?'

He sat down, a deep sigh emanating from his chest. 'I'm sorry. As you know, things between us were difficult anyway, but this pregnancy... it's thrown her, it's thrown both of us.'

'Does your mother know, about the pregnancy?' I asked in a quiet voice, not taking my eyes from the view.

'Yes,' he replied. 'She's worried.'

'I can imagine.' It hurt to think that he and Angela and Danni all had this big secret and didn't tell me, they had their own bubble that I wasn't part of. But since Scott and I had reconnected, he'd asked if he could come home, if we could get back together. I'd allowed myself to believe we could pick up where we left off, a little bruised and bloodied, but still capable of a happy marriage, a future together. But now...

His eyes were still staring ahead. He hadn't looked at me, he was still thinking about her, while I stood in the wings, waiting and hoping. I could see it now, I'd been a fool, he would never leave her.

'I mean a new *baby*, she's all over the place, unpredictable. Even her driving is erratic. I even wondered if... if she had something to do with the hit-and-run?'

'Really?' I replied, intrigued by this theory.

'I'm not saying she *did* it...' Seeing my interest piqued, he backtracked. 'I'm just saying that at this stage, nothing would surprise me with Danni,' he added with a sigh.

'But if she'd done anything like that it would be the end. I would demand custody of *both* children immediately,' he said, almost to himself. Deep down I'd always known I wasn't part of any future plan, he had no interest in patching up our marriage or our family. I'd just been a port in the storm for him, someone from his safe old life to comfort him on days when the new life was too much.

Before we could talk further, Angela joined us.

'Mum, I can't find Danni, I think she may have gone for a walk, but I'm worried,' he said, sounding like a child.

Angela didn't really react, then suddenly said, 'Oh yes she was up early this morning wasn't she? Very early if I remember rightly.'

We both turned to look at Angela. 'You *saw* her this morning?' Scott asked.

'Yes, must have been about five thirty, I'm not sure, but it was still dark. I couldn't sleep, the lighthouse was flashing in my window, it's like a searchlight, going round and round, I feel like I'm being interrogated in my sleep.'

She stopped talking. I saw the frustration on her face as she tried to remember what she'd just been saying.

'So you saw Danni – was she in here, or the kitchen?' I asked, to jog her memory gently without embarrassing her.

'No, she was out there, on the decking.' She pointed through the window, where the hot tub bubbled, on the expanse of frosty decking.

On cue Olivia started crying. Scott picked her up from her travel cot, and setting her on the floor, handed her a toy in an attempt to placate her. It didn't work.

'What was Danni *doing* on the decking, was she on her own?' I asked, as Olivia's crying became louder, more insistent.

'Yes, alone. Sitting. She was just sitting, all curled up on one of the garden chairs. She had a jacket and scarf on, her knees were covered in a blanket.'

'Was she asleep?' Scott asked, trying to calm Olivia by rubbing her back.

'Hard to tell... I offered her tea, but she didn't answer. Perhaps she *was* asleep?' she said, like it had just occurred to her. 'When she didn't answer me, I assumed she was just in one of her moods.'

Olivia's cries were becoming louder, more angry.

'She's teething,' I said. 'Do you have anything for teething?' I asked, thinking of Danni sitting there on the decking in the cold, dark morning.

He looked nonplussed, he obviously didn't.

'So, Mum, Danni didn't say *anything*?'

Angela shook her head.

'And how did she seem?' he asked loudly.

All she said was, 'She seemed... asleep.'

The colour had drained from Scott's face. 'I'm really worried.'

'Scott, she was up early, she's hormonal, couldn't sleep, so went for a walk,' I tried to reassure him.

'It was pitch *black*,' Angela pointed out, looking at me, her voice tinged with irritation. 'She was sitting out there in the pitch black. I mean that's not normal, is it?'

After several days locked up there with those people, I was beginning to wonder what normal *was*.

'Christ,' Scott murmured, as he continued to struggle with Olivia. It was as if the baby had picked up on the tension in the lodge. 'What if she *didn't* get up early to go for a walk?' he said loudly over Olivia's wailing. He was looking up at his mother and me from the floor where he desperately tried to comfort his daughter.

'What do you mean?' I asked.

He stood up, now holding Olivia in his arms as she fought to break free. 'What if she went out early this morning planning to do something stupid... and what if it's already too late?'

Angela's hand flew to her mouth. 'Don't say that.'

'Well it's the truth, Mum, she's been behaving weirdly lately, and it's odd that she'd sit out there in the dark. Was she... planning it?' He could barely say the words.

'Don't say that, she could walk through that door any minute,' I said.

Scott was shaking his head. 'If anyone went out there alone at dawn, they won't be coming back. The temperature is below freezing, and there's no one around, if she tripped and fell she could be lying in the snow for hours. Or worse she could fall into the sea.'

'You know Danni, she's very good at looking after herself,' Angela said. 'I wonder if we're worrying too much, overthinking it all. It might be that she's gone somewhere and is safe,' Angela offered.

'I have to agree, Danni wouldn't put her unborn child in danger,' I murmured uncertainly.

'No, she wouldn't,' Angela replied, sounding equally unconvinced. 'Mark my words Scott, it's probably one of Danni's dramas. I bet she's sitting in another lodge in front of an open fire telling some poor souls that her husband doesn't understand her.' She raised her eyebrows at Scott as she said this. Angela was now hiding none of her strong opinions regarding Danni.

He sighed, shaking his head, still patting Olivia's back to no avail.

Angela's face was suddenly screwed up, with tension. 'Scott, does she need feeding?'

'I don't know.' He looked from her to me, and I wondered if perhaps he hadn't changed after all. Scott still wasn't quite the hands-on dad he'd made himself out to be.

'So,' Angela continued, 'I suggest we all have breakfast, then call the police.'

'The police can't get down here, and I can't wait, Mum, I need to go and find her, even if she *is* sitting by a log fire in another lodge. I can't eat breakfast not *knowing*. No one could survive in these temperatures for long and she's *pregnant*.'

'But if you go out there searching you're putting yourself at risk,' I reminded him. 'You have Olivia to think of.'

He shook his head. 'I also have Danni and the new baby to think of. There's already been one murder near here, and the police are still looking for whoever did that, what if he's still out there?'

NINETEEN

FIONA

Scott checked the outside of the lodge, wandering around nearby and calling her name, but Angela and I managed to convince him not to head out any further into the treacherous weather. We reminded him that Olivia needed her daddy there, and he agreed to wait to hear from the police and not take any stupid risks. Everyone seemed concerned about Danni not returning, and they all had a theory they had to share. This was played out against the background noise of Olivia's wailing, and screaming. At almost twelve months she was on the verge of walking and in her primal need to explore she constantly wrestled Scott to release her each time he picked her up to comfort her. But when he put her down as she wanted, she'd crawl around, picking up on the tension in the room, and screech to be picked up again. Tension was high, everyone was on edge, we jumped at every text ping, and the melting snow falling in clumps off the warm roof of the lodge sounded like someone banging on the door. My heart was in my mouth waiting for the police to arrive.

'I just tried her again,' Sam said, his phone in his hand, where it usually was. 'Now her phone's completely dead.'

At this, I heard Scott whimper, like an animal in pain.

'What if she's just gone for a walk and decided to visit one of the other lodges?' Jenna suggested.

'Why would she do that?' Angela replied, clearly irritated by this.

'I think what Jenna is saying is has Danni disappeared for a reason? She sent a text to Scott telling him not to look for her, is she just trying to scare us... well, scare Scott?' I turned to him, and the others all followed my eyes. 'Do you think she might have any reason to want to... scare you?'

My ex-husband's expression was sheepish, his eyes shifty.

'That might be a possibility. As you all know,' he started, awkwardly, 'Danni and I had a few words last night. I slept in here with Olivia, and she slept in our bedroom,' he said. 'Yes, we were both angry and it isn't beyond the realms of possibility that she's gone somewhere and she's now hiding to teach me a lesson. But surely she wouldn't be so cruel?'

'Oh she *would* be,' Jenna muttered under her breath.

'I don't think she'd be cruel.'

'No, if she has gone somewhere to hide, it isn't out of cruelty,' I said, not wanting to play the bitter, jilted wife. I looked at Scott. 'It's probably confusion, insecurity, just a misunderstanding?'

'I think we should call the police and tell them just that,' Angela said. 'We don't want to waste their time, but we can't just sit here assuming she's fine, she's not fine, she's quite mad really.' Angela gazed ahead, like she'd just said something perfectly fitting.

Before she could say anything else, I reiterated to Scott that we had to call the police, and he agreed, albeit grudgingly. 'Okay, yes let's call them. I don't think we need to mention our disagreement or the text, it might just complicate things.'

'No, we should tell them *everything*,' I insisted. 'Let's not hide a thing, if it helps them find her,' I added firmly, and stood up to get my phone off the coffee table.

'Of course we should,' he replied, and being Scott, took his own phone from his pocket, and made the call himself. He was always the fixer, the one to sort everything and not knowing where she was or what to do, frustrated him. He liked to be in control.

So he dialled, and waited, and waited, until eventually someone answered. He kept it simple, told the person on the other end of the line that his wife had gone for a walk six hours before, that she'd sent a text to say don't look for her, but that was hours ago, her phone was now dead and no sign of her. He didn't offer any more information, and the police officer on the other end just asked basic details like her name, age, weight, height and the location, and time she left.

He put down the phone, disheartened. 'They didn't sound too alarmed, they'll get back to us if anything comes up, but at the moment they are inundated with problems caused by the weather, including missing people. Plus they just can't get here, we're still completely cut off,' he said with a sigh. 'They said under no circumstances must we go out and look for her.' He stared out through the huge window onto the white expanse that seemed to go on forever.

The afternoon was the longest of my life. Scott paced, Olivia screamed, Georgia and Angela cried on and off and Sam tried to comfort them. Jenna joined us every now and then but seemed to spend a lot of time either in her room or the kitchen. She offered to make sandwiches, brought some in on a tray with coffee, but none of us had an appetite, and just chewed on them to keep our strength up. Who knew what was ahead?

* * *

By three thirty the snowy sky was surrendering to darker evening skies, and we were all feeling extremely nervous. Any kind of hope had faded with the day, and we now faced the oncoming darkness with no news. The police hadn't been back in touch, Sam and Scott had stood outside for a while calling her, but there was no sign of her, just nothing.

'Where could she possibly be?' Georgia asked, while Angela just kept shaking her head.

'I know the police said we mustn't leave, but I'm going to go and see if I can find her.' Scott was shaking despite it being warm inside the lodge.

'It's dangerous, Scott, you mustn't,' Angela said.

'I have no choice, Mum, I have to,' he said, standing up.

'You're not going on your own, Dad, I'll come with you,' Sam said, and with that we all agreed to do the same.

'No, I don't want you all out there in this,' he said.

'It will be safer if we're all together,' I said. 'Danni went out on her own, we don't want you doing the same, it would be stupid of us to let you, so no arguments.'

We all started to get our outdoor stuff on; boots were by the door and our coats and jackets hung on the rack.

'But what about Olivia?' Jenna suddenly said. 'We can't leave her here. I'll stay with her if you like?' She was usually keen to go outside. Jenna seemed to have this need to belong and I couldn't imagine she'd want to miss out on joining in the search, even if it was for Danni. I wondered fleetingly why she offered to stay and look after the baby, was it genuine, or did she have an ulterior motive?

'No. I'll stay behind with Olivia,' Angela said, which was obvious really, she would be no use out there in the snow, especially now she'd lost her walking stick. And someone had to stay with Olivia, it made sense for Angela to look after her granddaughter.

'Of course, thanks, Mum,' Scott replied, plucking his thick

jacket from the hook in the doorway as we all started to move around, getting ready for the search. We had lights on our phones, and once dressed to go out, we turned them on and I also found some torches in a hall cupboard for backup.

The icy blast hit us as soon as the door was opened. Outside, the cold was unbearable. My teeth chattered, and I shivered, trying to walk as fast as possible to try and warm up. But the snow was still coming down, the ground was frozen and hard with layer upon layer of snow and frost. My boots sunk into the crispy ground, the snow sometimes reaching my knees. Walking was almost impossible, like wading through cold concrete and with the swirling snow, the blasting wind and the fading light, it was difficult to see ahead.

We walked for a while, calling her name, but as the darkness came, it felt really creepy, like we were the only people left in the world. The snow soaked up every sound, the silence thick, the ground unyielding, and despite having torches on our phones, shadows gathered around, like we were dragging the darkness behind us.

There were five of us, and I was beginning to realise how horrible it must have been for Danni. Wherever she was, and whatever game she might have been playing, this would be even scarier and more dangerous alone. Perhaps her intentions were genuine, she just wanted to take a walk, get away from the stuffy, claustrophobic atmosphere and other people. She might have started walking, realised it was a mistake, and found it impossible to find her way back. Approaching the coastal path with the sheer drop where I'd clung to Angela only a few days before, I was reminded of the dangers of slipping, and immediately called out to the kids to be careful. I was far more scared for them than I was for me, I just wanted to hold on to them, to keep them close, but they would, I'm sure, have been horrified. They were young and strong and healthy with better eyesight and better balance than me, but then again, Danni was also younger and fitter, and where was she? We continued to call her name loudly, following Scott and his light, our own flashing as and when we needed them. We were all aware that if any of us were to get lost we'd need the lights on our phones, and soon this theory was tested, when I followed what I thought was Scott's light, and it turned out to be Jenna's.

'Where is everyone?' she said.

'How did you lose them, you were just ahead of me?' I said, frustrated.

'I have no idea, one minute they were here, the next they weren't, and Scott's the only one who really knows his way round here, he used to holiday here when he was a child.'

'Yes, I know,' I replied testily. Why was she telling me this? I was his former wife for God's sake, I knew more about his childhood holidays than she ever would. I looked up and my heart jumped. She had put her phone torch under her face to light it up. It looked eerie in this setting, especially as there was just her and me. She was behaving weirdly. Was this her idea of a joke?

'Jenna, don't waste that torchlight,' I said. 'If we are lost, we'll need that.'

She continued to hold it under her face, it was disturbing.

'Jenna, we might be lost,' I said, injecting urgency into my voice. She always had trouble reading the room and now she was really being thick. 'It's cold and we can't find the others and I'm worried we might not be able to find our way back.' I called their names loudly, but she didn't move, just stood there, her face lit up like a ghost. What was wrong with her?

'They aren't calling back,' I said, feeling nervous. I didn't want to be alone on this dark coastal path in freezing conditions with snow swirling all around and the sea swirling beneath me. I wanted to be here with Jenna even less, and thinking about the last time I stood there, I moved as far away from the edge as possible.

'I'm not sure what to do,' I confessed, 'I was following Scott, I assumed he was leading us around the path and back again.'

'Silly you,' she said, 'you can't trust Scottie, you should know that by now,' she warned, still uplighting her face with the phone torch.

'So do you have any ideas?' I asked, irritated by the bloody torchlit face, the truth in her words and the fact she wasn't taking this seriously. 'People die in these temperatures,' I cried, feeling the rising panic, angry at Scott for putting our kids in danger.

'I say we go back,' she said. 'I've looked as far as I want to for Danni Watkins.' She used her maiden name, her voice cold, fringed with hate, then she turned and started walking in a different direction.

'Do you know where you're going?' I asked, trying to catch up with her. I was reluctant to be with her in this potentially dangerous situation. I'd seen a different side to the sweet young woman and wasn't sure I trusted her, but the alternative was to go off alone and try and find the others, which might be even more dangerous. She continued to walk on ahead, and I had no choice but to follow her. She could lead me anywhere, abandon me anywhere.

'She's unhinged!' I heard Danni's voice in my head as we walked side by side.

I felt really uneasy, panic slowly rising in my chest as I carried on trudging behind her blindly.

But as my teeth chattered in the freezing cold, and the sea roared beneath us, she continued to walk into the oblivion. And I had no choice but to follow.

TWENTY

FIONA

I walked with Jenna for about half an hour. I had no idea if we were going in the right direction. I checked my phone but the signal was down again. I couldn't call anyone, or work out the route from the map on my phone. But Jenna seemed to plough on into the darkness, head down, snow swirling around us. 'Are you *sure* you know the way back?' I asked anxiously between breaths.

She stopped suddenly, so suddenly I nearly banged into her.

'See that over there?' she said, and I looked to where she was pointing. At first, I couldn't make out what it was, then through the mists of snow and darkness saw the lighthouse.

'As long as it stays on the right, that's to the east of us, we should be heading back in the right direction.'

I was impressed, and felt a little calmer knowing she had a vague idea of how to get back. 'I didn't have you down as a girl guide, Jenna.'

She laughed. 'I'm not. I came out early yesterday morning with Scottie, and he told me about the lighthouse and how it can work for people as well as boats.'

'Oh. Really?' It sounded just like Scott, to turn a walk into a lesson, and using the lighthouse as a compass was something he'd probably done as a child on his summer holidays there. But I had no idea he took early morning walks, and it made me wonder about Danni's early morning walk and if she was alone after all. This was still on my mind ten minutes later when, to my great relief we saw the lights from the lodge in the distance. I'd been contemplating how to bring the subject up again without alerting Jenna to my obvious concerns that Scott was outside at the same time as Danni before she went missing.

'Did you and Scott go for a walk this morning?' I asked, as casually as I possibly could.

She stopped again. 'You really *don't* trust him, do you?' she said, turning to me. In the light of the lodge, I saw her face, a smile not of amusement, but more mockery.

'No more than I'd trust anyone else.' I shrugged, wondering why she'd say that. Was my mistrust so obvious? We trudged on silently, until we got closer to the lodge and heard Angela's voice.

'Hello, hello, is that you, Scott?' She was calling from the open lodge door, and waving.

'It's Jenna and Fiona,' I called, but she didn't respond, no doubt disappointed it wasn't her son.

As we got closer, she asked, 'Is Scott okay?'

'Yes, he's fine,' I said, 'he'll be back soon.' I hadn't a clue how or where he was, but didn't want to worry her yet.

I could hear Olivia's screams as I walked through the door, and my stomach churned. Poor little thing, this was distressing for her. She'd definitely picked up on the tension and despite being tiny, she must have been aware on some level of her mother's absence. My heart went out to her, and instinctively I went over to the travel cot and lifted her up.

'I need help with her when she's like this,' Angela said, apologetically. It was hard to hear this from the lively, loving and fun grandma she'd always been, and it saddened me to see her frail, and challenged by her beloved granddaughter.

Jenna went to her room to change, but I suspected the real reason was she didn't feel like doing any childcare or catering, which was fair enough. I sat down on the floor with Olivia and took out a bag of soft toy bricks and started to build with them. She loved this, and soon stopped crying, and joined me in my endeavours as Angela looked on from the edge of the sofa.

'I hope Danni's okay,' I murmured. I felt I should say something, I didn't want Angela to think I didn't care.

'I hope Scott and the kids are okay, I'm not sure *how* I feel about Danni.'

I was again surprised by this new candour coming from Angela. She'd finally lost her filter and I wasn't sure if it was the old Angela being honest, or the new, confused mother-in-law who'd lost her purse that morning. Fortunately Jenna had saved the day, and found it on the floor in the kitchen.

'But I haven't even been in the kitchen,' she'd said. Clearly Danni going missing had filled her head, this whole trip had been bad for Angela's seemingly deteriorating mental health.

'Despite being an intelligent woman with a good career, I find Danni's need for attention to be quite immature,' Angela said, which seemed like a pretty lucid, accurate comment. I nodded slowly in agreement. Danni's immaturity showed in her eagerness to hand responsibility to others and her pursuit of personal pleasure at the cost of everyone else – especially me. She handed her baby to Angela on her arrival, expected Scott to take over the childcare so she could play in the hot tub with the kids – well, with Sam. Then there was her tantrum over Angela's birthday cake, and even though the cake was smashed she presented it to us wanting attention and praise.

'Angela, I'm sorry,' I said, looking up from the soft pastel bricks I was piling up for Olivia to knock down. 'This weekend has turned into a bit of a nightmare, hasn't it?'

She sighed. 'I invited you all here because I wanted us to be together. I wanted to call a truce, to have family time before it's too late. But it's been a disaster, and mostly because of Danni.'

'It hasn't been a total disaster, it's been good for the kids to spend time with Scott,' I offered, not sure if I really meant that.

She raised her eyebrows. 'Scott's too stressed to enjoy spending time with anyone at the moment. I should have thought about it, so complex, different people's feelings to consider.'

'Yes, but the reason we all came here wasn't about *us*, it was about *you*.'

She looked at me with a puzzled smile.

'You said that it might be your last birthday.'

'Yes, yes I did, didn't I?' she said, like she'd forgotten. 'Well, I suppose *anyone's* birthday could be their last?' she replied, logically. She was looking down at me, smiling. That's when I noticed, her eyes were dark, like she was looking but not seeing me. I felt the hairs rise on the back of my neck.

'Angela? Are you okay?' I croaked, standing up slowly, with one eye on the baby.

'I'm fine, dear.' She sat down where I'd been sitting and reached for a soft brick.

'Angela, look out!' I yelled as Olivia started to topple, and I lunged towards her, catching her soft baby head before it crashed onto the floor.

'Oh God, what happened?' Angela squealed, suddenly springing to life as the baby started to cry. We were both down on the floor now. I was holding and comforting Olivia. Her head had landed in my arms, but the floor underneath was hard, so I checked for a lump. Nothing yet, she was probably screaming because the fall and my catch had just caught her by surprise. I'd keep an eye on her.

It had all caught Angela by surprise too. Was she suffering from seizures? I remembered what Jenna had told me about her slashing open a cushion. And now she was reaching for Olivia, which alarmed me, and I instinctively held on to her, unwilling to hand her over. I gently moved away, horrified at my own feelings, but I just didn't feel the baby was safe with her, though I was concerned she might pick up on this.

'You relax a while, Angela, she's fine, she seems to find this comforting.' I started walking slowly and rocking the baby as I did. If what Jenna told me was accurate and Angela was capable of cutting up a cushion without realising it, what *else* was she capable of?

'I'm perfectly fine, you know. I can look after Olivia,' she said indignantly.

'I know, I know.' I used my soothing voice. 'Why don't we have a nice cup of tea?' I suggested. Angela could never say no to a nice cup of tea, it was her answer to everything.

'That's a good idea.' She wandered off to the kitchen, and I stood at the window still holding Olivia to keep an eye on her. It was then that I suddenly saw flashlights far away, just dots in the distance, but two of those tiny dots were my kids, and relief flooded through me. As they came closer, I could just about make them out in the darkness. Scott leading the way, the other two slightly behind him, their shoulders drooped, heads down as they made their way through the freezing night. I thought about the pictures people posted on Facebook. Photos of kids, partners and pets at garden barbecues, holidays and Christmases, most of them captioned as, *my world*. And here they were now, my kids, *my world*. I watched them trudge through the dark, snowy landscape, staggering along the coastal path, one slip away from a fatal plunge, a walk away from being lost in the snow. My children putting their own lives in danger to save the woman who'd destroyed us.

'My world,' I murmured under my breath.

Those two were everything, and Danni had not only split Scott and me but come between me and my kids. Sam had broken my heart with the flirting and whispered conversations I'd witnessed between him and Danni on that long weekend. And now Georgia had recently softened towards Danni, who she'd always accused of being a homewrecker and a husband stealer. But things had clearly changed. I'd seen them in town enjoying girls' shopping trips together, giggling while carrying bags of new clothes for Georgia that I could no longer afford to buy her. Danni had done so much damage when she slept with my husband, but so much more since.

* * *

Olivia fell asleep in my arms as I stared out into the darkness. I had been reluctant to come to the lodge, but even I couldn't have imagined the terrible things that would happen.

I thought about Angela, still making tea in the kitchen, singing to herself – or was she talking to herself? I recalled walking up towards the edge of the coastal path with her by my side, her eyes gazing out to sea like she was a million miles away, like I couldn't reach her. And I remembered the fear in her eyes, the warning in her voice. 'Be careful... don't trust her, Fiona.' Was this a kind of madness, or a warning? If it was the latter, just who was she warning me about?

It bothered me then and it bothered me now, as she joined me at the window, smiling.

'They're on their way back,' I said, smiling back, and pointing at the three figures, now lit by the lights from the lodge, struggling through the snow.

'Who, dear?' She looked up at me, her eyes glassy and empty.

'Scott and the kids,' I answered.

'Oh... yes of course.'

I discreetly glanced over; her face was a blank.

Soon they were at the door, talking and banging their boots

on the step to get all the snow off. I longed to go to them, open the door and hug my kids, but I had another child in my arms, and I couldn't leave her with Angela.

Eventually they came in, bringing in an icy chill, and the sound of roaring sea and wind.

'No luck?' I asked.

Scott shook his head.

'Call the police!' Jenna said. She'd appeared as if from nowhere, having changed and put make-up on. Despite the panic in her voice, she looked very together. 'We have to let them know she's *really* missing.'

She moved forward. 'Come inside and get warm,' she instructed, then manoeuvring Scott past me, she looked up. 'Scott's in shock, I think.'

'No sign of her?' I asked the kids, who both shook their heads wordlessly and began to take off their thick jackets. 'Oh dear, hope she's okay,' I offered, but in that moment my children's safe return was all that mattered to me.

'We've looked everywhere, Mum,' Sam said with a sigh, as he and Georgia came into the sitting room. Their demeanour and the expressions on both their faces was just pure fear and sadness.

'It's just so sad,' Georgia said, stuttering the words through tears. She'd taken Danni's disappearance badly. I knew she'd grown fond of her stepmother, even though she had tried to hide it from me. It was heartbreaking to see her so upset, and still holding Olivia, I put my arm around her.

Jenna was now punching out the police's phone number which Scott had thoughtfully left on the pinboard earlier. Meanwhile Angela fussed around Scott, who just sat there shaking his head slowly.

'Do you think she might have taken something?' Georgia asked, tears streaming down her face. I cringed slightly at my daughter's insensitivity. She was only saying what was on her mind, but it was obvious Scott was stressed. He didn't respond.

I handed Olivia to Sam, and guided Georgia to the sofa to sit down next to him. I really didn't feel safe giving the baby to Angela; her wild eyes were darting everywhere and she looked even more confused than she had earlier. I put my arm around Georgia, while Sam hugged Olivia, distracting her by pulling faces and tickling her. It was touching to watch him, and I remembered how when she was born he'd told me, 'I've got two little sisters to look after now.' As much as it stung to hear that at the time, I was proud of him. He'd always been a good brother to Georgia, they were great friends, he'd do anything for her. I'd never got used to my kids being part of a family that didn't include me, but watching him with Olivia, I was reminded again of my children's relationship with this baby, and how they were a family too. I was ashamed that it was only then that I felt any sadness and regret for Danni having gone missing.

Jenna finally got through to the police to tell them that Danni was still missing. Scott still hadn't spoken as she put the phone down, shaking her head.

'What did the police say?' I asked.

'Same as before, they can't get here, they're struggling themselves. Said they'd call back when there's someone available to speak to us. Sounds like they have loads of other shit to deal with,' she added, clicking on the TV with the remote control.

She was right – according to the TV news, the area was in chaos: road accidents, missing people, and others stranded in remote areas due to the storm. As this was a coastal region, there was concern that anyone unaccounted for might have been swept out to sea.

'I guess the police are only able to help the people they can get to?' I offered.

'Are there wolves out there?' Angela asked, not taking her eyes off the screen.

'No,' I murmured, while Jenna looked at her, then me, like she was mad.

'I just wondered if she might have been mauled by a wild animal?' Angela suggested, and we all sat stiffly in uncertain silence, not knowing how to respond. This was random, and insensitive to Scott who was a mess. It certainly wasn't the Angela we knew, she seemed okay one minute then bewildered and confused the next.

Scott had obviously heard her comment, and stood up saying he didn't feel well. He headed straight for his bedroom where we heard him throwing up in the en suite.

'Oh God, poor Scott!' Angela cried, standing up from the sofa to go to him, but Jenna ushered her back down.

'Leave him, he just needs a few minutes,' she said, then turned to Georgia. 'Why don't you and Angela make us a nice hot drink, while I wait for the police to call back?'

'You only spoke to them a minute ago, and they were busy, they won't call back any time soon,' Georgia snapped, looking peeved at Jenna's request. She really wasn't as enthralled by Jenna as I'd thought she was, there'd obviously been some kind of falling out. Jenna *was* being rather assertive, perhaps she felt we needed someone to take charge? I would happily have done so, but was keen to stay under the radar, and avoid any conversations with the police.

Eventually Scott returned to the living room, and Jenna leaped up and guided him to the sofa, like he was unable to walk. He sat down, and I noticed her hand on his back, but he seemed unaware of anyone or anything. Whatever kind of state Scott and Danni's marriage was in, he was obviously worried about his wife. She was the mother of his child and of his unborn child, and it must have been tearing him apart not to know where she was. Scott adored children, and I knew in his heart he wanted that baby.

'Come on now, Scottie, I'm sure she's okay,' Jenna was saying firmly.

Was it my imagination, or was Jenna enjoying this? She had suddenly become the self-appointed person in charge, and that sweet, meek little girl had transformed into someone apparently quite fierce.

Georgia and Angela eventually returned with a tray of tea. They put the tray on the coffee table, while Angela poured the tea and Georgia handed round mugs.

'Oh I usually have Earl Grey,' Jenna said.

'I don't think there is any, it's just ordinary,' Georgia replied, monotonous, not even looking at her as she handed her the steaming mug.

'There *is* some Earl Grey, because I bought it when I shopped,' Jenna said firmly. Georgia was still holding the mug by the handle, and Jenna now had hold of it around the top.

'Do you want me to make you some?' Georgia answered, making this offer sound like a threat, while maintaining her hold on the mug.

'No, it's fine, I'll make do with this,' Jenna continued to hold the mug. It was turning into a tug-of-war, until Georgia eventually released it, unsmiling.

Those two had been quite friendly up until then, but something had happened between them. I doubted it was significant, Georgia was young and fell in and out of love and friendships very quickly. I was never quite sure who was 'cool' and who wasn't in Georgia's book, but it certainly looked like Jenna had lost her status.

Scott was gazing at his phone, like he was willing Danni to text him again.

Jenna looked around, and addressing Georgia said, 'Sweetie, would you mind just getting me some of those chocolate chip cookies, they're in the far cupboard in the kitchen.'

'Can't *you* get them?' Sam said, leaping to his sister's defence.

I was slightly concerned about the power dynamic that Jenna seemed to be imposing on Georgia. Perhaps it was just the brusque way Jenna made her requests, but I didn't like it. Sam had clearly picked up on this too.

'No, Sam,' Jenna started. 'I can't get them because I'm speaking to the police.' She waved her phone in the air, which she'd had held to her ear. She wasn't speaking, she was waiting for someone to answer, but to avoid any conflict, Georgia got up from the sofa, to do as she asked. It was then I decided it was time for an adult to step in.

'It's fine, you stay there and get warm in front of the fire, Georgia,' I said, in an attempt to take back some control from Jenna. 'I'll get your cookies, Jenna.' I half-thought she might be shamed into telling me not to go to the trouble, but she just nodded in an offhand way.

I walked into the kitchen, went straight to the cupboard and opened it. I was just reaching for the cookies, when I noticed a black, plastic bin liner had been pushed to the back of the cupboard. It wasn't full of rubbish as one would expect, but pressed quite flat, which was slightly puzzling, so I gave it a little tug and pulled it out of the cupboard. At first sight the contents of the bag were just card and paper packaging presumably meant for recycling, but I couldn't understand why they were hidden at the back of a cupboard. But as I opened them up, the reason became all too clear. The packets were ready meals, microwave friendly, probably expensive *French* ready meals. Boeuf bourguignon, white sausage with black truffle, caramelised apple, celery root puree and calvados sauce, coq au vin, the list was endless, and accounted for all the suppers we'd eaten since arriving there. I recognised some of the boxes, I'd seen them in one of the more expensive supermarkets. I was shocked, I could understand a few bits and pieces, but she'd made nothing; the boulangère potatoes were from a packet, she hadn't made the chocolate mousse, or the tarte Tatin. Nor had she made the croissants from scratch, and she'd told us quite a story about how she'd been taught to make the buttery pastry by a Parisian pastry chef who'd asked her to marry him! She'd sat at the head of the table every evening presiding over her fine cooking, accepting all the compliments when she'd merely popped them straight into serving dishes and in the oven. This wasn't in itself a terrible crime, but she'd landed this job with Angela to join us on the holiday, on the pretext that she was a Cordon Bleu cook. But why go to such lengths to lie, and what else was Jenna lying about?

TWENTY-ONE

FIONA

I returned to the sitting room with the cookies and put them on the coffee table. Jenna didn't acknowledge or touch them, it had clearly been a power play. But letting me go into that kitchen alone had done her far more harm than if she'd gone in herself to get her own cookies.

'They said they still can't get vehicles down here, the roads are blocked off, but they've called the other four lodges and she isn't in any of them,' she was announcing. 'They said there's nowhere to shelter along the coastal path, it's open and exposed to the elements, but there are sea caves along the shoreline, she may be sheltering there? They'll start searching as soon as they can, and will stay in touch with us.' She said this like she was reading it from a script. She really was loving being centre stage, which made me feel a bit sorry for her; she'd obviously never been praised or given any kind of encouragement, or responsibility. I could see why she was drawn to Scott, who was kind and fatherly, and I wondered if perhaps Georgia was jealous of that?

'Danni has her enemies,' Jenna was saying darkly, as I sat

down. This made my face go hot. I was obviously *one* of those enemies.

'I mean she *adores* you two,' she added, pointing at Sam and Georgia, like she was speaking on behalf of Danni, 'but you've had your ups and downs, haven't you?'

I turned to my kids, who were completely blindsided by this evaluation. Jenna didn't know them that well but seemed to be doing a weird debriefing of the situation after speaking to the police. Who was she to make those comments?

'I've never had a problem with Danni,' Sam replied firmly. 'She's a cool stepmum, I can talk to her about anything, even stuff I can't tell my parents.'

I bristled slightly at this but was keen to hear what else he had to say.

'There were no *ups* or *downs*, I really don't understand why you'd say that, Jenna?' Georgia added, hurt in her voice. 'She was like a big sister to me...'

'Was?' Jenna asked, her head to one side, like she was making a polite enquiry, not accusing Georgia of knowing something.

'You *know* what I mean, Jenna,' she said through gritted teeth.

'Sorry, I just thought...' She paused for a few seconds, then continued. 'It's just that Danni and I were friends when she first got with your dad.' She glanced over at me. 'And it was hard for her because you were really mean to her, weren't you, Georgia, it cut her up...'

Georgia's face crumpled even more through her tears.

'Jenna, I really don't think we should be discussing this, it's the past, a lot has changed and it isn't helping anyone,' I said.

She looked from me to Georgia, eyes wide, like she had no idea how she'd upset Georgia. 'God I'm so sorry, Georgia, I didn't mean to upset you,' she said, standing up and walking towards her, then awkwardly reaching out and touching her shoulder.

Georgia immediately shook her hand off, and looking at Jenna with barely concealed hatred, said, 'It's true, I blamed Danni when Mum and Dad divorced. I hated her and totally refused to go and stay with her and Dad because I thought she'd broken up our family.' Her chin was trembling, her face still wet from tears, her eyes filling with more. 'But then I got to know her and she told me she'd never try to replace Mum, she wanted to be my friend, and to think of her as my big sister. I'd never had a sister, and Danni was the best sister anyone could have!' Georgia crumpled again into noisy sobs, real raw pain made worse by the guilt she'd been made to feel by Jenna's mean remarks.

'Hey, hey.' Jenna now moved closer to her. 'Don't use the past tense, Georgia,' she said. 'As far as we know she's still alive. You have nothing to worry about.'

'Everyone here had an issue with Danni at some point,' I stepped in. 'Especially you, Jenna!' I tried not to allow the tremor in my voice to reveal the depth of my anger but I was sure my eyes gave me away.

The shock on her face at receiving her own treatment was deeply pleasurable.

'I mean I know she had you fired from your job, and *understandably* you harbour some resentment. But surely the fact that you and Danni fell out and you blame her for losing your job really isn't relevant to her going missing, is it?' I asked, unable to hide the sarcasm in my voice while pointing the finger directly at her.

She visibly paled, and looking down, stuttered, 'No, of course not.'

I smiled at her, but she must have seen the glint in my eye. Did she really think she could make those comments casting doubts on my daughter and I would sit there and let it happen?

I stared at her and didn't speak again, but my face said: *Go after me or my kids and you are dead.*

'Fiona's right, we've all had our moments with Danni. She's my wife, and like all relationships we've had our difficulties.' For some reason in the midst of all this blame and finger-pointing, Scott seemed to feel the need to defend his own, rather frayed relationship with Danni. 'She isn't the easiest to work with, or be married to...' He struggled a little to continue. 'But then neither am I.' He paused a moment... 'and it's my fault she's not here with us now. I *should* have treated her better. I *should* have realised how unhappy she was, but I didn't, and now she's gone,' he continued, as my heart began to break all over again realising that even if Danni wasn't in our lives, his love for her was *never* going to die.

His face looked like it would explode into tears any moment, but he was desperately trying not to cry. Angela touched his arm, tears streaming down her face witnessing her child's pain. His words about Danni seemed heartfelt, real, and everyone in the room seemed touched by what he'd said. Except me. I wondered what this looked like to an outsider, to the police coming into that room and asking us about our individual relationships with Danni. They might see that she was in the way of someone's happiness, that she'd caused pain and suffering, that she'd wrecked lives and careers and hurt feelings. And all of the above applied to me, Scott, and Jenna, even my kids and Angela who might have seen her as the catalyst of our family break-up, and therefore bringing sadness and destruction into their lives.

'I feel so guilty about this morning. I should have gone outside to ask if she was okay,' Angela muttered, reminding us that she was the last person to see Danni.

'I think we're all putting too much store by the fact she sat on the decking before going for an early morning walk. Don't beat yourself up, Gran, even if you had asked her if she was

okay, she'd probably have said yes, and still left for her walk,'
Sam said comfortingly. 'So there's really nothing to feel guilty
about.'

'Well I *certainly* didn't see her, I didn't get up until late,'
Jenna announced defensively. I thought again about the early
morning walk she'd told me she'd taken with Scott the previous
day. He'd apparently told Jenna he often went for a walk that
early, and I wondered if he'd been up and about this morning,
while Olivia slept?

'It doesn't matter *who* saw her,' Sam said sharply, 'we just
need her to come back.' He could barely get the words out.

* * *

That night we stayed up very late, waiting, talking and thinking
about Danni, asking ourselves and each other, *where is she?* But
looking back, I think everyone had their own suspicions about
why she'd gone, and they all wondered if someone among us
knew *exactly* what had happened to her.

'It's easier for us to think she may have taken her own life or
had an accident, but by the time she'd texted Scott it was
daylight,' I pointed out. 'The snow had almost stopped
throughout the morning, so even if she took a walk along the
coastal path, it was light and as long as she was careful she
would have been fine. She's young and fit, I don't understand.
What happened *after* she texted Scott?'

'You think someone did something to her?' Jenna asked,
looking around the room. I found her comments insensitive and
unhelpful, and still wasn't sure if she was being sarcastic, lying,
or just not emotionally intelligent. But she just kept on. 'I mean,
who knows who might be roaming around out there?'

'Oh no,' Angela said, 'there could be someone out there
now?' She clasped her cheeks with both hands. 'Poor Danni!'

'Unless... unless... it's *not* someone out there,' Jenna

announced, 'and it's someone in *here!*' Her eyes glittered. She was playing with us all and having dropped the bomb, looked around the room waiting for the explosion.

No one flinched.

I could feel her eyes burning into me, and wondered if, in Jenna's opinion, I was the prime suspect. It was obvious, I was the betrayed wife seeking revenge, and in all good thrillers I would be a prime suspect. But the more she snuggled up to Scott on the sofa, the more I wondered if sweet little Jenna had more than one reason to want Danni out of the way. I was still shocked from finding her stash of meal packaging, it was clear she had quite a talent for elaborate lies.

Watching her look into Scott's eyes and stroke his arm, I questioned the nature of Scott and Jenna's so-called friendship. I'd initially thought they were simply former colleagues, acquaintances at best, but her familiarity towards him suggested something more. Was he a father figure to her, and was she a student to him? Whatever it was, it seemed closer than I'd first realised when she'd turned up as the sweet young woman who Angela had befriended at the local café. I started to look at this more closely. I'd been too keen to see Danni's remarks about them being together as simple jealousy. I'd assumed too much and hadn't questioned why a young school lab technician would become friends with the headteacher anyway, let alone address him by his first name? She'd even warned him about his weight and teased him about having a second portion at dinner the evening before. They apparently went for an early morning walk alone together the previous day, and then there were the eggs. I still didn't quite understand why they'd both disappeared outside for seventeen minutes to get eggs from the car, when there were plenty in the kitchen.

I thought of Scott working late for weeks on end to 'help' new teacher Danni with her lesson plans. Her phone calls to the house to ask if she could have a quick word about a school event, the way I'd watched from a distance as she'd embraced him at sports day when he'd won the teachers' race.

Recalling these painful memories, I watched the way Jenna now lovingly handed Scott a glass of water. Was I just being irrational, and suspicious because of everything that had happened? Or, like the embrace from Danni on sports day, had I missed something that was playing out right in front of me – again?

TWENTY-TWO

FIONA

Wednesday

The morning after Danni's disappearance, we woke up to more snow. I looked out of the tiny window in my little single room at the endless white, and felt homesick for colour, and streets and cars and life.

Walking into the bathroom I shared with the kids, I was reminded again of the mess that came with family. There was all the emotional stuff, which was difficult enough, managing the kids through their hormonal lives, not to mention my ex-husband, whose hormones had also led him astray. But walking into a steam filled water-logged bathroom, with half-full plastic bottles abandoned to bleed expensive shampoo and body wash all over the floor, was also pretty stressful.

So before I could even think about having a bath or shower, I had to open the window to let out some of the steam, and clean the bathroom, including splashed mirrors, tiles and shower glass. Then I picked up the kids' towels and opened my toiletry bag to take out the bubble bath I'd treated myself to. As I took it out, I saw Nick's cricket bat keychain, and my heart banged in my chest. I'd hidden it in there so I didn't have to see it, or think about him being in the lodge before me, checking it out, looking in the bedrooms, imagining which one was mine. I tried not to think about him, or what was going to happen next. But I was terrified.

I zipped up the toiletry bag and tried to push him out of my mind. I wanted to forget I ever knew him. I distracted myself by picking up Sam's socks off the floor, and cleaned the bath with bleach and scouring powder, scrubbing like my life depended on it. The bath wasn't even dirty, but I had to wash everything away, even though my nails bled and my hands were raw after that.

Finally, I ran the bath and climbed into it. My hands stung from the hot water, but I deserved it, I deserved the pain. Within seconds all... well, *most* of my worries and fears were temporarily soaked away, and I was just drifting off, when I felt a chill and remembered I'd left the window open to let out the steam from whoever used the bathroom last. Despite the hot bath water, the air on my face was freezing, and I was just about to get up and close it when I heard someone say, 'Please don't tell the police. I beg you, Jenna...' They were just outside the window.

It was Angela's voice. What the hell was she talking about?

'Angela, can't you *see*? I have no choice, if I don't tell I could get into trouble myself, and I don't want to be dragged into this.'

'Perhaps you were mistaken?'

'Angela, I'm telling you there was blood in the snow.'

What? I sat very, very still. I barely breathed in the hope I could stay quiet enough to hear more. I couldn't let the slightest sound alert them to the fact that someone was in the bathroom and might be listening. I slowly lifted myself up a little higher and closer to hear more clearly.

'Is there anything, *anything* I can do? Do you need money?'

Just at that crucial point, Georgia's voice came from outside the bathroom. 'Mum, are you in there? I need to go to the bathroom.'

Christ.

I couldn't answer, if I did they'd know I'd been listening. I just sat quiet, hoping Georgia would go. 'Sam?' she called. 'Did you say Mum's gone for a bath?' I heard her trying the door.

'Shit. Someone's in the bathroom,' I heard Jenna say.

'Oh no!' Angela cried.

'Move away from the window, Angela,' she urged. I waited and waited, but then silence. I was trying to work out what the hell I'd just heard but had to pack it away for later because Georgia was now banging loudly on the door.

'Mum, I'm worried, are you okay in there?'

Like everyone else, my daughter had been scared by Danni's disappearance, and now she was extra protective of me, like I might be next.

'I'm fine, darling,' I called back. 'Fell asleep in the bath,' I added, just in case Jenna or Angela heard me and guessed I'd been listening.

'Oh thank God, you had me worried.'

'Sorry, darling.'

Georgia was a worrier, and I was concerned our time here had made her more anxious. My daughter wasn't the only one, I was also feeling more claustrophobic by the hour, Angela seemed more confused, Olivia was fretful, Scott was a mess, and Jenna had taken over. I asked Georgia if she fancied some fresh air and we sat outside on the decking, wrapped up in our coats and scarves. No one wanted to go in the hot tub anymore but it was nice to sit outside, get some fresh, cold air in our lungs.

She had no one to talk to about what was going on, and I wanted her to feel she could open up to me, that it might help her anxiety. 'You're very fond of Danni, aren't you?' I said.

'Danni's okay,' she muttered.

'Look, it's fine to say you *like* her, I won't be offended. I admit, when Dad first moved in with her and you were expected to stay over with them I worried I might lose you. But I was being stupid, I'm your mum, and now I know that nothing and no one will ever change that.'

She looked at me. 'You never *said* you were worried about losing us.'

'No, because it wouldn't have been fair on you guys for me to tell you that.'

'I knew you felt lonely when we went to Dad's.'

'I wasn't lonely, just sad we couldn't all be together.'

'I know, me too, I felt like you were being left out. And I was so sad for you when Danni was pregnant and then we had to go to the wedding and... I was excited about having a little sister but couldn't tell you.'

'I'm sorry I made you feel that way, Georgia.'

'Mum, I never told you, but Danni took me with her to choose her wedding dress. I had a glass of champagne with her and her friends and her mum,' she added guiltily.

'Good. I'm glad you had a lovely time, I just wish perhaps I'd been a bit more grown up myself and appreciated that despite what happened, Danni loves you. As a parent, the more people who love your kid, the better and richer their lives,' I added, putting my arm around her.

'I got to like her the more I knew her, she was kind. But she was sad.'

'What do you mean?'

'I think she worried that Dad would leave her like he left you.'

I'd sensed Danni's negative feelings towards me, the hatred was real, and yet I'd never seen it for what it was – insecurity. Danni knew I was a threat, and I saw her in the same light. We were both victims of what had happened, both unhappy, on edge, not trusting each other, when in truth, it was Scott we couldn't trust. *He'd* done that to us.

'I got the feeling your dad and Danni were going through a difficult patch, but perhaps that's all it was?' I offered, feeling guilty, questioning my own behaviour now in all this.

Georgia shrugged, then her face filled with doubt.

'What is it?' I asked.

'I don't know, it's just... I was staying over one night and Dad was working late. She asked me to babysit while she went out.'

'Okay.'

'But when Dad got back, he went mad about her being out. Then when she got home, he was asking her if she'd seen *him*?'

'Who?'

'I don't know, just *him*.' She shrugged. 'But Dad was really pissed off.'

'When was this?'

'A few months ago, early summer?'

This was interesting, Scott and I had recently reconnected, after Nick. Had Danni met someone and Scott found out and turned to me on the rebound? What a mess. Seeing our behaviour through my daughter's eyes made me feel ashamed. Scott had torn the family apart, but in my clumsy attempts to put it back together again, I'd tried to tear apart what he had with Danni. Meanwhile the kids had started to finally adjust to the new normal, and I was dead set on flipping it back again. If Olivia was picking up on tension then I was damned sure my seventeen- and eighteen-year-olds were too. No wonder Georgia was so anxious, and Sam so willing to fall into Danni's man-trap. He was confused, he wanted attention, and she'd given it to him.

Suddenly the door opened out onto the decking from inside, and Sam popped his head round. 'Dad's just had a call from the police, about the hit-and-run,' he said. We both started. My heart was thudding in my chest, could I take any more of this?

'What are they saying?' I asked.

But Sam shrugged. He either didn't know or couldn't be bothered to relay the information, just beckoned for us to go inside.

'Dad's doing an assembly,' Georgia turned to me, rolling her eyes, as we trudged through the kitchen still in outdoor clothes. We arrived in the sitting room to be greeted by Scott.

'I have news,' he was saying almost perkily. He was obviously finding Danni's disappearance distressing, but here was something he could distract himself with for a moment. Scott always needed a project, a problem to solve, and the hit-and-run was providing just the distraction he needed.

'I've just been called by Detective Chief Inspector Freeman,' he announced, in his headteacher's voice. 'She says there's been a development on the hit-and-run investigation.'

'Okay, what *is* it?' I asked, impatiently.

'The hit-and-run might be connected in some way to...' He faltered slightly. 'Danni's disappearance.'

My fingertips tingled with fear.

'In what *way*?' Sam asked.

'But we don't know anything about what's happened to Danni, how can they connect a murder and a disappearance, it's nonsense.' I shook my head in disbelief. 'I can't see how—'

'I know, but basically what seems to be two unrelated incidents have strong similarities. They both happened in this area and involve people from Worcestershire.'

'So you're saying they knew each other?'

'Either that or the killer knows them both, in which case I'm even more worried about Danni.' His voice faded for a moment, then he rallied, and in his headteacher's voice said, 'The police have asked that we are vigilant, that we keep doors locked at all times and no one is allowed to leave.'

'So you're telling us there's a fucking psycho on the loose, roaming around and killing whoever happens to get in their way?' Sam looked terrified.

Scott pulled a doubtful face. 'I wouldn't put it quite like that, Sam. And please don't swear like that in front of Grandma,' he added as an aside. 'From what the police are saying, they don't know *who's* responsible or why.'

'Oh, Scott, you don't think that he and Danni were...?' Jenna offered. God, she was twisted.

'No I don't,' he snapped, and she recoiled slightly as he took a moment to compose himself. 'Until they know anything more, let's do as they say, and keep ourselves safe.'

'We'd be safer just leaving, not sitting here waiting like bait,' Georgia snapped. 'Let's just go, what can they do?'

'They can do a lot – for a start they can arrest us, Georgia?' Scott replied sharply. Her face crumpled.

'Georgia, I know it's upsetting, darling,' I soothed, 'but we're all together, and even if we were allowed to leave, there's been so much snow overnight it's impossible to go anywhere, we'd never get a vehicle out of here.'

'Mmm and having looked at the forecast, that'll be the case for at least another twenty-four hours,' Scott said.

'Shit,' Sam murmured. 'Not another twenty-four hours stuck here.'

'Oh I'm sorry, Sam, did you have a hot date?' Jenna teased. Nobody laughed.

TWENTY-THREE

FIONA

Thursday

The next morning, I sat in the darkness thinking about Nick, and at the same time trying to push him from my mind. Having felt somehow protected in the quiet warmth, with the sound of the kettle bubbling, I suddenly felt vulnerable, and on checking the back door, was horrified to discover it was unlocked. I immediately found the spare keys kept in the cupboard and double locked it, as I had the previous evening. Once I'd made a mug of tea I wandered into the sitting room, and as I sipped, looked out onto the huge expanse of darkness outside. It was lit by snow, and I could hear Jenna's voice in my head telling Angela, 'There was blood in the snow.' What had she been talking about? It made me shiver and I wondered for the millionth time what had happened to Danni. Outside, the snow fell, light and pretty like a Christmas card, but in its silent stealth it was slowly covering more ground, more clues, and erasing vital evidence. It seemed determined to keep us here together in this place, making us wait while it continued to control us, without us even realising.

I felt a tear run down my face as I thought again about Nick, the way he'd made love to me the first time, gentle, caring, filling me with new life and hope. I'd hungrily consumed his whispered promises of days of endless sunshine. I recalled lying in the afterglow, embracing a future without Scott and daring to hope that here was someone to love. He bought me flowers and wrote me poems, and his love was like a sugar rush, the more he gave the more addicted I became. This was what I'd been looking for, here was the antidote to betrayal, a soothing cream on an open wound.

The longer I stared out, the paler the sky became; daylight crept in on a darkness that refused to give in, clinging to the shadows. And suddenly, from those shadows, something flickered across the window. Was there something or someone outside? I heard the voice of the newsreader in my head: 'Is there a killer at large in Kynance Cove?'

I thought my heart might stop, and put down my cup before I dropped it, while desperately looking around for a weapon. In the dim room, I spotted a bottle of wine on a shelf, and turned away from the window to grab it, walking back cautiously, my eyes trying to see through the darkened glass. My own reflection, my face looking back at me, but to my horror, the arms belonging to that reflection were moving. But my arms were still. In that moment the face came closer, just a shadowy outline, angry movements. Panic rose in my chest and I just started screaming, and screaming, until Sam came running into the room, swiftly followed by Georgia.

'Mum, what happened?' They both looked terrified. Georgia put her arm around me as I told them what I'd seen. Sam walked towards the window, pressing his face right up against the glass. 'I can't see anyone,' he muttered, then walked towards the door.

'Where are you going, Sam?' I asked.

'Outside to see if they're still there.'

'No, no,' Georgia whimpered.

'You are *not* going outside,' I hissed, as I grabbed him by the arm. 'It could be anyone out there waiting. If it's some psycho, they won't care who or what, they'll just pounce, you heard what the police said, stay inside.'

I was now standing in front of the door, barring his way. I was not allowing my son to walk out there in semi-darkness. 'If there is someone out there, they know as well as we do that the police can't get here.'

'Mum, if I see him, I'll scare him off.'

'No, you *won't. He* isn't scared, *we* are! We only have each other and we can't overpower anyone, the minute you open that door you could be letting someone in...' Before I could finish, we all heard a noise, coming from the kitchen.

'Christ, they're trying to get in the back door,' I whispered. I hadn't realised until then, but fortunately I was still clutching the bottle of wine, so I showed the kids my weapon, telling them to stay while I went to see what the noise was. Of course, neither of them were prepared to let me go alone, so all three of us crept quietly through into the kitchen, where it seemed someone was trying the back door. We stopped at the far side of the kitchen, and from that distance could only see the shadow of *someone* trying the door handle. The lights from the hot tub glimmered, from outside, ghostly pale, turning the figure at the door into a dark silhouette.

'Turn on the light,' I hissed.

'I don't know where the switch is.' Sam's voice was sheer panic. I heard Georgia whimper, and in my fear I couldn't recall where the switch was either.

'We've called the police!' I yelled. 'We have a weapon, and if you don't go away we will use it.' I lifted the wine bottle high into the air.

Suddenly, whoever it was on the other side of the door started shouting, and we all stepped back in fear.

'Oh, for fuck's sake!' Sam exclaimed.

'What?' I could barely speak.

He started walking towards the door, then remembering where the keys were, he opened it.

'No, Sam!' I yelled, as he unlocked the door and opened it.

'It's Dad!' he said, as Scott almost fell in.

'What's going on?' Scott asked.

'We might well ask you the same, you scared us half to death,' I gasped, my whole body was thrumming with relief and fear.

'I left the door unlocked so I could get back in.'

'Well, you shouldn't have. You put us all at risk by doing that, the police told us the doors have to be locked,' I snapped. The kids were both groaning with relief.

'What the hell were you *doing* out there?'

Before he could answer, Angela appeared in her dressing gown, understandably surprised to see us all in the kitchen.

'I thought I'd heard something going on, thought I'd better come and check,' she said, looking from one to the other.

'Scott was outside, we thought it was...' I didn't want to frighten Angela with what or who we thought it might be, so I shut up.

'I just... I just needed some answers,' he said.

'By going out there alone, and leaving the door open? Not only did you put yourself in danger, you compromised all our safety!' Again it occurred to me even as I spoke, that he'd put Danni before *everyone*, even his own kids. He'd done it before, and he'd do it again, he could never give her up.

'I was trying to retrace her steps,' he said. 'I was looking for clues, to see if I could work out what happened, see if I could find her.' He was standing in the dark, leaning against the kitchen cupboard like he might fall over, his voice tearful, croaky.

'Come on, Dad,' Georgia said, putting her arm around his waist, and her head on his chest.

Seeing them hug, I felt guilty for my anger. Of course it made sense to me that he probably just wanted to walk where Danni had, perhaps he wanted to feel close to her, walk with her and their baby?

'You're wet through, Dad,' Georgia said. 'Come and get warm by the fire.' Sam turned on the kitchen light so he could see where he was walking. He was a wreck, his hair messed up, his jacket so wet he looked like he'd been rolling in the snow. This had destroyed him.

Angela and I followed them into the sitting room, putting on lights and stoking the fire while the kids helped him off with his wet jacket and boots, then sat him down. Angela went off to make tea, and we sat around him, telling him it would all be fine.

'It won't be fine, I can't do this,' he murmured.

'You *can*, Dad,' Sam urged. 'We *need* you to be strong.'

'Yes, Dad, we all need you, we always have, you've always been there for us. What would we do without you?'

I felt such pride listening to my children, as they comforted and encouraged him, as he always had them. This role reversal was so moving I couldn't stop the tears. I reached out and touched Scott's arm. I was about to offer my own words of comfort, and that's when I saw it. Something red on the cuff of his pale Aran jumper. The shock went through me like electricity, and my chest tightened. It was *blood*.

I sat for a few minutes trying to take it in, my mind whirring. I didn't know what to do or say. Was it nothing and I was jumping to conclusions? Should I address this in front of the kids? Should I leave it for now, and mention it privately later? But over the next few minutes as the kids continued to care for him, and Angela brought in a tray of tea, I couldn't help it, and heard myself ask, 'What's that stain on your cuff?'

Scott looked at where I was pointing and the kids followed our eyes, as silence descended. I instantly regretted asking. The kids looked stunned. They both paled, and I hated that I'd done this to them, but I clearly wasn't alone in my fears.

'I... I...' He was staring at the mark, like if he looked at it long enough it might disappear and he could convince us it was never there. But the more we looked at it, the more stark and scarlet it seemed to be on the pale wool. As he struggled to come up with an explanation, I felt sick. I prayed he would have an obvious explanation, like ketchup or red ink – something, *anything*.

'I must have cut myself shaving,' he eventually said, with a half-shrug.

I knew when Scott wasn't telling the truth, he'd told me enough lies in our years together for me to pick up on them. I'd always given him the benefit of the doubt, even when he was seeing Danni, I believed him when he told me there was no one else. But the way he had denied her made me sure I was right, and he'd run straight to her, when I'd thrown him out of the house and demanded a divorce. And that morning, as the sun started to rise on another day in hell, I saw it again when I looked at him, and thought, *you liar*.

TWENTY-FOUR

FIONA

On the surface, we all accepted Scott's explanation for the blood stain and moved on. But I knew he was lying. And I was terrified. The police were concerned and thought there might be a killer somewhere in the area. And against police advice, my ex-husband goes wandering off in the early hours of the morning and comes back with blood on his cuff. It was a lot to take in, and I found it hard to concentrate on anything after that.

Later, when Scott went for a lie-down, Angela voiced the same fears and confusion as the rest of us. 'I don't understand what made him go out there this morning, it was freezing, there might be a dangerous killer waiting to pounce,' she announced dramatically.

'He's beside himself with worry, Angela, we all do strange things when we're worried.' Jenna smiled regretfully as she rubbed the old lady's arm.

'It was a stupid thing to do,' I snapped. 'He put himself and everyone else in danger.' But as I said it, all I could see was the blood stain, it filled my waking hours.

'Mum, just chill, no one was hurt. It's Dad, remember? He

does shit like that. He thinks he's a master of the universe and nothing can hurt him.' Sam, as always was keen to defend his father, his hero. I seriously hoped Scott wasn't going to let his son down again.

We were all zombie-like, tired and scared, but a little later, Angela asked Jenna if she could make some breakfast for everyone. She wasn't too chuffed about this, but smiled through gritted teeth and disappeared into the kitchen for a long time, eventually emerging without the pastries and croissants of the first few days that she'd insisted on baking fresh (she said).

'I thought it was inappropriate to eat croissants and jam given what's happened,' she announced, plonking a trucker's pile of bacon sarnies in the middle of the table. I doubted appropriateness came into it. The real reason was, that as the days had gone on, she was running out of fake French food, and at this rate it would probably be deemed inappropriate to eat anything if we stayed there longer and her packets diminished further. And as for fresh croissants 'baked from scratch,' any layering of warm butter onto fine bread dough had been done in a factory some time ago. My husband wasn't the only liar in the lodge that week.

After breakfast, we had a call from DCI Freeman who informed us she'd 'commandeered' a four-by-four vehicle that should be able to get them through the snow.

'We have started a search, we have equipment that can get us down to the bay,' she said. 'The snow's lighter now so we'll try and get to you at your lodge. We'll call when we arrive so you know it's us and safe to open your door.'

Two hours later, after calling us to let us know they were there, Freeman and a couple of her men were standing on the doorstep. I held my breath as Sam wandered to the door to let them in.

'It takes ten times longer, we're not used to weather down here,' she joked, as she stamped the snow off her boots in the porch. She'd asked if everyone could be present as she wanted to give us updates, but I think we all knew in our hearts she was there for something else.

'Is there news about Danni?' Scott asked urgently as Freeman stepped into the lodge.

'Sorry, Mr Wilson, nothing yet, forensics are still working on the area where we think she may have walked. I just hope if we find her we can get an ambulance out here. The weather's causing no end of problems.' She bent down to unlace her boots. 'There's a shortage of staff and ambulances, the NHS is dying on its feet and every bed is taken with some poor bugger suffering from flu,' she added rather bluntly, slipping off her snowy boots and placing them neatly by the door.

'Have you found the *driver* yet?' Angela asked, sitting on the edge of her seat, twisting her handkerchief between her fingers. It wasn't the obvious question given that Danni was still missing, but poor old Angela seemed to be finding it harder to make sense of anything.

Freeman shook her head. 'No, nothing as yet, but on that...' She stood up straight, and walking across the room, said, 'Can I just ask again did anyone see *anything* on Friday night?'

'I think it's been mentioned before, but I was almost run off the road by a car full of young men,' I offered.

'Yes, we have that in the statement, but the only young men we can locate are in a nearby lodge. There are just two of them and they're saying they didn't leave their lodge that day at all. This has been substantiated by their partners who are also staying at the lodge.'

'Well, someone was going fast enough to almost run Mum off the road, even if it wasn't those particular guys. So why aren't you looking for someone else?' Sam butted in, aggressively. I cringed.

'We *are* looking for someone else, and until then, *everyone* is under suspicion, sir,' Freeman said slowly, weighing him up with her eyes.

'So, what about Danni? Can you tell us *anything*?' Scott asked. He wasn't really interested in the hit-and-run, only how it might be relevant to Danni's disappearance.

'That's the main reason we're here, Mr Wilson,' she replied. 'We still haven't ruled out a connection between the two incidents. We've interviewed all the guests at the other lodges, and around the time of the accident they can all confirm where they were—'

'As can *we*,' Scott reminded her, his voice laced with slight indignation.

'Yes, of course. It's just a little difficult to establish times and whereabouts to tie in with the hit-and-run as you were all travelling, mostly alone. And the same with your wife's disappearance, when she left, everyone was sleeping separately.'

'And that means?' Georgia asked, puzzled.

'No one can corroborate anyone else's statement that you were all asleep in bed.' I waited for Angela to mention the fact she'd seen Danni that morning, but she didn't.

'Look, DCI Freeman, I don't mean to be rude, but in my opinion you're wasting valuable time,' Scott said. 'No one here would do anything to hurt Danni.'

Freeman took a deep breath, her expression unfathomable, which suggested to me that she might just not believe that. I wouldn't.

'I can assure you, Mr Wilson, time-wasting is not on our agenda,' she added, a hint of sarcasm in her voice. 'We are concerned about your wife, she is pregnant, and not familiar with the area, this makes her medium to high risk, given the weather and the terrain. We have helicopters looking for her, along with some of our team, but the snow is making the search very difficult. So I'm here to talk to her family, in the hope that we might also approach her disappearance from every angle.'

We all knew what that meant – they obviously thought one of us, or some of us might know more than we were letting on. They were going to interview us in the hope that someone might slip up. 'So, we would like to take statements from all of you,' she announced.

'Statements?' Angela said, like she'd never heard the word before.

'Yes, this will involve speaking to you all individually, and in private – now normally this would be done at the station, but that isn't possible at this time. We'd hoped by now the weather would have improved, and we could interview you all there, but today it's taken us more than two hours to get down here in a police weather vehicle. Without your statements, we can't move on any further with the investigation, and we need to pin down times and dates and facts in writing now. So, we would like to interview everyone separately, in a private space. We will record all interviews and have two officers present who will double check everything.'

We all visibly slumped. As if things weren't bad enough, we now had three members of the *police* stuck in there with us. This was going to be a long day, and as Scott and Jenna sprung to their feet to facilitate some kind of police interview room, the rest of us looked at each other with barely concealed dread.

After consultation, Scott and Danni's room was chosen for the interviews. It had a desk and chair and plenty of room for the recording equipment and three members of Cornwall police, plus an interviewee.

'This is cool, like we're on a true crime show,' Sam said, a twinkle in his eye.

Georgia rolled her eyes. 'If you think this is cool you need therapy,' she murmured sulkily.

'It won't take long,' Angela tried to reassure them. 'When we had a theft at the art club the police interviewed us all about it, and we were a matter of minutes.'

'It's hardly the same, Mum,' Scott said, as he walked into the room with Jenna in tow, having helped the police set up.

'No, gosh I'm not saying it is, they just asked us about the artist equipment and who had access to the store cupboard.'

'I think it will be quite different,' Jenna said, emulating Scott's knowing air, leaning on the wall next to him, as they both stood at the edge of the room.

'Well, you'll know all about it, Jenna, from when they had that theft at the café...' Angela said.

Instinctively, Jenna moved away from the wall, like she was ready to run. 'Yeah, it was nothing though.' She didn't look at Angela as she said this.

'Oh, I heard there was a lot of money stolen from the till.'

'I don't know, *was* there?' Jenna smiled, but it didn't reach her eyes, she really didn't want to pursue this line of enquiry.

'You all had to give police statements, didn't you?' Angela pushed on, determined. I wondered if she was as oblivious to Jenna's discomfort as she appeared to be.

'Yes, I think so.'

'It was several hundred pounds. My friend Fran the owner was devastated, they don't make much profit. They only sell snacks, and coffee, you know?' She addressed us all.

'Ooh that reminds me, I promised the police a coffee, I'd better get on with it,' Jenna blurted, as she disappeared into the kitchen – quickly followed by Scott. I caught a glance between Georgia and Sam, and was intrigued to know what they had made of all that.

Suddenly the bedroom door opened at the end of the little hallway, and an officer poked his head through. 'We're going to start the interviews, we'll be as quick as possible and try not to detain you all for too long. Can everyone stay out here? And we'd prefer if you didn't discuss your interviews before or after,' he said. I was aware, as were my kids, that Scott and Jenna were now in the kitchen and probably doing just that.

'Angela, could we speak with you first?' he asked, reading her name from a list. Poor Angela looked like she might cry. She really shouldn't have had to go through something like this in her current condition. I also wondered just how useful her interview would prove to be, she was lucid one minute and confused the next. But she stood up, still clutching her twisted handkerchief, and in her fluster almost fell over her handbag. I leapt to my feet, but Sam got there first.

'Whoa careful, Gran.' Sam grabbed her by the arm. She smiled and patted his face, as he lifted his arm out to her. 'You're a good boy, Sam,' she said, slipping her arm through his as he escorted her down the little hallway to Scott and Danni's room, where the police were waiting.

He wandered back seconds later, raising his eyebrows as he sat down.

'Is she okay?' I asked.

'Think so, she wasn't quite sure why she was being interviewed by a detective in Dad's bedroom, but then I'm not sure why we are either.'

I nodded, it seemed ridiculous. They'd brought audio equipment and live feeds and a special technician. I wondered why they didn't just wait until the weather had improved and we could go to the station, but it seemed there was some urgency, which bothered me.

Angela was 'released' more than an hour later, and informed us all she'd had her DNA taken, which was a surprise. Scott queried this with Freeman, who explained, that if no charges were made, the information would be disposed of.

'I was concerned,' Scott said. 'I don't want a police record.'

'None of us do,' I reassured him, and despite Freeman's reassurances, felt uneasy having my fingerprints taken and my mouth swabbed.

The interview process continued throughout the afternoon, and to make it less nerve-wracking, I told myself this was just like a job interview – it certainly felt like it was. The 'candidates' were called in to return later in silence, unable and unwilling to even hint at what had been said inside the room. After the kids, Scott was asked in. I wondered if the order was relevant and if so why they hadn't interviewed Scott first, or last? They say the husband or wife is always the main suspect in a missing or murder investigation. I didn't think Scott had done anything to Danni, but of all of us, surely he would be the prime suspect. I just wish I knew what he'd told them about *our* relationship, because I didn't want to tell a different story. Nor did I want to lie about anything, because it could drop me right in it if his story differed.

Scott was in there a very long time, and when he eventually emerged, he looked ten years older than he had when he went in. I felt sick. Now it would be my turn to be quizzed, and having had a relationship with the missing person which consisted of hatred from afar then combative in the flesh, I wasn't looking forward to it. After Scott's interview, the police officer wandered down the hall with his list. 'Thanks for your co-operation, we're almost there now,' he said. 'Just two more interviewees. Jenna, would you come with me please?'

She looked surprised. 'I'm not a family member, I barely know Danni,' she lied.

'But you were here when she went missing?'

'Yeah,' she shrugged, clearly irritated. I was surprised at her reaction to this, did she think she was above police suspicion? I thought of the story Angela had told me earlier about money stolen from the café where Jenna worked. Was Danni really lying about Jenna dealing, or was Jenna the liar? I wasn't sure who I believed, and now I was also disturbed by the way Jenna looked at Scott. Why hadn't I seen this before? She gazed at him constantly whenever he was around, it was like she wanted to fold herself into his arms for ever. How I'd love to be a fly on the wall for Jenna's interview with the police – it would definitely be the most interesting of all.

But my prevailing, and most terrifying thought throughout this ordeal was that the police must have *something* on one of us, and they weren't hanging around on this. My knowledge of police procedure was limited, but I questioned why they were going to the considerable trouble of setting up a room, and interviewing us at the lodge, rather than wait the twenty-four hours or so to ask us to the station? I came to the conclusion that they must have had undisclosed information or evidence regarding Danni's disappearance, and/or the hit-and-run. So what or who had led the police to the lodge – and *who* was their prime suspect?

TWENTY-FIVE

FIONA

I sat for over an hour waiting for Jenna to come out of the 'police interview room,' at the end of the hallway. It felt like a lifetime. My nausea rose every time a door opened, or a chair scraped on the wooden floor, each time a false alarm, one of the children going into their rooms, Scott dragging the travel cot along the floor, someone emerging from the kitchen with yet another cup of tea or coffee. The police had told us not to share any information regarding our interviews with the other guests. Disappointingly, Angela was sticking rigidly to the rules, barely speaking to me, like a child who's been told not to tell. I couldn't help but wonder what she'd said about Danni, given her recent lack of filter, but I doubted it was complimentary.

Eventually, after an hour and forty-five minutes, Jenna emerged, looking pretty beaten yet defiant. My heart sank. She struck me as a survivor, and if she was on the ropes would say anything about anyone to save herself. I had to hope I wasn't a casualty of her desperation.

I was the final interviewee to be called, and when the officer said my name, I thought I might faint. The sheer tension of waiting and thinking and worrying had completely drained me.

If, just a few days before, I'd been told I would be being interviewed by detectives in my ex-husband's bedroom, I wouldn't have believed it. Life really can punch you hard in the face sometimes, as I'd discovered in different ways over the past few months and years.

I followed the officer down the hallway, stepping into the room cautiously, my whole body thrumming with nerves. But Freeman smiled pleasantly, even commenting on the beautiful view from the bedroom as I walked in, which helped put me slightly at ease.

'Yes, it's a lovely view,' I replied. 'It's such a stunning view.'

'And this was Scott and Danni's room?' She seemed to be asking me to confirm this.

'Yes, they are the only couple, so they had the double room. Angela had the other double.'

She looked down at her notes. 'Yes, Angela said you wanted *this* room?'

Whack! That came from nowhere. 'No, that's not quite...' How the hell to explain this without sounding like the bitter ex-wife? 'I assumed Angela was showing it to me because it was mine...' I started.

'So you were disappointed?'

'No, not at all,' I lied. 'I was happy to have a single room, it made sense.'

'Ahh yeah, it made sense to *them*, but not to *you*.' She frowned. 'I mean there he is, the prodigal returning with his new wife and baby while the ex is pushed into some Barbie-pink kids' room, quite a come down?'

I didn't respond.

She then looked up at me and smiled. 'I'm divorced too, it's not easy to go from a double to a single, is it?'

I felt so uncomfortable at this. 'I'm fine, I don't mind at all.'

She leaned back in her seat, and paused for a beat, presumably working out how to pitch the next line to me. 'Look, I'm going to be honest with you here, no one would blame you for resenting Danni.'

'Oh I wouldn't say that I—'

'Hey, I get it.' She spoke over me. 'And from what your former mother-in-law told us, it was pretty brutal, they had an affair, it went viral, he left you and he married her.'

'I don't think it went... *viral*, and he didn't leave me, I kicked him out. But none of that's relevant now, it was in the past.'

She glanced down at her notes. 'It was only three years ago when you split. I bet that was tough after being married for *seventeen* years.'

'Yeah.' I heard the tension in my own voice and tried to soften it. 'It was, it's sad when marriages end, but I've moved on, well we both have.'

'Really?'

I nodded, afraid that my voice would give me away.

'It's just that your mother-in-law says you haven't.' She looked up at me again, I wanted to shield my eyes from her glare. She took a breath. 'Your mother-in-law, sorry *former*,' she added, rubbing it in. 'Now she reckons you still have feelings for your ex-husband.'

I was stunned. I knew she was confused, but what the hell was Angela trying to do, didn't she realise that remarks like that could be harmful to me? 'He's the father of my children, I'll always care about him, but it's nothing *more*,' I replied firmly, wondering if Scott had mentioned our recent affair. It wouldn't look good now, for either of us, but as we hadn't been allowed to talk before or after the interviews, I had no idea what he'd said. Or *not* said.

'So, you and Danni,' she returned to the questioning. 'I hear there were quite a few little spats?'

Had Angela also filled her in on mine and Danni's gladiatorial moments? Perhaps, but I could only imagine Jenna's glee at regaling Freeman with those.

'Thing is, I *did* resent Danni, I resented Scott too, of course I did *at the time*. Their affair came out of the blue, and it took me a while to accept the huge changes imposed on me. I had to sell the family home, the kids had to move with me and were made to go and see their father and... Danni.'

I saw something flicker across her face; she knew how I really felt about my replacement. She was a professional people watcher, and I'd just given myself away.

'I don't blame you for hating her...' she murmured.

There was no point in hiding from her, she could read me, it was her job.

'I'd be lying if I said I like her, I don't. But I don't *hate* her, if I did, I would never have agreed to this family trip.' I wasn't sure I believed this myself, the only reason I'd agreed to go away with my husband's new wife was for Angela.

'Yes,' she said, doubt etched all over her face, 'but Angela says you only came along because you thought she was ill...' She looked down at her notes. 'She'd said, this might be her last birthday, which you took as meaning she was perhaps terminally ill?'

'Yes, I did, it was a logical conclusion,' I replied trying not to let my impatience leak into the words.

She took a sharp intake of breath while shaking her head to imply empathy. 'Now *that* is a big ask of anyone to be under the same roof as their ex-husband with his new wife.'

'Yes, it was, and as I have already said, I was okay with that. I'll admit I was surprised Angela asked it of any of us, it must have been as hard for Danni as it was for me. But out of respect and love for Angela, I was prepared to come here, I was also prepared to accept Danni and her place in this family,' I added, though this wasn't true. I wanted to see her with Scott, observe them like one would observe animals on a safari – and then I wanted to usurp her and destroy her, as she had me.

'It must have been hard to see them together, them with

their new baby,' she was saying, moving on. 'And with your own children too. Georgia and Sam both said they didn't share stuff about their weekend visits with Dad because it upset you.'

I'd never directly said that to my children, but it must have been implicit in the same way Georgia couldn't tell me she'd been with Danni for her wedding dress. I felt ashamed, and very guilty about that, but this wasn't a therapy session, so no need to get into it. I wasn't quite sure what to say. How could I address any of this without looking like I was guilty? I was convinced Freeman thought I'd dragged Danni out at dawn and pushed her off the coastal path into swirling rough seas in full-on *woman scorned* mode.

'I know how this might *look*,' I said eventually. 'I'm the wronged wife, therefore the obvious suspect, I presume?' I was trying to play reverse psychology, presenting her with my obvious guilt, which might make me seem innocent. It was a technique we sometimes used at work when interviewing job candidates.

She stared at me for quite a while, taking me in, without responding or reacting to what I'd just said. She was good.

She took a long breath, then went in for the kill. 'Your ex-husband says that Danni is *intimidated* by you.' I was shocked at this, didn't Scott and Angela realise that by saying these things about me that they were making me look guilty? This, and the kids implying that my rage towards Danni was so bright they couldn't even mention her in my presence, was making it look like I was involved in her disappearance.

Okay, I thought, *if everyone else is going to be brutally honest I need to do the same and tell the truth, if only to save myself.* I had no choice. If Scott was somehow involved in Danni's disappearance because he wanted to be back with me, I had to cover my back. Telling the police I intimidated his wife wasn't a good look, and if he was going to throw me under the bus, then why shouldn't I do the same to him?

'I want to be completely honest with you, Detective,' I started. 'It wasn't *just* the fact that I believed Angela was ill that brought me here this weekend.'

'Oh?' Her interest was piqued.

'No, there's something else.' I paused a moment, not sure how to say this. 'Scott and I have recently... reconnected. I wanted to spend time with him and the kids and Angela too,' I replied, without mentioning that I was also keen to leave Worcestershire and Nick Cairns, who'd turned out to be someone quite different than the man who'd charmed me on our first date.

'Scott was going to end things with Danni,' I continued. 'He said he'd made a mistake and wanted to come back to me and the kids, and I was considering this quite seriously. So any motive you might think I had to get rid of her just doesn't exist.'

'So you and Mr Wilson are back together?'

'Not yet. He hasn't had that conversation with Danni, he was going to talk to her after this holiday, but of course she's gone missing, so he hasn't had the chance.'

'He does seem pretty cut up about her going missing, he implied to me that they were very happy.' She shifted slightly in her seat. 'He didn't mention getting back with you.'

I shrugged. 'Well, he wouldn't, would he?'

So now it might be his word against mine and I could end up looking like an insane fantasist. In trying to save myself, I might just have thrown *me* under the bus.

'I don't want to upset you, but your ex-husband told us that Danni's pregnant.'

'Yes, I know about that, it was a mistake.'

'Oh? He seemed pretty excited about it when I spoke to him, said they're looking forward to a bigger family.' God, the woman was mean, she picked up on everything we said and twisted it.

'He told me it wasn't planned, that's all I know,' I replied listlessly.

She gave a doubtful look as if to say *that's not what he told me*.

Why was Scott pretending everything was fine with Danni, why hadn't he told them about us, and why did he say Danni found me intimidating? It was all so damning.

'I'm surprised Scott hasn't told you about us.'

'No. He didn't.' She looked at me, waiting for me to somehow add to this, and the pleaser in me felt I needed to.

'We weren't going to abandon Danni, we didn't want to hurt her.'

'Like they hurt *you*, you mean?'

I paused; I wasn't taking her bait. 'I just want you to know that there's no motive here. We have a plan, Scott and I will get back together, he'll share custody of the children with Danni, and *she* can go back to work. She's very ambitious, it would *suit* her...' I was rambling now.

Freeman didn't seem convinced, but she didn't pursue it, and after that I felt like she was rushing to finish the interview. She looked at her watch and to my deep relief, before I dropped myself in it even further, she wound up the interview. But just before I stood up to leave, she said, 'Oh hang on, one more thing.' She put both elbows on the table, and leaned forward.

'Nicholas Cairns?'

A bolt went through me, but I tried to look composed. 'Who?' I replied, hiding the tremor in my voice and putting my hands under the table so she couldn't see them clench.

'The hit-and-run victim? We've just released his details. He lived in Worcester, not far from you actually?' She said this matter-of-factly then looked up at me like she was waiting for an explanation as to why he lived near me.

'Oh, I saw on the news that the victim was from Worcestershire...' I replied, pointlessly.

'Know him?'

'No,' I blurted, then smiled awkwardly to try and recover, which seemed to pique her interest.

'Oh, none of your party know him either, yet you all live quite near, just a couple of miles.'

She was searching my face, I was convinced this woman could see into my soul. Lying to her about knowing Nick wasn't a good move, but if I'd told the truth I'd immediately look guilty, besides, it was too late now, I'd denied knowing Nick, and I had to stick with that.

'I had to let the family know first, his wife and kids are devastated,' she said.

I felt like I'd just been shot in the face. I didn't flinch, at least I tried not to, but was sure I'd turned white at the mention of his name.

'Oh...' was all I could muster. I had no *idea* he was married with children.

'I really felt for the wife,' she was saying, 'turns out he was on dating sites, shouldn't speak ill of the dead I know.' She was slowly shaking her head, then looked directly at me. 'But what a slimy bastard eh?'

'Awful,' I managed to say, while shaking my head vigorously.

'Yeah, another good old family man eh?' She smiled conspiratorially. I wanted to run.

She took a deep breath, as I continued to hold on to mine, until she spoke.

'Okay, well that's all for now, thanks, Mrs...'

'Fiona, please call me Fiona,' I gushed, relieved, desperate to escape.

She smiled. 'Thanks for your time, Fiona.'

I left the room feeling like I really hadn't got the job. In fact, in my effort to be transparent and truthful, I'd blabbed too much and provided information that she didn't even ask for, seriously implicating myself in Danni's disappearance and probably the hit-and-run along the way. I walked down that hallway on wobbly legs feeling exhausted, and very scared.

* * *

Later, when the police had gone, we sat around talking, and before long the inevitable happened and we broke the rules and ended up revealing some of the interviews. We all kept our cards close to our chests and only offered snippets, but listening to what the others had to say about Freeman, her demeanour, her questions and remarks were like pieces of a jigsaw. And the final picture concerned me.

'The police think one of us knows what happened,' I said, walking into the living room and sitting down with the others. It was only what everyone else was thinking. I just wanted to get it out there. I also wanted to see their reactions, but they *all* looked shifty, even my own kids. By then we were all paranoid, and trying to convince ourselves that whoever was involved in Danni's disappearance, and the hit-and-run – it wasn't one of us. My head was still spinning about Nick being married, and I was also now very concerned that the police would find me on the same website where I'd met him.

'They wanted to know everything – but it *wasn't* one of us, why can't they just get that in their thick heads?' Georgia sounded stressed and tearful.

'They asked about my birthday cake, the one Danni made,' Angela said.

'What did they say?' I asked.

'They wanted to know who spoiled it. I said I thought it was you, Fiona.'

I knew she was confused, but... 'Why did you say that, Angela, it just isn't true?'

She turned to Scott. 'I think it was Scott who told me.'

I was expecting Scott to deny this, but instead he stuttered and stammered and flushed.

'Scott, did you say that?'

'I... Danni said she *thought* it might be you. I mean you can't blame her, you'd always made Mum's cake and she thought you were jealous that she'd usurped you.'

'Christ! She did a lot more than make Angela a bloody *cake* to usurp me,' I spat, angry now. 'And you told the police this?' I looked from Angela to Scott. Their reactions told me all I needed to know.

'They asked *me* about the cake too, I told them it was probably you,' Jenna offered, like she'd done me a favour. Were they all just being naïve and thoughtless saying things like this to the police, or was there something going on here?

'Why did you *say* that, Jenna?' I asked, keen to know what the hell was going on here.

'It's what I thought. I mean, who else would *do* that?'

'*You* might.' I was lashing out childishly now.

'Well, I *didn't*.' Jenna shrugged at this, was it bravado to hide her nervousness?

'Neither would I!'

'I'm sorry, Fiona, but I had to be honest, especially when they asked me about your relationship with Danni,' she added.

My stomach dropped. This girl had no understanding of our relationship, she knew *nothing* about me or the situation, and yet there she was damning me to the police with her stupid mouth. And why would she suddenly target me like that, was she also trying to detract from her own relationship with Danni like Scott was? Unfortunately, Freeman hadn't asked me anything about Jenna, now I wished she had, because Jenna looked a damn sight more guilty than anyone. In my opinion she had *several* reasons to want Danni gone.

But what really hurt was that she wasn't the only one who seemed to be pointing the finger at me. Scott had hidden the truth about us being back together, Angela had told the police I'd only gone to the lodge because I thought she was ill. Even my kids had told the police they didn't share stuff about Danni because it upset me. All this was true, but under the circumstances, every little nugget of information became potentially damning. But everyone seemed so afraid of looking guilty, they kept moving the focus – and it kept landing on me. This was what happened when people tried to save themselves, they threw each other under the bus, we'd turned on each other. But I seemed to be the only person that *everyone* had implicated in Danni's disappearance.

I looked around the room as I sipped my coffee. The fact everyone had been so keen to point the finger at me made me think that someone in that room might know more than they were letting on. After those interviews the police would have a full picture, and whether it was accurate or not, the net would close in – and I was terrified that it was about to close in on *me*.

TWENTY-SIX

FIONA

Angela was the first to go to bed the night of the police interviews. I thought perhaps the brandy had made her tired, but when she'd gone, Scott gave me a concerned look.

'Is your mum okay?' I asked. I wanted to say so much to him, to ask about his real feelings for Danni, talk about the kids, and ask about his 'friendship' with Jenna. I also wanted to ask about the hit-and-run, ask if he knew Nick Cairns, but I couldn't. We had secrets between us and secrets from each other, and now wasn't the time to open up. He was distressed about Danni, and Angela was giving us both cause for concern, I couldn't think straight with everything going on. No, now wasn't the time for any frank conversations.

Jenna and the kids had gone out to the hot tub, and though they were old enough to look after themselves, I watched from a distance. Under the circumstances, I didn't feel comfortable them spending time outside alone, especially around Jenna; besides I thought the friendship with her had soured, which made me even more curious as to why they were spending time with her.

'I'm worried about Mum,' Scott was saying. 'What

happened to Danni has really upset her. She blames herself for having us all here.'

'I find it hard to look at Olivia and not feel guilty.'

'Why?'

He paused for a moment, fighting tears. 'Because if things had been different we'd have been sleeping in the same room the other night. Even if she *had* decided to go hiking at dawn, or whatever she did, I would have *known,* and I might have asked her not to.'

'We can all think back and wonder if things might have been different. I wasn't particularly nice to her,' I said, my feelings mixed. I was concerned for Danni, but hurt that Scott seemed to be completely dismissing what had been happening between us. Had that all been erased now Danni wasn't here?

'I think she felt alone here, especially once you and Jenna became friends.'

I was surprised at this. 'I wouldn't describe Jenna and I as friends.'

'I think Danni thought you were, she said she felt like you were both talking about her.'

'That's not fair, it's just her paranoia.' I felt a shimmer of anger at her playing the victim. 'I'm getting really pissed off about how Danni's hurt is being used to lay some kind of weird blame on me. Danni's happiness or unhappiness was not my responsibility, and if she *was* insecure or paranoid that people were talking about her, perhaps *your* closeness to Jenna had more to do with it than *mine*! I suppose you told the police this theory of Danni's that I ganged up with Jenna?' I said sharply.

He looked confused. 'I was just honest with the police, Fiona, I told them the truth. I told them... everything.'

'You didn't tell them about us!'

'No, I didn't because I don't think it's relevant to her disappearance.'

'You only told them the so-called truth when it made

someone else look guilty. What about the truth that puts you in the frame? Like the fact you were married to her and having an affair with me, and that you wandered out at dawn looking for her and came back with blood on your jumper?'

He paused. 'Look, there are things you don't know, worse things than me being found guilty of hurting Danni.'

This was unexpected. 'Like *what*?'

'Nothing... nothing, I shouldn't have said anything.'

'I'm sorry, Scott, you can't just change your mind, you said something then and...'

He took a deep breath. 'The night before Danni left, she threatened to leave me and take Olivia.'

'Oh?' I wasn't completely surprised at this, Danni had seemed unhappy, but the threat to take away Olivia and the child she was carrying would have killed Scott; he had his faults, but he adored all his children – they were everything to him.

'There's something else too,' he said, his voice so tight with emotion, he seemed to struggle to release the words. 'That night, she told me the baby wasn't mine.'

I was stunned.

'No? Did you have any idea?' I gasped.

He shrugged. 'I had this feeling that she was seeing someone, she'd become bored being on maternity leave, and she was looking for something new. I think the charm of the older man had worn off for her,' he added sadly.

This explained what Georgia had told me about the conversation she'd overheard when her dad asked Danni if she'd seen 'him'.

'So what happened?'

'She told me the other night that she met up with an old boyfriend, one thing led to another and they slept together once – *apparently*.' He shook his head sadly. 'That was about three months ago, at a time when she and I were estranged, and well, you do the maths.' I felt for him, but then again, he'd slept with me numerous times in recent months, so it wasn't one-sided. This did change the landscape somewhat though, and I could see why he was worried it might incriminate him in Danni's disappearance.

'And you told the police all this?' I asked.

'Yes, even if it does make me look guilty as hell.'

We both sat for a few moments while I processed this, then I asked, 'Does *Jenna* know about the baby, or about Danni threatening to leave?'

'*Jenna?*' He seemed genuinely surprised at this. 'Why would she? I *certainly* haven't said anything to her. I only told Mum the day she went missing.'

'Mmm, I wonder if your *mum* let it slip to Jenna? She seems very confused at the moment, and she might have repeated what you told her.'

'I hope not, hadn't thought of that. But what interest would it be to Jenna?'

'I don't know, Danni didn't trust her, I guess information like that in the wrong hands could be embarrassing, and Jenna seems to be in everyone's business. I heard her talking to your mum the other day, saying she had to go to the police, said she'd seen blood in the snow. I think your mum was trying to stop her.'

'What?' He looked horrified, then seemed to change tone slightly. 'As you say, Mum's confused, she probably didn't understand.'

'No, I heard the conversation myself. Your mum *has* been a little confused lately, but the conversation was pretty clear to me. Jenna was threatening to go to the police, and your mum was begging her not to. She offered Jenna some money, Scott.'

'Christ, she really is going gaga, isn't she?'

'I think she is, and I don't think being around Jenna is help-ing. I get the feeling Jenna might be playing your mum, I don't know if it's for money or work or just to be part of a family. I know Danni didn't trust her, and the more I get to know Jenna, the more I think Danni might have been right.'

I thought again about Angela's warning the day we all went for a walk in the snow: 'Don't trust her...' *Was* it just a confused old lady getting mixed up, or was she talking about *Jenna*? Did she also feel that Jenna was up to something?

'No, Jenna wouldn't play Mum, she's a nice girl.'

'She likes you.' I threw this in to see his reaction.

'What do you mean?' He looked flustered.

'I think you have to be careful you don't give her the wrong impression, Scott. She seems to misinterpret your interest in her, she told me you went for an early morning walk together, and you taught her so much. I've also seen the way she looks at you.'

He was horrified, and I couldn't help but notice he flushed slightly. What wasn't he telling me? 'No, we have a friendship, and that's all. She is looking for guidance, and I give her that. Danni had her reasons for disliking Jenna, she didn't *understand* her.'

'Mmm, I'm beginning to think Danni might have had a point.'

'Why, what do you mean?'

'She isn't who she says she is – or what she says she is. She didn't cook any of those meals Scott, I found wrappers and boxes, they were all ready-meals she re-heated. She is no more a Cordon Bleu chef than I am.'

He paled slightly, again I felt uneasy at his reaction; 'I'm sure she is... you must be mistaken, perhaps she just had back-up food, in case we ran out?'

'No, she didn't, the empty packs from all the meals we'd eaten were there,' I replied. Again I was surprised at his strong defence of her, and pressed this. 'I don't trust her Scott, if she can lie about the meals, what else is she lying about?' But then again, I wasn't sure of anyone or anything anymore. 'I feel like I can't trust *anyone.*'

'I know,' he said softly, 'it's been a difficult time for all of us. But you can still trust me.' And as he put both arms around me, I believed him, and fell into his embrace, I'd missed the warmth and safety of my husband's hug. I hoped this meant that the two of us hadn't been erased, that once we discovered what had happened to Danni, we'd be able to regroup again. We held each other for a long time, until Sam came in, causing us to spring apart guiltily.

'Oh God, get a room, you two,' he said, smiling as he dripped hot tub water all over the floor.

'Sam,' Scott reprimanded his inappropriate comment, but Sam just kept smiling. He was drying his hair, still as blond and curly as when he was tiny and I'd wrap each curl around my fingers to get him off to sleep. Hard to believe this was the same person as the six-foot man before me, beaming, and pretending to be nauseous at the affection between his parents. I could see he was secretly pleased.

Just then the baby monitor started screaming, or rather Olivia did, and after patting my knee affectionately, Scott slowly stood up to go and tend to her.

'Where are Georgia and Jenna?' I asked Sam, glancing out of the window, seeing the empty hot tub and immediately panicking.

'They went to bed, you obviously missed them when you were snogging Dad.'

'We were just comforting each other,' I said seriously. 'Don't joke, it's disrespectful to Danni.'

'Wow! And she wasn't disrespectful to *you*, sleeping with Dad while you were married?'

This surprised me, I hadn't heard my son talk this way before.

'It's water under the bridge now, I don't bear any grudges.' I trotted out the same old lie. Perhaps one day I *might* be able to forgive them for the pain they caused me, but I'd never forgive them for the pain they caused my kids.

'So, you and Dad? Are you guys hooking up now?' he asked, sitting down next to me on the sofa.

'I told you to stop joking about it. It isn't funny or appropriate, poor Danni could be out there badly injured or...' I stopped. 'And get off the sofa, you're wet!' I exclaimed.

He smiled. 'You can be such a mum sometimes.'

'Sorry about that, blame my kids.'

'Do you still love Dad?'

His question hit me like a bullet, and I needed a few seconds to answer it.

'You went there, didn't you?' I said.

He smiled.

'Do I love Dad?' I repeated the question slowly. 'I don't know anymore,' I replied, truthfully, only just realising this.

'I just feel a bit weird about stuff.'

'What do you mean?' I asked.

'Well, Danni disappeared the day before yesterday, and Dad and Jenna suddenly start being like the mum and dad of the house, Grandma's going a bit insane, and now I walk in on you and Dad.'

'Don't say it like that, Dad and I go back a long way, he's in pain, love.'

'I know, this has really got to us all, hasn't it?'

I nodded. 'It's turned everything upside down. It's the uncertainty, is she okay? Is she in pain? Has she simply run off or...'

'Is she dead?' He finished off my sentence.

'Yeah, I suppose the longer she's missing, that's something we have to consider.'

'Yeah, I was, she's someone I can talk to. I like her a lot.' His voice broke as he tried to pretend he wasn't crying.

'Do you think we'll ever find her? Or will the police just give up one day and move on?' he asked, wiping his eyes quickly with the back of his hands.

'Who knows? But I have my suspicions.'

He looked really interested at this. 'What? Who?'

'I don't know but all I'm saying is the person I trust least is Jenna.'

He considered this. 'I can see that, she hated Danni, and has a weird "daddy" thing going on with Dad.'

I cringed slightly at this expression. 'I don't know about that. I think she just sees him as her mentor. I know your dad, he wouldn't go there.'

'Mmm, when Jenna worked at the school, Georgia said she was always in Dad's office, that's what used to piss Danni off.'

'He *was* mentoring her,' I said defensively.

'Yeah, but I think Jenna thought it was more than that. She can get a bit clingy, you know?'

'Really?'

'Yeah, a mate of mine's older brother went out with her a couple of times. She was *well* clingy, so he dumped her, then she started writing stuff about him on Facebook. She told everyone she was pregnant when she wasn't.'

'Oh dear. From what you say, it sounds like Jenna has some issues. And as none of us can prove where we were when Danni went out into the snow the other morning, who knows if someone else followed her, or went along with her? I could see Jenna and Danni getting into an argument, and Jenna lost her temper?'

He raised his eyebrows. 'Maybe? But I reckon Danni was unhappy, and just ran off into the snow.'

'Yeah, she could have, but there's obviously something that is making the police think it's suspicious. And I heard Jenna talk about seeing blood in the snow.'

'Oh shit. When did she say that?'

'I overheard her talking to Grandma.'

'What the hell?'

'I don't trust her.'

'I don't either,' he murmured. 'I just can't imagine *anyone* wanting to hurt Danni,' he said.

'If something *has* happened to Danni, I can't imagine anyone hating her enough to *kill* her,' I said, not sure I believed this myself.

He put down the towel he was holding and picked up the box of chocolate mints Angela had received for her birthday and started eating them.

'Danni's so attractive, it must be hard for you to *see* her as a stepmum?'

A smile slowly spread across his face. '*You* think I have a thing for Danni, don't you?'

'No, I... look, you wouldn't be the first son to have thoughts about...'

'Mum, I really thought you knew. I thought you were just waiting for me to *tell* you.'

My stomach dropped. 'About you and Danni?' I breathed.

'No. No she's my stepmother and it would be creepy, and I was *never* interested in Danni.'

'I just assumed that—'

'You really don't know, do you, Mum?'

'Don't know what?'

'Mum, I'm *gay*.'

This was not unwelcome, but it *was* a huge shock. My son the big, butch member of the rugby team, who'd protected me and his sister when Scott left. The boy who could have his pick of young women.

'But you've always had girlfriends and...' I looked at him. 'So the girlfriends that you took up to your bedroom, lovely Kara, the one you're always with at uni?'

He was looking at me with half a smile.

'They are all girl *friends*?'

'Yeah. I'm not interested in them in any other way. I've had *sex* with girls, but it just never felt right, like I was doing it to be one of the lads on the rugby field, you know?'

I nodded slowly.

'Sam, why didn't you tell me?' I was hurt to think he'd kept it from me.

'I was going to tell you this weekend, or whenever I got the chance. I met this guy at uni, and we're together, and it's... it's just *right*, you know?'

'Oh, darling, that's wonderful.' I hugged him. 'I feel bad that I didn't know, that I never guessed.'

'Why should you?'

'Because I'm your mum, shouldn't mums know these things?'

He smiled.

'Who else knows, does your dad know?'

He shook his head. 'Georgia does, she guessed – which is why I thought you had.'

'Wow, well I'm happy you've found what you're looking for,' I said.

'I don't want this to upset you... but Danni knows.'

'Oh?'

'I knew you'd be pissed off that I'd told her before you.'

'I'm not, I *promise*.'

'I told her the other night when we were sitting in the hot tub, she said she'd wondered. But after I told her I lay awake worried she'd tell Dad. I know he'll be fine with it, but I wanted to tell him, and I didn't want him to feel like I told her first.'

'I understand.' And I thought again about all the complications and guilt we passed on to our kids without realising it. We tried our hardest to protect them from divorce, and they tried not to hurt our feelings, but sometimes we had to be hurt to become better parents.

'So the next day I made her promise not to tell Dad,' he continued. 'And while we were talking, she thought you were listening at the door, which was actually quite funny.'

'Yes, very funny because I wasn't!' I replied indignantly.

'Mum, you are such a *liar*!' he laughed.

'Okay, I may have heard the odd word, but frustratingly I didn't hear enough!' I joked – my son knew me well. I reached out with both arms and hugged him. 'I'm proud of you, love,' I said into those blond curls. 'So who's this great guy?'

'His name's James, he's doing law like me. You'll love him, Mum.'

'I'm sure I will, but as long as you love him, that's all that matters.'

So Sam and Danni's friendship was just that, there were no secret trysts, no inappropriate behaviour. Danni's stroking and touching was just her way, and Sam, unlike Georgia, had always been comfortable with physical affection. I was comforted to know he was happy, and I now had peace of mind regarding Danni's behaviour towards him. Perhaps I could trust Danni with my children after all?

In all the madness and sadness and blood and darkness, Sam sharing this with me was a golden moment, a brief respite from the fear. I treasured it and would always keep it close in the locket of my heart. My boy really had grown up, and I was so proud. And for the first time, I didn't resent Danni being close, and knowing first – in fact, her acceptance and love had helped my son along the way.

TWENTY-SEVEN

FIONA

'Mum?' Sam said. 'I want to ask you something.'

'Okay? What do you want to ask me?'

He played with the last of Angela's birthday chocolates left in the box, holding one between two fingers. 'You know the guy who was killed, the hit-and-run?'

I felt my chest tighten. 'Yes.'

'I googled him, his photo was in the local news online. Nicholas Cairns was the same Nick you were seeing, wasn't it?'

I shook my head; it was an instinctive reaction, but I knew it was hopeless.

He took a breath, looked away in frustration, then came back to meet my eyes. 'Mum, I *know*. Remember I met him once when he came to collect you? His photograph is online, it's definitely *him*.'

I couldn't speak, I just looked at him, panic rising in my throat.

'When I'd seen the news, I just had a feeling, and went out to look at the car. I wiped away the snow, and saw the damage, the car hood and the driver's side door were dented...'

'Shit, there's damage?' I'd been in shock, and in my desperation to get off the road, to the lodge and park up without being seen, I hadn't noticed the damage in the dark. I think I'd tried to put it all so far out of my head I didn't even allow myself to think about the car, just parked it and left it outside the lodge.

'No, there was very little damage to the car, apart from the hood, which had a dent in it. I hammered it back out, you can barely see it... It's not perfect, but you'd have to really scrutinise it to see the damage. Hopefully the police won't go looking.'

'Thank you,' I hear myself say, knowing if the police *were* to find me on the same dating website, they'd be straight to the lodge to look at my car.

He hesitated. 'From what they said on the news report – about the car being... reversed?'

I nodded, hearing the screech of tyres, feeling the bump of his body as I backed up over him, again and again. I stared at my son in horror.

'When I saw his name online and realised that Nicholas Cairns was the guy you'd been seeing.'

I breathed a heavy sigh.

'Why, Mum, tell me what *happened*?'

I looked at him for a long time, trying to work out what to say, if anything. The last thing I wanted to do was tell one of my children the horrible secret I'd been holding on to for days. But it was like a poison eating away at me from the inside. I was torn between relief and guilt and self-loathing. Sometimes I felt like Nick Cairns' name was inked on my forehead and everyone could see it.

'Mum? Tell me what happened.' My son was looking at me, he'd discovered my secret. And whatever the consequences, I owed him an explanation. This time, the truth.

* * *

Nicholas Cairns was someone I thought I loved once, for a short time. I met him through a dating app, it was sheer madness on my part, I was pretty messed up after the unexpected end of my marriage. It had been a while, I was now divorced and Scott had married Danni, and I knew it was time to move on. What I didn't acknowledge, even to myself, was that this new relationship with Nick was driven by my feelings for Scott, and in an attempt to wipe away the hurt, I threw myself into it. I didn't ask enough questions, I didn't listen carefully, and as Scott now had his relationship, I saw this as mine, tit for tat, a volley back at him to say, 'If you can do this, so can I.'

But in truth my heart wasn't really in it, and though at first Nick seemed like the perfect partner, bringing roses, writing me poetry, telling me how beautiful I was, after a while it paled. I just told him it was over and expected us both to go our separate ways, but with a man like that you can never go separate ways.

I'll never forget it, Georgia had been away on a geography field trip for a few days. I'd really missed her and was looking forward to her coming home that evening. I was due to collect her from the coach at 8pm, and I'd planned a nice dinner together so she could tell me all about her trip.

I was thinking about shopping for Georgia's welcome home dinner as I was walking to work, it was summer, the weather was warm and I was beginning to feel happy. I had this stupid hope that everything was going to be fine, that I could be alone and love my kids and live my life. But as I walked, I was suddenly aware of a car driving slowly along next to me, then pulling up. I knew it was him, and started walking quickly, my breath catching, my heart racing.

'Hey, Fiona, I called you, why didn't you call me back, where have you been?'

'Nowhere, just don't think it's a good idea to stay in touch,' I gave him a smile and walked on.

'Hey, don't be like that, surely we can still be friends? Hop in, I can give you a lift to work.'

'Thanks, but I'm fine, I'd rather walk,' I replied, without even looking at him, but he just continued to pull along beside me which was quite intimidating.

'Oh come on, Fiona, it's not like I'm a stranger,' he chuckled. 'It's a five-minute drive, I just want to talk.'

'No, thanks.' I said over my shoulder.

'If you let me just explain, I promise I won't bother you again. I know it's over, I just want to say goodbye properly, please, Fiona, I need some kind of closure.'

'It's over Nick.' I felt so guilty, but had to be firm, aware I mustn't give him any mixed messages.

'Yeah, I know it's over, but if you could give me five minutes, I promise I'll be out of your life, we can be mates can't we, please? I can't believe you don't even want to talk to me. Honestly, I don't want to get back together, I met someone, she's really nice.'

'I'm glad,' I replied, relieved about this.

'I just don't want to be hurt again Fiona, I just wanted some advice, I don't want to lose her like I lost you. Please, I need you to tell me where I went wrong?'

After a few more minutes of this, I thought, 'It's broad daylight, what can he do?'

So, believing this might just be a way of helping him, of stopping him from being so obsessed with this new person, and seeing him finally leave me alone, I got in the car.

As we'd been dating for a few months, he knew where my office was, so he just drove towards it. He chatted away as we went along, saying he missed me and I'd always have a special place in his heart. 'But I get it, I really do, and I know we can't be lovers, but can we be friends?'

I shook my head.

'I don't mean best friends, I just mean if we met in the street you wouldn't cross the road to avoid me, because that's what you do.'

'Can you blame me?'

'No, my behaviour has been unacceptable, and I admit I got a bit obsessed with you back there, but I'm okay now. I've met someone.'

This was music to my ears, and I relaxed a little as he told me about his new girlfriend.

'It's early days, but I know she's the one.'

I smiled with relief, and we talked as he drove, light rain began pattering against the car windows. 'I'm glad I had a lift, I would have got wet,' I said. It was small talk, my way of saying thanks for the lift.

'Yeah. I'm good for a lift so you don't get your hair wet, but apparently I'm not good enough for you, Miss High and Mighty.'

I thought he was joking, it was a remark that came from nowhere and I tried to work out from his facial expression what was happening. But he just looked straight ahead, both hands on the wheel. It was only then I realised that he was driving past my office.

I pointed this out calmly, but he turned to me and said slowly, 'Shut your filthy mouth.'

I felt my stomach drop. I'd got into a car with a psychopath, and the doors were locked.

'Nick, just stop the car, and drop me off,' I said, desperately trying to unlock my door, imagining I might be able to just hurl myself out. But as I said this, he put his foot down and as we were moving out of town, he was able to drive faster and faster until we were way out of town. I asked him several times more to stop, but each time he would turn to me, taking his eyes off the road and putting his foot down to go faster. Several oncoming cars swerved to avoid us, and I screamed – which seemed to shock him, and before I knew it, the back of his hand smacked hard across my face. I yelped in pain, then ducked as his hand came back across my face, and from then I was silent, because any kind of noise would land me another. I was in agony, my nose was bleeding and I was trying desperately not to cry while finding a tissue in my handbag, but when he saw this, he assumed I was looking for my phone and grabbing the bag, he threw it onto the back seat out of reach.

We were driving down country lanes, and I was so terrified I couldn't speak. The blood was drying all over my face, and I looked down to see my cream blouse was red. Eventually, he stopped the car and pulled up on a quiet country lane.

'Now,' he said, in what I thought was meant to be a kind and gentle voice, but given the circumstances sounded sinister. He leaned towards me and I flinched. 'Hey, I'm not going to hurt you, as long as you're good to me...' His hand, the one that had bloodied my face, was now caressing it. How could one person be so different, so split? I looked down, unable to bear the sight of his face, the feel of his hand on my cheek. Blood had run from my nose onto my cream blouse, blooming onto the silk like a full-blown red rose.

I told him again that I had to go. 'They'll miss me at work and if I don't turn up they'll call the police,' I tried, unable to hide the terror in my voice.

'That's such an overreaction,' he said, 'you always did enjoy the drama didn't you?'

Now his other hand lifted to cup my face, I flinched as he gazed into my eyes, both hands now holding my head firmly. I couldn't move.

'I'm sure your colleagues wouldn't phone the police cos you're a few minutes late.' He smiled, bringing his face closer to mine and lowering his voice, 'They'll just think you're a lazy bitch and you're having a lie-in.'

With that, he took the keys out of the ignition, put them in his pocket and told me to get into the back of the car, where he raped me. Ten minutes later, he threw me out onto the side of the road, *covered in blood, and half-dressed. I was so scared he might come back, I hid for hours in a thicket on the side of the road, just staying quiet and playing dead, like a hurt animal. Eventually, when I came to my senses, I found my phone in my bag, but the battery had died so I had to make my way to the nearest house where a young woman let me in. She was nice enough, but didn't want her kids to see me standing there covered in blood, and just wanted to call the police and get them to deal with the mess I was making in her kitchen as my nose started to bleed again. I was so distressed, almost hysterical at the prospect of her calling the police that she let me call a friend from her landline, while she took her kids to school, asking me to close the door when I left.*

My friend Maureen turned up in her car, and after taking me straight back to her house she tried to call the police, but I literally wrestled the phone from her hand. She begged me not to take a shower. 'His DNA will be all over you,' she said, 'it's the only way of getting this bastard.'

But all I could think was, he knows my kids, he's seen them at my house, he knows where Georgia goes to school. What if he did this to her? I remember crying, thinking about her coming home from the school trip that evening. I couldn't let her see me like that, it would be too distressing. I never wanted her or Sam to know about what happened. So I called Scott, told him I had to work late, and could he collect Georgia and take her back to his and Danni's. He was always a good father, and he agreed immediately. I was so disappointed not to be able to collect her, but grateful to Scott, because I knew she'd be safe with him.

Maureen continued to battle with me about reporting Nick to the police. She was angry with me and had every right to be, I was angry with myself. But I couldn't live my life knowing that he knew where we lived, and one day, when I was late from work, and one of the kids was there on their own, he could pounce. Maureen was so concerned at my fear and what had happened to me she insisted on photographing my injuries when I came out of the shower.

She then told me to text him the photos. 'Text them and threaten to tell the police if he ever comes near you again,' she said. 'If you don't stop this now, what's to stop him from throwing you in his car, or turning up on your patio and breaking in?'

I was so scared of a future with him in it, I thought perhaps this might work. So I sent the photos telling him I'd go to the police if he came anywhere near me or my kids. I hoped if he thought I had something on him, some proof of what he'd done, he might just go away. But men like Nick don't just go away, a threat like that from a woman is a challenge. My message had the opposite effect and just seemed to ignite his fury at what I'd done to him by ending the relationship. He responded by saying if I went to the police, he would hurt my kids, that he would follow them or go to my home when I was at work and wait for them. I didn't know what the hell to do, which was why I was so glad to get myself and my children away to Cornwall. It was only a weekend, but I felt it would be a good opportunity to think straight, and work out what to do – which would have been to call the police the minute we arrived home. I'd driven to the lodge at the end of a long week of abusive text messages, phone calls and threats to me and my family, and I was exhausted and scared. I'd encouraged Georgia to spend a few days with Sam in Bristol because I knew she would be safer there than in Worcestershire with me – I had this feeling he was watching us. I was even prepared to put up with the presence of my nemesis Danni, if it meant I was miles away from him. The lodge was remote, the weather was bad, it couldn't have been better, and I relished the idea of a few fear-free days. I worried I was becoming paranoid, imagining him staring in my windows, loitering around corners and waiting nearby in his car.

Arriving in Kynance Cove I felt this huge weight being lifted, and for the first time, I seriously considered calling the police on my return from Cornwall. But just a couple of miles from the lodge, I saw it: his car behind me, following me down the road, pulling up too close on the icy ground, almost causing me to skid. It was a late winter afternoon and the light was fading, but I'd know his car anywhere. I kept driving, making sure my doors were locked, and started to cry. Fear sat in my chest since that terrible day in his car, and just knowing he was close by, that heightened that fear. I knew there was a chance I might not make it to the lodge, because he'd told me he'd kill me, and here was the perfect place. No one was around, the weather was so bad you could barely see ahead, and when he drove past me, then swerved and pulled up in front of my car, I had to brake, and stalled the car. I turned the key in the ignition, but I was in such a state, I couldn't get it to start, and now he was climbing out of his car and walking towards me. In my headlights I could see him smiling in the swirling snow. He came closer and stood in front of my car, laughing. He had me trapped, like an animal, and in that moment I screamed and screamed. My headlights were bright, and still laughing, he covered his eyes with one arm, gesturing with the other for me to get out of the car. For a second, I almost gave in, I almost opened the car door climbed out, and surrendered to the hell he had in store for me. If I did that he would surely kill me this time, but if this was the only way I could free myself from him, and keep my kids safe from his prowling and his vile threats, then so be it. This had been my deepest fear, and I could face it and finally get it over with.

But thinking about my kids, the survival instinct kicked in, and my terror turned to rage, mind gave way to body, as every sinew and nerve urged me to start that car. And suddenly, the engine spluttered to life and I put my foot down on the accelerator to make my escape. But as I surged forward at speed, I didn't turn sharply enough, and he didn't get out of the way in time, and bounced off the hood of the car. I immediately put on the brake, screaming in horror. I kept the engine running as he *emerged in the headlights like a ghost rising from the dead. He staggered a little and I thought he'd fallen, but suddenly he grabbed the handle of my car door, desperately trying to open it. I moved around his car, and pushed down harder on the accelerator, going forward, staring straight ahead, stifling my screams and whimpers, aware his face was too close to mine, pressed now against the glass. I kept on going as his fists banged on the window, and in the corner of my eye his contorted face, like a wild animal spewed anger and hatred, silenced only through the glass. He was banging his head hard against the car window, thud, thud, thud. It made me feel sick, but I didn't stop, I couldn't stop, if I did, the doors would automatically unlock and he'd have been inside, his hands around my throat. This time I knew he would kill me. But the faster I drove, the tighter he held on, and I wondered if he'd ever fall, if he'd just stay with me clutching at my car door, his face in mine forever. And when, out of the corner of my eye he eventually seemed to slide down the glass, I kept going, and going, too scared to stop and let him rise again. And when I finally found the courage to put the brakes on, I sat for a few moments in shock. Instinctively, I wanted to keep on driving, but I knew I had to stop and check on him. I was a mess and had no idea what I was going to do, but I realised the right thing would be to turn around and drive back. I could call an ambulance, say it was an accident, not give my name and leave. I turned on the engine, checked my rear mirror, and my heart nearly stopped. He was on the ground, moving like an animal, desperately trying to get to his feet. With his injuries, I don't know how he was still breathing, and I doubt he would have got very far, even if he could get to his feet. But I thought about my kids, and how, if he survived, he would still be a shadow over our lives. I knew then what I had to do to rid us all of this evil waiting around every dark corner. So I put the car into reverse, and put my foot down.*

I kept my eyes closed, and screamed so loud as I reversed into him at great speed. He had no chance, I can still feel the impact of his body as the car whacked him, and he was mowed down in an instant. And then, I did it again.

Afterwards, I sat for a long time in the gathering darkness, shaking, my car doors locked, all the lights off, and the engine dead. I couldn't move. I still had this fear that he might get up and stagger towards the car again, and he does – in my nightmares. I knew the shock of what had happened and what I'd done would always be with me. And yet I felt no regret, and no shame. I'd had to save myself, and my kids and for that I was prepared to kill. Eventually, I stepped out of the car, I wish I could say it was to check his pulse, call an ambulance, say goodbye. But this time it wasn't. I wanted to make sure he was dead, and that there were no traces of his blood on the car.

The oncoming darkness shrouded me as I stood in the freezing wind staring at the body before me, blood seeping into the cold, white snow. The ripped jacket exposing bare flesh on the frozen ground, and the silence, the deathly, tortuous silence.

Suddenly an arm reached out, fingers stretched in shock and pain. A pointless move, a final twitch of life, then nothing. I had to look away. It was hard to see what I'd done, the mess I'd made, but this was the only way I could move on and live my life. This was my revenge.

Standing in the winter wonderland of white, with only twisted skeleton trees as my witness, I called out to see if anyone was there. I waited and waited, but only the wind and the sea answered. Then I walked away.

TWENTY-EIGHT

FIONA

Icicles had begun to drip from the lodge doorway as they melted, and the snow slowed down. Sam and I had talked for hours about what had happened with Nick Cairns and the final, horrific moments of his life. He was so understanding, so forgiving and compassionate, and once again I was proud to call him my son.

'You had no choice, Mum, and if I'd known any of this, I'd have wanted him dead too.'

'He would always have been there, a shadow in our lives. I couldn't ever let him near you or Georgia, after what he did to me. I couldn't sleep or eat or rest, I felt permanently on edge, because I just knew he would be back. I tried to hide my anxiety, because I didn't want to worry either of you, but when he put himself in my way, it was my chance to rid the world of evil.'

I felt lucky to have Sam in my life, he had always been kind and caring, and after we'd talked, I felt so much better, so less alone.

'I don't think the police have any idea,' he said. 'There's no CCTV around here, and it was dark, the weather was bad, we all just drove down that road trying to see ahead, wherever he was, I didn't see him. And Georgia and I were the first to arrive after you, and you were already at the lodge by then.'

'Yes, he was on the side of the road, and as the snow came down presumably he was covered anyway.

'I think we just have to stay cool about it, and never tell anyone else,' Sam murmured.

I thought about DCI Freeman mentioning the dating website. I wasn't on there for long, but surely if the police checked the archives they'd find me and put two and two together. I didn't mention this to Sam as I didn't want to worry him. 'It's not right, I should tell the police, but then I'd be locked up and Georgia would be alone, and you'd never get to be a lawyer. But if one day the police should come and ask questions, or arrest me, you must promise you'll tell them you never knew about it,' I said. 'I don't want you involved in any way. This was my crime, it wasn't yours.'

He agreed, and we both swore to never mention it again. It was bittersweet, I wasn't proud of what I'd done, but being able to tell my son made our relationship stronger and deeper. Talking to him helped me to begin to come to terms with what I did, and it gave me some sense of redemption, however small.

* * *

It was midnight when Sam went to bed, and I was just tidying up before going myself, when Scott appeared in the doorway.

'I thought I heard someone,' he said, 'I was checking all was okay.'

'It's fine,' I said, feeling fragile but happier and calmer for sharing my secret with Sam.

'How are you feeling?' I asked.

'Devastated.' He plonked himself down on the sofa next to

me. 'I can't eat or sleep, I just keep seeing images of her lying in the snow.'

'I know, but she may not be, she might be okay somewhere. We have to cling to that possibility and not give up.'

'No, she's gone. I can feel it, she was the light and it's gone out.'

I put my arm around him. He felt fragile, thinner, like he was fading.

'I just can't accept that she's dead, that Olivia and I will have to go on alone without her.'

'You *won't* be alone,' I reassured him, 'you'll have me, and Sam and Georgia.'

'I've been thinking, I might move away. There's a vacancy for a headteacher in a school in Scotland.'

What? 'You can't...' I was horrified. 'I can't move up there, Scott, it's too far, I have my job – and what about the kids?'

He seemed surprised at this and looked at me questioningly.

'You wouldn't *have* to, Fiona, I would go with Olivia. I could take Mum with me, she could do the childcare.'

This was strange, why was he saying this?

'Your mum couldn't look after a baby, she's suffering from some kind of dementia.'

'Yeah, yeah, I know, I'm going to make an appointment with her GP when we get back, but I'd still take her with me.'

'But if you stay here, you won't have to move your mum, and you'll be nearer to me and the kids...' I hesitated for a moment, then said, 'Scott, I thought you and I were going to get back together? I thought the plan was for you to leave Danni?'

'*Leave* her?' He seemed genuinely surprised.

'You told me you were coming home.' My throat was suddenly blocked with tears. He'd told me he was unhappy with Danni, that he wished he'd never left me.

'I'd like to, of course I would, but it isn't that easy, Fiona, I can't just *abandon* her, or Olivia.' This was like a stab in the heart. I understood Olivia was the pull for him, but how could he completely disregard me in his plans?

'But we said we could make a nursery for Olivia at mine, we talked about it endlessly, I thought—'

'Yes, we talked, we talked about how it would be great to do those things in an ideal world.' He stood up, and walked towards the window. 'But that's all it was, Fiona – talk. We don't *live* in an ideal world.'

This took my breath away, and we stood in silence, staring out of the window at the endless white as I swallowed back my tears and worked out what to say. 'I slept with you, how could you lead me on like that knowing you had no intention of seeing it through?'

'I... I made a mistake with Danni. I don't want to make another mistake, I need to be on my own for a while, perhaps in the future we could talk about being together?'

'Perhaps in the future? When you're desperate and bored or fed up of your latest affair, perhaps *then* you'll come back?'

'Don't be like that, Fiona, you know I love you, I always will.'

'You don't love me, you've just been using me, you were using me for most of our marriage, and I mistook it for love. I was your comfort, the one you could run to but didn't have to share real life with. The reason you left me for Danni was because you didn't *live* with her, real life never touched you with her, until Olivia came and you both got bored – that's when Danni and I unknowingly swapped roles.'

'I don't think it's as simple as that, Fiona—'

'Don't!' I warned. 'Don't you dare speak down to me. If ever we had problems in our marriage you'd run to your mother – and with Danni you ran to me. Well, I'm not your shelter in the storm, Scott. This is *your* life, and *you* need to learn how to live it! I'm not going to hang around the lucky one, because I can just walk away!' I spat.

'I'm sorry, I don't want to lose you, Fiona.'

I spun round. 'You lost me the day you kissed *her*, the day you risked our marriage and everything we'd worked for. You took out my heart and you squeezed it in your hand, you broke it, because you could – but never again.'

I started to cry, and walked quickly back to my pink, eight-year-old girl's room. There among the unicorns I reflected on what a fool I'd been believing his promises, listening to his lies – again. I thought about the madness of him planning to move to Scotland, taking his mother and Olivia and leaving everyone else behind. But apart from my hurt in all this, what about Danni? He couldn't take Olivia to Scotland if Danni came back, and we still didn't know that she wouldn't. I suddenly felt a chill go right through me. Scott was planning the rest of his life as if Danni had died, why was he doing that? Did he know something about what had happened to her?

Perhaps it suited Scott more than anyone to get Danni out of the way, not because he was planning to leave her for me, but because he was leaving her for someone else? I felt shocked again at my husband's behaviour, at his cavalier attitude to his loved ones. He'd shattered our family just three years before, for the human equivalent of a pretty bauble. And now he seemed to be moving on from her before he even knew her fate. Which begged the question, did Scott *already* know what had happened to Danni, and was that why he felt free to move to Scotland with his new, pretty bauble?

I found this hard to process, but the more I thought about it, the more it all began to make sense. And I had to ask myself if I'd ever really known the man I'd been married to, and what he might be prepared to do, to get what he wanted?

TWENTY-NINE

DANNI'S LAST DAY

It's such a relief to be out here in the cold. Sounds mad I know, but I would so much rather be out here wandering in white solitude than stuck inside that bloody lodge. I woke up alone with that heavy feeling in my chest, why does everything have to be so complicated and messy?

I've never been able to sustain a relationship, but I really thought with a reliable, steady man like Scott I wouldn't have to try, and he'd steer me to a safe harbour. But I hadn't reckoned on my ex Pete turning up a few months ago and reminding me how much fun life could be. Scott was working long hours, and I felt insecure wondering what he was up to while I was at home all day.

I adore Olivia, and have longed for Scott to be more involved, but he seemed distant, and always seemed to be hanging out at Fiona's with her and his older kids. So cue Pete with his cheeky smile and flirty eyes, who invited me out for a drink, and later, whenever I could find a babysitter for Olivia I'd go to his flat.

Ironically, my marriage to Scott had been all about getting away from the 'Petes' of the world. I'd wanted to grow up, and settle down with someone dependable who would love me and not mess me about. I really didn't need a fling with my ex – an out of work musician with no money, no commitment and no future. But that's what I've always done, I ruined anything good that I had. I'd aim for something or someone, then once I had them, I'd smash everything up. My mother said I was self-destructive, and she should know, she was the same, we lived like nomads when I was a kid. Mum said we were both free spirits and like her, I'd never settle down, so I guess Scott the straight headteacher was my weird rebellion against my crazy, bohemian mother.

Being trapped in a beautiful lodge might seem like a dream come true to some, but I feel like a bird in a gilded cage. I was seduced by the warm wood, the crackling log fire, the beautiful seaside in a winter setting. But like everything else in my life, once it's in my hands it all turns to sand. I had to destroy it, I didn't even realise I was doing it until now when it's too late.

I hadn't been exactly overjoyed to spend time here with Fiona, but the nightmare started on this holiday the moment I saw Jenna; from experience I knew it was going to go downhill from there. Jenna has this way of snaking around people, squeezing them until she gets what she needs, I can see her doing it with Angela, and Georgia, she's even found her way around Fiona, now they cook together like mother and daughter. Then there's Georgia and Angela, who keep whispering then going into rooms and closing doors, and I feel like everyone's talking about me. And just when I thought it couldn't get any worse, Jenna or Fiona – or both – ruined the birthday cake I'd made for Angela. They must have *punched* it hard to cause that much damage, and it's made me even more jittery, because whoever punched that cake was punching me. It's frightening to think that someone here at the lodge hates me that much, and I'm scared about what they'd do to me if they got the chance. But who is it? It could even be both Jenna *and* Fiona, and I really don't know where benign, smiley Angela stands in all this, because during this weekend away I've seen another side to her. And last night I've never felt more alone and attacked than I did at dinner, it felt like they were ganging up on me. Perhaps I invited it, but Jenna's getting away with her ridiculous charade and I had to call her out. It seems that was a big mistake, because everyone now thinks I'm a total bitch. But it's not *me* who was selling drugs to vulnerable teenagers, not *me* who put vile comments online on the school website.

I'm still angry that even after I reported Jenna to Scott he didn't call the police. He wanted to brush it under the carpet, which confused me, it wasn't like him. He's always been his own man, and wouldn't do something just because someone *else* felt he should. Jenna must have some kind of hold on him because he only fired her when I threatened to go to the police. He begged me not to, and I said only if he stopped her, so he gave her three months' pay and 'let her go.' That didn't stop Jenna and Scott staying in touch though, he must have felt he owed her something because he asked Angela to have a word with that poor café owner and give her a job.

I wish I'd never met Jenna, she's been nothing but trouble for me since the day she started at the school. She was trying to get some crisps out of the staffroom machine, and I heard her swearing at it, so I wandered over and gave the machine a kick. Several crisps landed, and she laughed at this and said she owed me a drink.

Despite her being much younger than me, we were soon friends – she was bright and bubbly and more fun than most of the crusty old teachers who sat around the staffroom moaning all day. So when she found out I loved cocktails, she suggested a new cocktail bar, and after that we went out together a lot. We were both officially single – though I was seeing Scott secretly, and the more I fell for him, the more I wanted to share my secret. And who better to share my secret with than my lovely new friend, who wouldn't judge me as other staff members might. So one night after too many drinks, I told her about our affair, and she seemed as excited for me as I was.

Thinking about that time reminds me of how I used to feel about Scott back then. Those early days of our affair, the magic, the longing – when did it all turn so sour?

He started out as my boss, but he wasn't like any other boss I'd ever had. He had this kind, reassuring, authoritative manner which was a poultice to my insecurity, and lack of confidence in the new job. He guided me down the rocky road between students and parents, resources and needs, league tables, exam results and targets. I knew with him by my side I'd hit every target, get inside the head of every student, and become the best teacher I could be. He played to my ambition, and I respected and admired him hoping his skill and experience might rub off on me. But for me, the nature of our working relationship slowly began to change, and I was suddenly excited for Monday mornings, thrilled when he invited me for a working lunch, or a mentoring session after classes. Until then I'd told myself it was innocent, harmless, that he was happily married and us working closely wasn't going to change that.

But now I am forced to ask myself, would a *kind* person abandon their wife and children for a woman they've known a matter of months? Was I just a palliative, a boost to his middle-aged ego? Have I been blind to who Scott really is, do I even know my husband?

I dreaded telling Scott I was pregnant the first time, it was so unexpected, even I couldn't get my head around it. But this second time I was even more nervous. I hadn't coped well with Olivia's birth, post-natal depression floored me for the first few months and we decided not to have any more, at least for now. So finding out I was pregnant sent me into such a panic I didn't know what to do, but Scott's reaction was positive, he said he'd give me all the support I needed and he was happy. But I've been living with this lie and last night I had to tell him the truth, that this baby wasn't his. And it broke him, he was absolutely devastated. He said he'd never forgive me, that I'd ruined his life, that he'd given up everything for me and now I'd gone too far.

'Do you care about anyone but yourself?' Scott had asked, he was close to tears.

'I care about Olivia,' I replied, 'she's everything to me.'

He'd looked at me with such hatred, his eyes were really dark and small and he said, 'She's everything to *me* too.'

I told him that if he couldn't forgive me and accept the baby I understood, but if I left, I was taking Olivia with me. At this he got really scary, he raged on and on about how I'd tricked him into leaving Fiona, how he didn't love me, and never had. 'It was lust and fear of mortality,' I'd said.

Then he pushed his face right into mine and said, 'You can think what you like, and do what you like, but Olivia's staying with me – and I don't care what it takes.'

He really creeped me out, I've never seen him like that, and I honestly dreaded going to sleep. I worried he might take a pillow to my face in the middle of the night. I was so relieved when he told me he'd be sleeping in the sitting room last night. I locked the bedroom door and put a chest of drawers in front of it. That's why I'm out here now, I didn't want to face his anger this morning, and I certainly didn't want him coming back to the room. Being alone with him, I wouldn't feel safe.

I'm not proud of myself, I've been sleeping with someone else and am now pregnant by him. I am totally in the wrong and I'm owning that. But Scott's been distant, he stopped looking at me, I mean really looking at me some time ago. I think Olivia's birth burst the bubble for Scott. I couldn't be spontaneous in bed like I used to be, and he complained I wasn't exciting anymore. Meeting Pete again made me feel wanted, and I felt myself drawn to him, but while I was sleeping with Pete, where was Scott? I've known for a while that he's been seeing someone else, and he's denied it, but having now witnessed his 'friendship' with Jenna, I wouldn't be surprised if it's her. I try not to imagine the two of them together and find it hard to believe she was once a friend. It scares me the way she was able to detach herself once she got what she wanted, which was access to Scott. She clearly adores him, hangs on his every word. Her daddy issues are definitely showing, and he loves the attention from a younger woman – as he once did with me.

My suspicions have been difficult enough to cope with, and Scott is fond of telling me how paranoid I am, but he doesn't know the half of it. When I found out to my absolute fucking horror that she knows Charlotte, I thought my heart might stop beating there and then. Weeks ago, I'd taken a pregnancy test in the toilets at work, as for obvious reasons I didn't want Scott to know. When the line appeared to confirm my fears, I was devastated because I knew the baby couldn't be his. On autopilot, I just stood there washing my hands at the sink; I started to cry just as Charlotte happened to walk into the toilets. She asked if I was okay, and I couldn't help it, I told her everything. I trust people too much, I always think that this time it'll be okay, but it usually isn't. I'd trusted Jenna, and I trusted Charlotte, I really thought she was my friend. And when I texted her asking if she'd delete the online message it never occurred to me that she wouldn't, that she'd let it sit there. But when at dinner, Jenna asked if I'd heard from Charlotte, I *knew* that Jenna had got to her, and that's why she never deleted the message.

Jenna knew that Charlotte and I were friends, so must have love bombed her so she'd tell her what she knew. And if Jenna is the one leaving damaging online posts, then she can now post anything knowing Charlotte won't erase it, her loyalty is now with Jenna.

I had to tell Scott about the baby, but knowing she'd be hell bent on posting about it, I wanted to plead with her not to put anything online. It was humiliating enough for both of us, but I didn't want him to find out like that, how cruel would it be? So, I went into the kitchen after dinner to plead with her. As I walked in, she turned around and her fake smile dropped as soon as she saw me.

'Can we talk, Jenna?' I asked. 'I hate this, it's horrible. I'm sorry you lost your job, but it wasn't personal, I just couldn't live with myself knowing and not acting.'

She was leaning against the kitchen cupboard, dark, dead eyes staring at me, shaking her head slowly.

'You are kidding me, right?' the hate emanated from her eyes. 'Why would I ever want to talk to you again? You are a selfish, entitled bitch who was jealous because I was more popular with the kids than you.'

'Yes, because you sold them drugs!'

'No, because I'm younger and cooler – and your husband thinks so too by the way,' she added, and turned back to the sink.

'Okay, I get that, it's too late, we can't be friends. But I guess Charlotte's told you, and that's why you're writing threatening messages on the school website?'

'Like I say, me and Charlotte go a long way back – she tells me everything, stupid cow,' she smirked.

'I just wanted to ask you, beg you... for old times' sake, could you not put anything else on the website – if not for me, for Scott?'

Her eyes shone, the smile played on those thin red lips. 'Oh the BIG secret you mean? You can't tell me what to do, I'll post it *whenever* I like!'

This was the real Jenna, mean and nasty and hurtful. I'm the only one here who sees who she really is. My husband thinks she's sweet and needs looking after, and God alone knows how that's manifesting itself, but she definitely implied that something is going on and after seeing them in Angela's room, I reckon it's full on.

Sam says she's a laugh, Georgia is clearly besotted, as is Angela and now Fiona. But I *see* her, and I know she came to the lodge for a reason, I just can't work out what it is. Something I have noticed is how close she's got with Georgia, and I've texted her to warn her not to trust Jenna. When she worked at the school, she always befriended the weakest, sweetest kids, and before you knew it, she had them in the palm of her hand. She was soon selling drugs to them and their friends, and making a fortune. I found out about this, and told her it had to stop. That's when our friendship ended, and she went to Scott saying I was bullying her, she said I was jealous, and lying about her and I still don't understand why Scott believes her over me. But Scott plays by the rules and perhaps he was scared she'd go to the school authorities and said I had no proof and shouldn't be accusing her of such things. Then one day, I saw her in town passing something to a young teen from school. I knew I had her nailed, I even took a photo on my phone, and went straight back to Scott. But his reaction was really weird, he told me it was in my best interests to delete the photo and forget about the rumours.

'Trust me it will do more harm than good,' he'd said. 'I'm telling you, forget it!'

But I *couldn't* forget it, my brother died from an overdose of drugs when he was just seventeen, he'd been using since he was twelve, having been sold drugs at the school gate. Jenna was even more dangerous, she was selling from *inside* the school, and as a lab technician she was a member of staff and kids trusted her. I couldn't let this happen under my nose and pretend it didn't exist, so I told him I was going to the police.

'It will ruin her life,' he said.

'But how many lives will she ruin if we let her continue?'

He just started pleading with me not to go to the police, and that's when I got suspicious of *him*. And I've held on to that suspicion for a long time, until tonight, when after telling him my secret, I asked him what he was hiding.

I wanted to know why he refused to report Jenna to the police, and why he stayed in touch with her after she'd left the school, why he found her another job at the café his mother frequented.

'What has been going on between you and Jenna?' I asked. 'What does she have over you, Scott?'

And that's when he told me – everything, and I'm now sitting on the decking at 5am in the morning, watching the moon sink into the snow, and knowing it's all too late.

I am at a loss, not knowing what to do, but I have this deep yearning to break free of the lodge, filled with its lies and secrets.

I get up and wander through the snow, I have to blow away the cobwebs breathe in the cold air, take in the beautiful, snowy landscape. The skies are navy blue, the sea swirls beneath me as I take my first, faltering steps on the rocky coastal path. Out here I can think clearly about my life, my future and what I want for Olivia and me.

I know if Mum were alive she'd be telling me I messed up again, that self-destruct button is never far away from my relationships, and this time I detonated it. But how was I to know what was really going on, and how strong and deep the hold Jenna had over my husband was?

I hope, when I return in a few hours, Scott will have worked through his anger and I will have come to terms with what he told me. Hopefully we can work out how we go forward from all this – but whatever we decide, it will be without the other. Our marriage is over.

As I wander through the flurry of snow, white sky above, icy water swirling beneath me, I feel free for the first time in years. Olivia and I will move to a flat, I'll have the baby, employ a live-in nanny, and go back to work. I can't go back to my old school where Scott is headteacher, but I can find a new town, a new life and finally move on.

I walk carefully, but with purpose, needing the exercise having been stuck inside for days. It's beautiful, but it does feel a little eerie, like I'm the only human for miles and miles. I probably am. It's deathly quiet, there isn't a soul around, and as much as I want that, it's making me feel a little uneasy. If I were to fall, or hurt myself in any way, no one would know where I was. And even if I screamed, or called out, no one would hear me in the thick snow-silence, because there's nobody here. That scares me and I walk a little faster. Perhaps I'll go back soon? I must bear in mind that I'm pregnant. I forgot how exhausting it is growing a baby, it's taking everything out of me, and all I want to do is sleep. I stop. Did I hear something? A twig breaking? I wait in the silence for more audible clues. I wait and wait. Nothing. Silence all around me. I spin around, everywhere I look is white. Snow is still falling, it's heavier now and the wind is whipping up, biting at my cheeks. I can't see more than a few inches in front of me, I almost lose my footing, and have to grab the bark of a wizened tree covered in snow. And as I do, I see someone walking towards me. I can't see who they are, just a dark figure striding forward, getting bigger. I want to turn round and go back, but that would mean going towards them, and I'm scared to do that. Instinctively, I start to run.

THIRTY

FIONA

Friday Evening

After being stuck at the lodge for a week, we were all beginning to wonder if our lockdown would ever end.

'It's like Covid all over again,' Angela observed on more than one occasion, which didn't really help lift the communal mood.

However, on that Friday evening, as we ate dinner, there was a loud banging on the door. We all looked at each other in shock. We'd talked ourselves in and out of so many scenarios, our imaginations had run wild, and I doubt I was the only one expecting a marauding serial killer at the other side of the door. But no sooner had Scott unlocked and opened up our beautiful prison, Freeman and Fry marched in. Freezing wind and radio noise intruded violently into the polite calm of clinking cutlery and quiet chat, reminding us how isolated we'd been from the world in those last few days.

'The snow's stopped but now we've got sleet, which is a damn sight worse,' Freeman announced, walking in and stomping her snowy boots on the door mat.

She continued to mutter to her boots as she stomped, before looking up, and seeing us all, waiting expectantly. It was as if she suddenly remembered why she was there, and gathering herself, she marched into the room followed by Fry.

'Mr Wilson? I'm afraid we have some news,' she spoke more formally and respectfully now – which turned my blood cold.

'What news?' Scott asked, with thinly veiled horror.

Everyone moved from the table towards where he was standing, clutching Olivia in one arm. Georgia moved close to him, touching his back as he placed his other arm around her shoulder. She was now propping him up. His face was white and he looked like he might fall at any second.

Freeman walked towards him, and said in a quiet, solemn tone, loud enough for us to hear, 'Mr Wilson, I'm afraid I have some difficult news. Would you like to talk in private?'

He shook his head, bewildered, yet like the rest of us, knowing what she was about to say would change everything.

Once he was seated, Olivia on his knee, Freeman began. 'We've found a body, just off the coastal path. A woman who looks to be in her thirties, we will need a formal identification, but want to prepare you. We believe it's your wife Danni, Mr Wilson.'

Olivia's little face looked from Freeman then back to her father. I remember thinking, she isn't aware of the meaning of this moment, when her father is informed of her mother's death, but it will now be part of her.

Sam and Georgia rushed over to console their father, but Jenna was already there, entangling herself around him like ivy, keeping the children and everyone else away. I shuddered, knowing she was probably enjoying the drama, the emotion, the attention. Scott, however, seemed unaware of everything and everyone around him, the blood had drained from his face, tears etched his cheeks, and it was only then I realised how much he loved Danni.

'Obviously we will need a family member or someone close to Danni Wilson who can come and formally identify the body,' Freeman said.

Jenna looked up from Scott's chest, concerned. 'You sure it looks like it's definitely *Danni*?' She clearly wanted confirmation.

'We can't say for definite, at this stage,' Freeman replied.

'I'll identify her,' Sam said. 'I don't want you to go through that, Dad.'

'No, son, I'd like to see her...'

'I have to warn you, she suffered a violent death,' Freeman said.

Scott nodded. 'I can handle it.'

'Okay, we'll make arrangements for you to go to the mortuary tomorrow.' She cleared her throat and taking a breath, said, 'This is rather sensitive. But we believe Mrs Wilson was murdered, and we have found the murder weapon.'

We all looked at each other. 'Initial fingerprint tests prove it was the weapon that killed Danni.'

The tension in the room rose and again and without speaking, we all looked at each other. Was Danni's killer in the room?

'I don't want to alarm anyone, but we would like that person to come with us back to the station where we can discuss the new evidence.'

Who?

Again, we all slid our eyes around the room to see who was squirming, if anyone's expressions gave anything away.

But Freeman shocked us all, when she said, 'Angela Wilson, could you come with us to the station please?'

There was an audible, communal gasp. Angela looked as shocked as the rest of us and stared from Scott to me to the police with a look of confusion and pain on her face.

'No,' Scott snapped. 'I know you have your theories – but I strongly believe this was a random killing. And while you're here scaring an old lady and her grieving family, the killer is roaming the hills out there looking for his next victim.'

'I'm sorry, Mr Wilson, I do understand, this must be distressing for everyone, including Mrs Wilson, but I can assure you we only want to talk with your mother. At this stage, we aren't arresting her.'

'*Arresting* her?' I thought he was going to have a heart attack, but I felt the same outrage and shock – no way did I believe Angela had done anything.

'You can't just demand my mother goes to the police station with you, without a solicitor.' Scott's face was crowded with anger and fear.

Fry stepped up at this. 'As DCI Freeman said, we *aren't* arresting her, Mr Wilson, but of course she can have a solicitor, if you think she needs one?'

Scott shook his head reluctantly. He probably didn't want to make her look guilty before she'd even been questioned.

'I don't need a solicitor,' Angela said, 'I'm not guilty of anything.'

'Okay, Mum, but I can't let you go to the police station on your own.'

'Of course you're welcome to come with us, obviously she will be interviewed alone – but you can be there for support, would you like that, Mrs Wilson?' Freeman asked.

'Yes please,' she said. Considering Angela was the one about to be questioned, she seemed a lot calmer than Scott. Within minutes, she was being gently guided out onto the slippery fore-court in front of the lodge and into a police car, while Scott climbed in after her.

Sam offered to go with them, but Scott rejected his offer gently. 'It's fine, son, you stay and look after everyone.'

Classic Scott. Who in a houseful of women could possibly look after themselves? In his world, all women needed a man.

But for me, it seemed my life would have been so much happier and less complicated without them.

Once they'd all left, a hush descended on the lodge. Jenna seemed upset, but Georgia was inconsolable, and Sam and I spent the next few hours comforting her.

'But Grandma might go to prison?' she hiccoughed through sobs.

We tried to reassure her but I was as dumbfounded as Georgia and had no idea if her grandma was going to be okay. I just couldn't *imagine* what had been found near the crime scene that had implicated her so strongly.

'She wouldn't hurt Danni, she loved her,' Georgia was saying.

'Everyone loved Danni.' Sam was the only one to confirm this. I wasn't going to lie, and even Jenna resisted joining in on *this* obituary. The evening rumbled on, the snow melted, drips everywhere, and we continued on the hamster wheel of conversation and tears. We'd been told about Danni, then immediately about Angela, and we were finding it all tough to process.

'Do you really think Angela killed Danni?' Jenna asked, her eyes sparkling.

'No, I don't,' I replied firmly. 'It's all a big mistake, I agree with Scott, it was a random killing and once they've cleared up the weapon and the DNA details, I'm sure she'll be back.' But I wasn't sure of anything, Angela *didn't* love Danni, and despite the sweet, batty old lady persona she portrayed, I'd seen a different side to her that holiday. And despite, or perhaps *because* of her confusion and mental deterioration – she was probably capable of anything.

By midnight, we still hadn't heard from Scott, Angela or the police, so Georgia, Jenna and Sam all went to bed. I locked the doors, seriously hoping I was locking the killer out, and not locking them in, and checked on Olivia, who was sleeping soundly. Then I went back to the living room, lay on the sofa and wrapped a fur throw around myself and drifted off to sleep.

I was woken around 2am by Scott and Angela returning. They were talking quite animatedly, and both of them seemed slightly better than I thought they'd be.

'Thank God!' I said, throwing off the fur and rushing to hug Angela, who looked perkier than Scott. His face was grey with tiredness and worry.

'What happened?' I asked.

'I'll let Mum tell you, I'm going to bed,' Scott said. 'Has Olivia been okay?'

'She's slept through,' I replied, and nodding, he wandered off to bed.

I made Angela and myself some tea, and buttered her a scone. Surprisingly she had quite an appetite despite the ordeal and the late hour.

'It was my walking stick, Fiona. Remember, I lost it on that day when you and I went for a walk?'

'I do remember that. Where was it?'

She pulled a face. 'Unfortunately it was near Danni's body.'

'Oh dear,' I said as we walked through and settled back in the sitting room. 'So is that why they interviewed you?'

'Yes, those buggers kept it, wouldn't give it back to me!' she growled, turning from sweet, bewildered Angela, to someone else.

'They probably need it for evidence,' I offered gently, but she continued to bare her teeth. 'That was my *mother's* walking stick.'

'Yes, I remember,' I replied softly, hoping to calm her obvious anger.

'I asked if I might be able to have it back after all this, but they said probably not as it was evidence. But it was a good walking stick, pearl-handled, it belonged to my mother,' she repeated. 'They knew how to *make* walking sticks then, solid, heavy, not these lightweight Perspex ones the celebrities use now.'

Her description sounded more like that of a weapon than a walking aid; perhaps it was?

Angela was definitely losing the plot. She was there one minute and gone the next. I mean, if that walking stick was the weapon that killed her daughter-in-law, who cared if it was a family heirloom – who would want it back?

'It was my DNA, Fiona, they found it on the stick.' She said DNA slowly, like they were letters she hadn't heard before.

'Well, it was *your* stick, it's *bound* to have your fingerprints on it.'

'Yes but there was no one else's DNA on it... except Danni's.' Again, she pronounced the letters slowly, carefully.

'Was it Danni's blood on the stick?'

'Yes. They found it hidden under some fresh snow. They saw the blood, a big red stain in all the whiteness.' She leaned forward, conspiratorially. 'Whoever killed Danni had hidden it. Her DNA was on it,' she repeated again.

It seemed implausible for Angela to walk as far as the coastal path alone, but then again, she was walking fine without her stick on the day we took the walk, or she wouldn't have forgotten it. It was her mental stamina that seemed to be suffering then – but she attended the gym, wasn't immobile, and as she'd said to me on our walk, 'I can walk for miles, I just can't do it quickly.'

But could she overpower a younger, stronger woman? I considered this as she nibbled on her buttered scone. Danni was pregnant, she might have been feeling unwell and weakened which made her easier to overpower?

'And so they let you go?' I asked. This all felt rather disjointed, they had her DNA on the weapon, so why was she back at the lodge?

'Of course. I didn't kill Danni.'

She sipped on her tea, then putting the cup back in the saucer, she said, 'I told them I couldn't walk that far. I was angry about the baby not being Scott's, but he said not to tell them that, so I said, "Whoever is the father of that baby, it was *my* grandchild,"' she went back to her scone.

'Is that what you really thought, or what Scott *told* you to say?'

'Yes, I did as Scott asked, but as far as I'm concerned that baby was nothing to do with me. It wasn't my Scott's, it was another man's – Danni was such a slut!'

I was shocked. I'd never heard Angela say a word like that; not only was she too ladylike and proper, she also respected women. This confirmed that she wasn't the woman I knew.

'I *could* have killed Danni,' she suddenly said, like it had just occurred to her. 'I *could* have hit her over the head with that stick many times, bang, bang, bang.' She gesticulated the action of bashing someone over the head with a heavy walking stick. Her eyes were half closed, her mouth tight, her face flickered as if she were remembering, feeling it all over again. I felt sick.

'I *might* have flung her phone in the sea, and as I'm old and insignificant, no one would think it was me, would they?'

'After all, no one knew it was *me* who smashed her cake. You always make my birthday cakes – not *her*.' She put her shaking finger to her lips. And my world turned upside down.

EPILOGUE

One Year Later

It's been a year since our long weekend at the lodge – hard to believe Danni's been dead a year.

Angela was ultimately arrested and tried for Danni's murder.

The police still aren't any further with their investigation into the murder of Nick Cairns.

Of course I'm relieved they haven't found anything to incriminate me, but worry it's just a matter of time. I try not to allow it to affect my life, and some days I manage to rarely think about it, but every time my phone buzzes or the doorbell rings, another little piece of me dies. I've seriously considered handing myself in, just calling the police and telling them everything. Perhaps under the circumstances the courts would be lenient? But the longer I leave it to confess, the worse it will be for me, and by now my crime would definitely land me in jail. Living with this is like having a slow-growing cancer that one day will have to be cut out, but I just keep moving on, hoping it will cure itself.

For me it always comes back to the children. Sam's in his second year at Bristol University, and still with James, his partner, who's also studying law. The boys dream of one day having their own law practice. And Georgia is now at Exeter studying medicine. She finds life a little harder than her more gregarious brother, and she's still in her first term, but medicine is her dream, and I think she's happy. I don't want to be parted from them, and if I can stay free until they are both settled with careers and families and their own lives, then that's all I ask.

As for Angela, all the evidence was there to lock her away for the rest of her life, and she confessed to Danni's murder in a police interview, but later she denied anything to do with the murder and accused Jenna of being the killer. But the walking stick, the DNA, and her rather outspoken criticism of Danni to the police regarding her 'sluttish' ways pointed to her being responsible. Let's not forget Angela was the architect of the weekend at the lodge, which looked very much like a device to get us all together, including Jenna – and then point the finger at her. It didn't help her case that we were all a little unsure about exactly *why* she'd arranged the weekend. I think in her lucid moments she'd realised what was happening to her and genuinely invited us thinking it might be her last, but then she got confused. The police acknowledged that Angela was not of sound mind, but believed she'd set up the whole weekend to kill Danni so that Scott and I could get back together. Despite our protests, the case went to court, where Angela continued to struggle with her deteriorating mental health. But after a long, protracted court case, she was finally found not guilty by reason of insanity, with jurors finding that her undiagnosed dementia had affected her.

Angela's now been hospitalised. She won't have to go to prison for her crime, she will live out her days in safety and security in a medical facility. She's still with us in spirit, still sporting those crazy earrings and rainbow trainers, we make sure of that. I visit her every week at the care home, but she isn't Angela anymore. Sometimes she's back with us briefly, like a few weeks ago when the kids and I took her a cake for her seventy-sixth birthday. 'I always love Fiona's cakes,' she said in her old voice. 'It isn't my birthday without a cake made by Fiona.' I imagined her smashing Danni's cake, and tried not to imagine her smashing Danni's head.

I still find it hard to think of Angela killing anyone, but her walking stick only had her and Danni's DNA on it, which was pretty conclusive. I still wonder how a seventy-five-year-old woman had the strength to kill a fit young woman, but apparently Danni was first hit from behind, so perhaps that knocked her out and gave Angela the opportunity to end her life. Sometimes I wonder if she had help?

It was a horrible time, we were all scared and mistrusting of each other. The lodge was beautiful, but oppressive and we all felt so trapped. Only recently have I started to recover, and begun to see a chink of hope, some light a little further down the line.

The kids are due home for Christmas today, they're travelling back together on the same train from Exeter, which Sam will board at Bristol. I am so excited to see them. I am clearing out stuff from one of Sam's cupboards when I find a rolled-up winter jumper that I remember him wearing at the lodge last year. I unroll it, intending to wash it; this jumper will be needed this winter with heating bills so high. As I do, something solid and sparkly emerges. I know what it is, and immediately let it drop to the floor like it might bite me. Then I stand over it as a whole sequence of possible events runs like a video in my head. It's Danni's pink, blingy phone with DANNI emblazoned across in fake diamonds. I look at it for a long, long time, unable to pick it up. It was never found – the theory was that Angela had thrown it over the cliffs into the sea after killing Danni. But it's here. And I have no idea why my son has hidden it in a winter jumper. But I am *terrified*.

My mind is blank. Acres and acres of white snow, a stain of blood. Angela's pearl-handled walking stick. Danni's phone lying on Sam's bedroom floor. It doesn't add up.

Angela wouldn't have had the foresight to take Danni's phone, even before her decline into dementia. Whoever took this from her or from her body, was someone who understood the *power* of a phone, and the secrets it keeps. I continue to stare at it, consider burying it, or burning it, or wrapping it up again in the jumper and putting it back. Should I pretend I've never seen it and forget all about it?

I presume the phone is broken, it must have been lying in the snow for a long time. Then again, if Sam... I can't even contemplate it. But if *someone* killed Danni, he may have taken her phone straight *after* he killed her? Unlike Angela, he'd know that things can be traced through a mobile phone. But why didn't he just throw it into the sea? I plug the charger into the wall and attach the phone on the off-chance I might be able to get it to work, and when I return a few minutes later it's charging. A photo of Danni and Olivia is looking back at me, Danni beaming, holding her baby. Why does Sam have this phone? I know he didn't kill Danni. Did he?

* * *

Weird thoughts are ribboning through my brain as I drive out of town to a small market several miles away. I have checked online and there's a phone stall here, and rather than go to a proper shop, I need this to be discreet, dodgy if you like. Their website says they unlock any phone, and as I walk towards the stall I just hope I'm in luck. The guy tells me he can do it for £50, he doesn't ask me any questions, but still, I feel the need to volunteer a long and involved story about this being my daughter's phone. 'She's asked me to get it unlocked,' I say. I'm too old to be a Danni with a blingy pink phone case and fake diamonds.

Later, as I drive home with the phone unlocked and in my bag, I'm tempted to just throw it away, hurl it into a field of tall grass or a river. But what if it turned up again? What if it was handed in and ended up with the police? Besides, I need to know what I'm dealing with, if only to protect Sam.

Once home, I sit down and brace myself as I open the phone and glimpse into Danni's last days.

Aware this is a huge intrusion into someone else's life, I will only look at messages that are relevant. I find the newest ones which happen to be between Danni and Georgia. I feel justified in looking at these, if only to protect my kids. The first from Danni, sent the night before she died:

Hey Georgie. I sent you a text earlier warning you not to trust Jenna, I guess I was too late, a few years too late! Tonight, your dad and I have had a talk. I told him some stuff I'm not proud of, but more importantly for you, he told me why he never told the police about Jenna, and why he stopped me from doing it too. The truth is he was protecting you. When Jenna found out I knew about her drug dealing, she told your dad if either of us went to the police then she would name you as the main dealer. Unfortunately she had photos of you handing stuff to other schoolkids, and she'd also saved some incriminating texts. I understand now. Your dad is one of the good ones after all – but I guess I found out too late. I don't want you to worry, I realise you must have been struggling with this for a long time, and I want you to know that I won't ever tell anyone that you were involved. You're young, you have your life before you and you've been conned by someone older, who doesn't have your best interests at heart. Please reconsider your friendship with Jenna, for your dad's sake. He's trying to be nice to her so she doesn't tell on you. But honestly? I think she's going to screw him over, and you if she gets the chance. Dad's not told anyone except your grandma, and as you know I wouldn't interfere normally, but I want you to know about this. I also want you to hear from me that your dad and I have decided to split up. So sorry to tell you like this Georgie, but I'm going as soon as I can and taking Olivia with me. Look after yourself darling, Danni x

Oh Danni, I'm so sorry about you and Dad. I know I wasn't very nice to you when you first came into our lives, but now I see you as a friend. When you and Olivia go, can I come and see you both? I love you and my little sister. But you're right about Jenna, I thought she was my friend, and didn't know she'd dropped me in it with Dad. I haven't done drugs for ages, but today she threatened to report me to the police if I don't pay her £500 by tomorrow morning, I don't have that kind of money. I can't think straight. If I get into trouble it will break Mum and Dad's hearts. I won't get into university, and I won't ever be a doctor.

Hey Georgie. It will all be fine. Don't do anything. I'll call the police as soon as I get out of here. I'd do it now, but I'd like to be as far away from Jenna as I can be when I snitch on her! Just leave it with me. Danni x

I put the phone down for a second to digest all this. How did Danni make things okay for Georgia? Is that why she was killed?

The phone messages are an insight, and put Scott's behaviour into perspective. They also explain who Jenna really is, a criminal. But I am still none the wiser as to what happened to Danni, and finding the phone in Sam's drawer and knowing there was other stuff going on with Jenna makes me question what really happened.

* * *

The kids are home, we've had a lovely dinner, and to Georgia's delight we share a bottle of wine between the three of us.

'Ooh I'm allowed wine now. You've finally realised I'm grown up, Mum?' she says.

'Mmm, having been at university for three months now, I imagine you've been drinking tequila slammers all week anyway.'

'Me? Drink?' she jokes, and I'm immediately back in those messages, I'd never even considered that my daughter might have taken drugs, and it still shocks me.

I serve dessert and we talk about what's been happening. The kids' stories are filled with friends and fun and lectures and all-night raves. My stories are a little less exciting, consisting mainly of days in the office and evenings alone with Netflix, and I'm okay with that. I don't want another relationship, and as much as I'm happy to go for a drink or babysit Olivia for Scott, I don't want him back. I need to live my life on my terms now. His plans to move to Scotland never materialised, but for a while back there I genuinely thought he was running away. It crossed my mind he might have had something to do with Danni's disappearance, but Scott is too law abiding. Sadly I can't say the same for Jenna; she did apparently have a thing for Scott, and he said it was all very difficult. She told him he'd given her mixed messages. Perhaps he had? He'd always been kind to her and seemed to go out of his way as had Angela, but he said she'd got the wrong idea and didn't take it well when he explained that he wasn't interested in a relationship. Now I realise he was just being nice to her to protect Georgia, and a little part of me actually feels sorry for Jenna. She was looking for love, but it seems she was also looking for money, and saw my family and all our secrets as a potential source of income.

After dinner, we sit at the table still nibbling, still laughing and I hate to do this, but I tell them we have to talk.

'I found Danni's phone,' I say, without pre-empting this, wanting to see Sam's reaction. He looks at me steadily, without speaking. So, I show them the text messages, which of course Georgia's already seen, and now Sam must have too – presumably he read them as he had the phone.

'Why have you got Danni's phone, Sam?'

He rests his elbows on the table, and puts his head in his hands.

'Was I was right all along?' I ask, breaking the silence.

He looks up at me, again saying nothing.

'After finding out that Dad had merely covered for Jenna because he was protecting Georgia, did it all erupt again? Did Danni say something to Jenna trying to warn her off, threatening her again with the police? So did Jenna follow Danni out into the snow and take Grandma's walking stick?' I suddenly think about this. 'She probably found it in the snow and just whacked Danni with it.'

'God, yeah, I think you're right, Mum. That must be what happened,' Sam replies.

'So you're hiding Danni's phone to protect Jenna?'

'No, no, I found it...'

'You found it? Where? And why didn't you tell us, tell the police?' I'm confused, I honestly assumed that there'd be a simple reason why Sam had the phone in his possession. But he isn't being clear, and I know my son, he's definitely covering for her.

'Answer me, Sam, were you hiding the phone here to protect Jenna?' I ask, loudly and firmly. 'I know what she's like, I think Danni was right, she's manipulative, untrustworthy, if she asked you to look after it, you need to come clean or you'll be the one in trouble.'

'Yeah... I guess...' He's shaking his head.

'I don't need to tell you, a law student, how bad this looks,' I snap, angry with him for being so naïve.

He doesn't respond, just stares down at the table, so when I realise he isn't going to engage with me, I say, 'Okay. I'm going to speak to the police first thing. I'm going to tell them it wasn't Grandma, it was Jenna.'

'Good luck with that, Mum,' Georgia says wistfully.

'Why?' I ask.

'She went to Thailand last February, no one's heard from her since,' she explains.

'Well, what about Interpol, they'd find her, wouldn't they?'

'Mum, she got busted in Bangkok with three litres of Molly in gin bottles,' Sam says.

'I'm sorry, I didn't understand a word of that, can you please translate?'

'*Drugs*, she got busted at Thai customs, she's already behind bars, so you've got your justice. We won't be seeing her for a long time, thank God,' Sam says, shaking his head.

'Yeah,' Georgia joins in. 'Jenna was dangerous, so toxic.'

I nodded. 'I agree, she came into our family that weekend and tried to pull it apart, but just because she's already in a prison doesn't mean she can escape some kind of trial for what she did to Danni?'

Sam seems to think for a moment. 'But then again, as you say, everyone thinks Grandma did it – she's already been tried, and she doesn't have to go to prison. She's beyond any kind of jurisdiction, so perhaps we don't rattle Jenna's cage, and just let it lie, eh?'

'Sam, how can you say that? I know she's poorly, but she's your grandma, do you want her to be remembered as a murderer? Surely you can see that for her sake justice has to be done—'

'We can't *do* that, Mum.'

'No.' My voice is raised, I'm angry on Angela's behalf, for

the woman she was. 'Sam, you want to be a lawyer, isn't this at the very heart of what you want to do?'

'Mum, you don't understand,' he says, irritated.

'STOP!!!! Just STOP, will you?' Georgia's now shouting.

We both turn to her.

'I can't do this anymore.' She's looking at Sam and shaking her head, tears streaming down her face.

'Georgia,' Sam says warningly.

I look from Georgia to Sam and back again for an answer.

He takes a breath, and I think he's about to speak when Georgia starts whimpering, then in a low voice that doesn't sound like her, she says slowly, 'I can't lie anymore.'

'Don't, Georgia. We can't tell anyone, Dad told us...'

Suddenly my world is moving and I'm losing my balance.

'I don't care what Dad said, I can't live with this inside me.' She's staring ahead, her face is twisted, her voice different, like she's possessed.

'GEORGIA, SHUT UP!' Sam's yelling at her.

'Dad? What has he done?' I'm raw, my nerves jangling. 'Tell me, did Dad kill Danni?' I look from Sam to Georgia and back again, but neither of them can look at me.

'Tell me!' I say loudly. 'You *have* to tell me...'

'I'll tell her,' Georgia says, looking sternly at Sam, who was about to step in.

'Thing is, Mum, I was so sick of her,' she starts, her voice louder now, 'so *fucking* sick of her.'

'Danni?' I ask. 'But I thought you...?'

'No, I was sick of *Jenna* ruling our lives.' She pauses, clearly not sure where to go with this. 'She was vile, always trying to manipulate, cause trouble, and she was *obsessed* with Dad.' She's breathing quickly. 'Danni once told me Jenna was evil – and now I believe that. She wrecked Dad and Danni's marriage, always trying to cause bust-ups between them, hinting to Danni that she had something going on with Dad.

And after Danni went, she started to blackmail Grandma. She told her she'd seen Dad digging in the snow, and she saw blood. She said *he* must have killed Danni. Grandma told me what she said, she was confused, but I understood, I knew Jenna was blackmailing her.'

'And was Jenna telling the truth?' I hear myself ask, my voice shaking with emotion, was Scott the killer?

'Yes, she *did* see him,' Georgia admits. 'He was out in the snow, and he had been digging, and...' She starts to cry. 'There was blood, there was so much blood... he was trying to hide the *body*!'

She's sobbing now, and Sam moves over to comfort her.

I am too shocked and upset to speak, so I just wait for her to talk again, and when she does, it comes flooding out of her.

'One night, I finished netball late and went to Dad's office to see if he'd give me a lift home, but when I got there the office door was locked. I don't know why, but I walked round to the outside, it was dark, and I was about to bang on the window, because I could see the back of his head.' She goes pale reliving this, and I can see it's hard for her, she's been traumatised.

'He and Danni were... together.' She wipes her eyes. 'And I was so upset, I told Jenna about it the next day, and she was kind and sweet and listened to me. I was only about fourteen and she was the lab technician at school, and she was kind to me, and seemed to really care. She said the way to stop their affair was to take photos as proof, then post them on Facebook and the forum on the school website. She said they'd be so embarrassed they'd stop seeing each other, and you and Dad would stay together. I didn't know what I was doing, I couldn't talk to you because I didn't want to tell you and hurt you, I thought I could finish it. So I did what she suggested, and I posted the picture.' She pauses, remembering the horrible fall-out. 'And of course it didn't work out and you found out and kicked Dad out, and it was all my fault.' She starts crying again.

'Georgia, NO!' I say, angry that our child is carrying this guilt. 'What happened between your dad and I was nothing you did, your dad was cheating, our marriage was over, and you did nothing, do you hear me?'

She nods. 'But it was all so awful, and I leaned on Jenna when you and Dad split, I realise that now. She seemed so understanding and sympathetic, and when I was worried because I couldn't concentrate in class, she said she could give me something to help me... and that's when it started. I took whatever she gave me, I trusted her and came to depend on her, depend on the drugs, and then she said I should really pay her because she'd been paying for them and had no money. I felt terrible, and when she told me how much I owed her, I said I couldn't afford to pay for them, so she said she'd do me a favour – if I sold the stuff to other kids, she'd let me have it for nothing.'

'Oh, Georgia,' I murmur, reaching across the table for her hand.

'I hated myself, so as soon as I felt strong enough, I stopped taking them and told her I wasn't doing it anymore. But she threatened to go to the police, and said I had to keep on working for her or I'd end up in prison.'

Sam clearly knows all this, and is just sitting with his head down while I gasp in horror.

'That night at the lodge when I got those texts off Danni and found out Dad had covered for me, and he was having to be nice to Jenna... for me!' She shakes her head in disbelief. 'I wanted to smash her to bits. She was hurting people I loved, and she was ruining my life. Then early on the morning that Danni... went, poor Grandma came into my room very early, so early it was still dark. She sat in my bed crying. "Jenna's going to tell the police about your drugs," she said. Jenna had told her she was going to make sure I wouldn't be a doctor, that I'd be a criminal with a drug conviction. Grandma still understood things then, but she was a bit confused and it was distressing for her. While Grandma was telling me this, I heard someone leaving the house. She heard it too, and she was saying, "That's Jenna leaving, she's going to the police now, she said she would." I totally panicked, and just threw on a coat and ran out into the snow after her. I could see her bright yellow jacket in the distance with my phone torch, I thought she was going out early because she was taking the coastal path up to the road. I thought she was trying to get to the police first thing before we were up, before anyone could stop her. I was *determined* she wasn't going to tell the police about me, so I ran after her, and as I got closer, she was aware I was behind her, and started running. But I was much faster, and the more she ran, the angrier I was and I almost fell over something in the dark, and bent down and picked it up. It was a stick, a big, heavy stick and I was going to threaten her with it. I was going to tell her if she didn't fuck off home now, I was going to hit her. And as I ran I was still thinking about what she'd done to Dad and Danni and Grandma – and how she'd given me drugs, then forced me to sell them to other kids. I understood after Danni's texts why Dad put up with her and why Grandma had found her a job, they were both trying to keep her happy to save *me*.' This brings on fresh tears, and she has to stop talking to wipe her eyes and blow her nose.

She is calmer now, retracing her steps along the coastal path, remembering her thoughts. 'It wasn't random, it wasn't an accident, I just *knew* I didn't want a world with her in it. And... and...' She stops a moment as she recalls every second. 'I got right up behind her, pulled back the stick and whacked her *so* hard, I'll never forget the noise she made, it was quiet, a short groan like an animal being shot. But I didn't stop, I just kept whacking her, and whacking her and even when she tried to turn to me, I kept on hitting her. My anger just swept me along, like I had no control over my actions, and she fell and only then did I realise what I'd done. And *then* I was scared, I was so scared my teeth started chattering. I flashed my torch and... now I was scared and wanted her to get up, or at least start groaning so I knew she was alive. I couldn't allow myself to think she might be dead. That I'd *killed* someone, even if it *was* Jenna. I couldn't let that into my head. But it was far worse than that. And I'll never forget it, I flashed my torch along the ground so I could see where she'd fallen, and saw *Danni's* name in little diamonds on her phone, it was lying on the ground. I just felt this cold horror creep through my body. And I suddenly realised what I'd done. I had to put my hand over my own mouth to stifle my own scream.'

'Oh God, Georgia,' I groan, tears rolling down my cheeks.

'And then I just ran and ran and ran, and when I got back to the lodge I went straight to Sam and told him.'

I get up and move around the table to comfort her. And it's only then she crumples, her body shudders, as a year of grief and horror comes pouring out of her, and I just hold her for a long time until it begins, finally to subside. Sam continues to sit silently, gazing down at the table, moving the wine cork from one hand to the other, again and again. Then he finally speaks. 'When Georgia came to me, I didn't know what the hell to do, but I thought *if she's still alive we need to get an ambulance*, I hoped there might be a chance she'd just been stunned or fallen and we could save her. So I told Georgia to take me there and we ran all the way. I kept praying that it wasn't as bad as Georgia said it was.'

'But when we got there she was still lying on the ground, all twisted,' Georgia says through her tears. 'There was blood seeping into the snow from her *head*.' Her voice rises to a squeal of horror.

'By then it was light, and I was close enough to see her eyes open, her face was pale blue, I'll never forget it.' Sam shudders, tears in his eyes.

I try not to react, to stay calm, Georgia is on the verge of hysteria. 'So what did you do?'

'What *could* we do? She was obviously dead. But then I saw it – her pink phone. Georgia had said it was lying next to her, she probably took it out of her pocket to call someone when she was being followed and it had landed on the ground. By now we were both freaking out. I panicked, thinking that somehow the phone might incriminate Georgia so I grabbed it and we ran.'

I don't know where to start with the questions. My mind is numb with shock, but I realise I'm the only adult in the room and we have to talk about what happens now.

'So Grandma had nothing to do with this?'

They both shake their heads.

'Then why are hers the only fingerprints on the walking stick?' I ask.

'Because I was wearing woolly gloves. I threw on my coat and the gloves were in the pocket – by the time I found the stick, my gloves were on,' Georgia explains. 'But Grandma had used the stick in the house, without gloves on, so her fingerprints were all over it.'

I nod, that makes sense. 'The body, you said *Dad* moved the body?'

They both look at each other, and Sam starts to clarify. 'I told Dad. Georgia didn't want to, she said he'd hate her, but I was alone outside and he asked me if I was okay. I tried to make out I was fine, but Dad, he just has this way of knowing things and he told me that the text he'd received from Danni was sent by someone else.'

'Who?' I ask.

'Me,' Sam says. 'But he knew it wasn't from Danni.'

'How did he know?'

'He said she'd signed her text D x, but she always signed her texts to us D x. To Dad she signed them S x. It was their little nod from the days when they were having the affair.' He looks awkwardly at me. 'She was in his phone as Steve.'

I shrug at this, it doesn't even sting anymore, it's all in the past, and I'm finally in the present, and happy – well, until today.

'So you sent the text from Danni saying not to look for her, that she wanted her space?' I say.

'Yeah, it was stupid, but I just thought if we could let everyone believe she was just being Danni and playing around, it would give us more time. I also hoped we could move the body and make it look like suicide. But Dad thought the text might be from you, he thought you'd hurt Danni,' Sam said to me.

I was horrified. 'Your dad really doesn't know me does he?'

'No, but I realised then that we had to tell Dad the truth or he might start pointing the finger at you. He was obviously really upset and I expected him to call the police there and then. But instead, he asked me where Danni was.'

'So that night we went out to search, with you and Jenna, we took him to the body,' Georgia adds, ripping her damp tissues into a pile on the table.

'You deliberately lost Jenna and me?'

'Yes, we had to, but we could see you in the distance. Georgia was lookout, she was making sure you didn't get lost or come and find us.'

'Dad's plan was to push Danni off the coastal path where she was lying, but it was dark and far too dangerous to see properly, even with torches. Her body was heavy and frozen and Dad said we risked slipping off with her, so we decided to cover her in snow. We figured the police couldn't get there and we had time to work out what to do.'

'The next day, Dad went out early, remember he came in by the back door, we thought it was an intruder?'

'Yeah, and scared the life out of us,' I replied. It's all making a strange kind of sense now.

'He'd been to see Danni, he wanted to check her body couldn't be spotted, he was worried about foxes and other animals. But when he got there the snow we'd covered her with was a block of ice.'

'So that explained the blood on his cuff?'

'Yeah, the body was rock solid with ice, but her hand was free, and when he tried to move her, he must have touched some blood that had melted in the snow.' Sam shudders.

'That's gruesome.' I groan in horror at the spectre of Danni encased in her own snow coffin. 'Did Dad never say that you should go to the police?' I ask.

They both shake their heads. 'He said we had our whole lives before us,' Sam says, 'and if anyone ever found the body, he would say *he* did it.'

I finally breathe out.

'And when Freeman came and told us they'd found Danni, Dad was preparing to confess. But Grandma beat him to it, she was confused.'

'Not *that* confused,' I say, realising that in her last few weeks of lucid moments, their grandma had saved her grandchildren *and* her son. Angela knew what was going on. Scott told her most things, plus she knew that Georgia had run out that morning in a rage. 'I guess we'll never really know, but I reckon Grandma confessed to the crime in order to save Dad and Georgia,' I say quietly.

We all sit for a little while, just getting to grips with the true horror of what happened. Eventually, I say what's on my mind.

'You know the *right* thing would be to go to the police now, and explain everything?' I say, aware of the irony of this, because I should also be doing the same about Nick.

'Yeah, we should do that,' Sam says half-heartedly, 'but then that would open another can of worms.'

Sam looks at me. He's thinking of the hit-and-run, but I

don't want Georgia to know. She's too fragile, been through enough. I shake my head and he nods.

'So that would be the right thing to do,' I repeat. 'But what would the consequences be? Georgia, you'd gone out that morning to hurt Jenna, picking up the walking stick and using it as a weapon on the victim. Despite it being Danni, who you didn't intend to kill, it would still be seen as premeditated, and though you were only seventeen when you committed the crime, you could have ended up in prison. It was murder, and in serious cases people of your age *can* get custodial sentences and be locked up in some kind of institution.'

Georgia nods slowly, terror on her face as Sam shudders. We both know Georgia wouldn't survive prison of any kind; she's fragile, an anxious child growing into an anxious woman, it would be the end of her, and I can't even contemplate it.

'And, as someone who found the phone and kept it, *I'm* also implicated,' Sam points out. 'So that's my future as a lawyer fucked, and Dad's implicated too because he tried to move the body, so no more teaching for him. None of us called an ambulance, or the police and none of us *told* the police any of this when we were questioned. In fact, we *lied* to the police,' he says. 'We could even end up with short, custodial sentences, and ultimately be jobless with police records and no future.'

'So, looking at this... mess... we could *all* be found guilty, one way or another,' I conclude. 'And if, as you say, some of us could end up in prison, we have to think about what that means for Olivia.' I leave that to hover over the table, so they can really think about this, then I say, 'But what is the alternative? I mean, can we live with ourselves if we *don't* go to the police and confess?'

They look at each other. Neither of them answers.

I wait for this to sink in, then ask, 'What would Grandma want us to do?'

They both react in the same way to this, with a regretful

half smile.

'I don't think Grandma would want *any* of her family to be in prison, and her youngest granddaughter in care, do you?' I offer.

They both shake their heads slowly at this. 'I think she'd want us two out in the world making it a better place,' Sam says. 'And she'd want Dad to carry on changing kids' lives, being headteacher, and looking after Olivia.'

I turn to Georgia. 'And what do *you* think? You're the one who's going to have to live with this more than Sam. If you decide *not* to tell the police and we keep everything as is – then you need to stay strong and be able to live with it.'

She sits for a while, her flawless young face damp with a lifetime of tears. She will struggle with this I know, but if she confessed and was charged, I truly believe my daughter's life would be over.

She sits for a long time, clutching at her damp tissues, her face a flawless study in pain and regret.

'I'll never do anything like that again,' she says quietly. 'I *want* to be a doctor, it's all I've ever wanted. Danni encouraged me to go for it, and it's what Grandma wanted for me too, and I know they would want me to continue on that path. I'll never get over what I did, Danni's death is the worst thing that's ever happened to me, and that won't ever change. And honestly? I'm not sure how long I can live with what I did, but as long as I do, perhaps I can give something back? And every time I *save* a life, I might be able to justify still being in the world, still being alive – when Danni isn't?'

I breathe deeply and touch her hand. I worry about Georgia, I always have and always will. In truth, I don't think she will ever rid herself of guilt like that, who could? I know she doesn't believe that she deserves to live while Danni died. I just hope her career brings her some balance, a kind of redemption that will help her get through the rest of her life.

'Okay, so we're agreed.' I stand up, take Danni's phone from the table, and walk into the utility room, where I find a hammer. After taking out the SIM card, I smash it to smithereens.

I can't ever justify this morally. What I'm doing is wrong. I'm a bad mother who's encouraging my children not to tell the truth, while also hiding my own shame. But believe me when I say, this isn't about me, it isn't about saving *my* skin, it's about keeping my children safe, and preventing more casualties. I know Georgia's a good person, I know she will save lives, and if she can bear to live with what she's done, then hopefully she'll go on to live a good life with purpose. I hope the same for Sam, and for Olivia who will also have her own struggles, but if we stick with the plan, Scott will guide her, and I will be in the background, the kind auntie who babysits sometimes when her dad works late.

I know I should call the police right now and tell them what I did, and I should tell them what my daughter did. And who knows, they might beat me to it, they might find some archived record of my dating profile on that same website as Nick Cairns, and it's all over for me. So far, there's been no call, but if the police should contact any one of us tomorrow, or if Georgia can't live with what she's done, then we will go to the police and confess together.

Angela always said she'd take a bullet for her grandkids, and I believe she did that. It was her final act of love for her family before she disappeared into the tragic oblivion of dementia. She sacrificed herself for their freedom, and I won't throw that back in her face. I don't take this decision lightly, but feel it's the *right* thing to do – for now.

And for anyone reading this and thinking I'm the worst mother, and the most morally corrupt woman in the world, you are probably right. But when you close this book, sit a moment, and just ask yourself: 'If my child murdered someone, and I could save them, what would *I* do?'

A LETTER FROM SUE

Thank you so much for choosing to read *The Lodge*. If you enjoyed it and want to keep up to date with all my latest releases, just sign up at the following link. Your email address will never be shared and you can unsubscribe at any time.

www.bookouture.com/sue-watson

This book was inspired by those beautiful ads for winter holidays that appear in our newsfeeds, and the back pages of glossy magazines. Pictures of perfect families in hot tubs, drinking champagne and smiling, their teeth as white as those snow-capped mountains. These gorgeous images made me think about how wonderful it would be to book a beautiful lodge in a magical winter setting and invite all the family for a long weekend. Three generations sitting by a log fire as the snow falls like white confetti outside – what could possibly go wrong? Well, that depends on the family, and if there's an old wife and a new one under the same roof, then anything could happen. Surely it's just a matter of time before all the resentments, jealousies and blame come bubbling to the surface, just like that luxury hot tub?

I loved writing this book, in fact, once the characters took over, it was easy – they did all the work. I sat back with a steaming mug of hot chocolate, and allowed things to get messier, and messier, while I enjoyed the scenery!

I hope you enjoyed reading *The Lodge* as much as I enjoyed

writing it, and if you did, I would be so grateful if you could write a review. It doesn't have to be as long as a sentence – every word counts and is very much appreciated. I love to hear what you think, and it makes such a difference helping new readers to discover one of my books for the first time.

I love hearing from my readers – so please get in touch with me on social media.

Thanks so much for reading,

Sue

facebook.com/suewatsonbooks
twitter.com/suewatsonwriter

ACKNOWLEDGEMENTS

As always, my huge thanks to the wonderful team at Bookouture who are amazing, supportive and expertly transform my ideas into books.

Thanks to my wonderful editor, Helen Jenner, who tames my writing, makes sense of it and makes my books the best they can be. Thanks also to Sarah Hardy, my book publicist for always doing an amazing job to get my books out there!

Big thanks as always to Harolyn Grant, my Canadian friend and reader who not only casts her forensic eye on the details and always finds stuff I miss, but gives so much more with her wonderful insights and take on life. Thanks also to Su Biela and Dawn Angel for fabulous first readings, and to Anna Wallace for a fantastic final tidy-up.

As always, a huge thank you to my long-suffering husband, Nick, my amazing daughter, Eve, my lovely mum, the rest of my family and all my wonderful friends.

And one final nod to a new member of the family. Sadly late last year we lost our 18-year-old cat Poppy, who would sit by me on the sofa as I wrote through the night, and should have had a co-writing credit for the hours she put in. She is greatly missed and for a little while those late nights on the laptop were rather lonely, until we inherited a rather beautiful, very fluffy boy called Cosmo. He's now taken Poppy's place, keeps me company when everyone else is asleep, and is always happy to help with those complex plot issues for a few tasty cat treats – whatever the hour.

Made in the USA
Middletown, DE
14 January 2024